Lincolnshire
COUNTY COUNCIL

discover libraries

This book should be returned on or before the last date shown below.

'T
in
by
W
liv
or

'Y
po
yo
W
hap

'P.
of
or

'N
ou
wr

'O
p

e
his
wr

'The incomparable and timeless
ages, shapes and sizes!' Ka

'A genius . . . Elusive, delicate but lasting. He created such a credible world that, sadly, I suppose, never really existed but what a delight it always is to enter it and the temptation to linger there is sometimes almost overwhelming' *Alan Ayckbourn*

'Wodehouse was quite simply the Bee's Knees. And then some' *Joseph Connolly*

'Compulsory reading for anyone who has a pig, an aunt – or a sense of humour!' *Lindsey Davis*

'I constantly find myself drooling with admiration at the sublime way Wodehouse plays with the English language' *Simon Brett*

'I've recorded all the Jeeves books, and I can tell you this: it's like singing Mozart. The perfection of the phrasing is a physical pleasure. I doubt if any writer in the English language has more perfect music' *Simon Callow*

'Quite simply, the master of comic writing at work' *Jane Moore*

'To pick up a Wodehouse novel is to find oneself in the presence of genius – no writer has ever given me so much pure enjoyment' *John Julius Norwich*

'P.G. Wodehouse is the gold standard of English wit' *Christopher Hitchens*

'Wodehouse is so utterly, properly, simply funny' *Adele Parks*

'To dive into a Wodehouse novel is to swim in some of the most elegantly turned phrases in the English language' *Ben Schott*

'P.G. Wodehouse should be prescribed to treat depression. Cheaper, more effective than valium and far, far more addictive' *Olivia Williams*

'My only problem with Wodehouse is deciding which of his enchanting books to take to my desert island' *Ruth Dudley Edwards*

The author of almost a hundred books and the creator of Jeeves, Blandings Castle, Psmith, Ukridge, Uncle Fred and Mr Mulliner, P.G. Wodehouse was born in 1881 and educated at Dulwich College. After two years with the Hong Kong and Shanghai Bank he became a full-time writer, contributing to a variety of periodicals including *Punch* and the *Globe*. He married in 1914. As well as his novels and short stories, he wrote lyrics for musical comedies with Guy Bolton and Jerome Kern, and at one time had five musicals running simultaneously on Broadway. His time in Hollywood also provided much source material for fiction.

At the age of 93, in the New Year's Honours List of 1975, he received a long-overdue knighthood, only to die on St Valentine's Day some 45 days later.

P. G. WODEHOUSE
Big Money

arrow books

Published by Arrow Books 2008

3 5 7 9 10 8 6 4

First published in the United Kingdom in 1931 by Herbert Jenkins Ltd

Arrow Books
The Random House Group Limited
20 Vauxhall Bridge Road, London, SW1V 2SA

www.rbooks.co.uk

www.wodehouse.co.uk

Addresses for companies within The Random House Group Limited can be found at: www.randomhouse.co.uk/offices.htm

The Random House Group Limited Reg. No. 954009

A CIP catalogue record for this book
is available from the British Library

ISBN 9780099514220

The Random House Group Limited supports The Forest Stewardship Council (FSC), the leading international forest certification organisation. All our titles that are printed on Greenpeace approved FSC certified paper carry the FSC logo. Our paper procurement policy can be found at www.rbooks.co.uk/environment

Mixed Sources
Product group from well-managed
forests and other controlled sources
www.fsc.org Cert no. TT-COC-2139
© 1996 Forest Stewardship Council

Printed and bound in the United Kingdom by
CPI Bookmarque, Croydon, CR0 4TD

Big Money

CHAPTER 1

On an afternoon in May, at the hour when London pauses in its labours to refresh itself with a bite of lunch, there was taking place in the coffee-room of the Drones Club in Dover Street that pleasantest of functions, a reunion of old school friends. The host at the meal was Godfrey, Lord Biskerton, son and heir of the sixth Earl of Hoddesdon, the guest his one-time inseparable comrade, John Beresford Conway.

Happening that morning to go down to the City to discuss with his bank-manager a little matter of an overdraft, Lord Biskerton had run into Berry Conway in Cornhill. It was three years since they had last met, and in his lordship's manner, as he gazed across the table, there was something of the affectionate reproach a conscientious trainer of performing fleas might have shown towards one of his artists who had strayed from the fold.

'Amazing!' he said.

Lord Biskerton was a young man with red hair and what looked like a preliminary scenario for a moustache of the same striking hue. He dug into his fried sole emotionally.

'Absolutely amazing,' he repeated. 'It beats me. I am mystified. Here we have two birds – you, on the one hand; I, on the other – who were once as close as the paper on the wall. Our chumminess was a silent sermon on Brotherly Love. And yet I'm dashed if we've set eyes on one another since the summer Peanut Brittle won the Jubilee Handicap. I can't understand it.'

Berry Conway shifted a little uncomfortably in his seat. He seemed embarrassed.

'We just happened to miss each other, I suppose.'

'But how?' Lord Biskerton was resolved to probe this thing to its depths. 'That's what I want to know. How? I go every-where. Races, restaurants, theatres, all the usual round. It seems incredible that we haven't met before. If you ask most people, they will tell you the difficult thing is to avoid meeting me. It poisons their lives, poor devils. "Oh, my sainted aunt!" they mutter. "You again?" and they dash down side-streets, only to bump into me coming up the other way. Then why should you have been immune?'

'Just the luck of the Conways, I expect.'

'Anyway, why haven't you looked me up? You must have known where I was. I'm in the 'phone book.'

Berry fingered his bread.

'I don't go about much these days,' he said. 'I'm living in the suburbs now, down at Valley Fields.'

'You aren't married, are you?' asked Lord Biskerton with sudden alarm. 'Not got a little wife or any rot of that sort?'

'No. I live with an old family retainer. She used to be my nurse. And she seems to think she still is,' said Berry, his face darkening. 'I heard her shouting after me as I left the house this morning something about had I got on my warm woollies.'

'My dear chap!' Lord Biskerton raised his eyebrows. 'These intimate details. Keep the conversation clean. She fusses over you, does she? They will, these old nurses. Mine,' said Lord Biskerton, wincing at the memory, 'once kissed me on the platform at Paddington Station, thereby ruining my prestige at school for the whole of one term. Why don't you break away from this old disease? Why not pension her off?'

'Pension her off!' Berry gave a short laugh. 'What with? I suppose I had better tell you, Biscuit. The reason I've dropped out of things and am living in the suburbs and have stopped seeing my old friends lately is that I've come down in the world. I've no money now.'

The Biscuit stared.

'No money?'

'Well, that's exaggerating perhaps. To be absolutely accurate, I'm better off at the moment than I've been for two years, because I've just got a job as private secretary to Frisby, the American financier. But he only pays me a few pounds a week.'

'But doesn't a secretary have to know shorthand and all that sort of rather revolting stuff?'

'I learned shorthand.'

'Golly!' said the Biscuit. It was as if this revelation had brought the tragedy home to him in all its stark grimness. 'You must have been properly up against it.'

'I was. If an old sportsman, on whom I had absolutely no claim, hadn't lent me two hundred pounds, I should probably have starved.'

'But what on earth has been happening?' asked the Biscuit, bewildered. 'At school you were a sort of young millionaire. You jingled as you walked. A twopenny jam-sandwich for self and friend was a mere nothing to you. Where's all the money gone to? What came unstuck?'

Berry hesitated. His had been for some time a lonely existence, and the idea of confiding his troubles to a sympathetic ear was appealing.

'Do you really want to hear the story of my life, Biscuit?' he said wistfully. 'Sure it won't bore you?'

'Bore me? My dear chap! I'm agog. Let's have the whole thing. Start from the beginning. Childhood – early surroundings – genius probably inherited from male grandparent – push along.'

'Well, you've brought it on yourself, remember.'

The Biscuit mused.

'When we first met,' he said, 'you were, if I recollect, about fourteen. An offensive stripling, all feet and red ears, but worth cultivating on account of your extraordinary wealth. How did you get the stuff? Honestly, I hope!'

'That came from an aunt. It was like this. I was an only child—'

'And I bet one of you was ample.'

'My mother died when I was born. I never knew my father.'

'I sometimes wish I didn't know mine,' said the Biscuit. 'The sixth Earl has his moments, but he can on occasion be more than a bit of a blister. Why didn't you know your father? A pretty exclusive kid, were you?'

'He was killed in a railway accident when I was three. And then this aunt adopted me. Her husband had just died, leaving her a fortune. That's where the money came from that you used to hear jingling at school. He was in the jute business, I believe. All I remember of him is that he had whiskers.'

'What a gruesome mess you must have been at three,' said the Biscuit meditatively. 'You were bad enough at fourteen. At three you must have made strong men shudder.'

'On the contrary. Hannah has often told me—'

'Who's Hannah?'

'Hannah Wisdom. My old retainer.'

'I see. The one who gets worried about your woollies.

I thought for the moment you were introducing a new sex motive.'

'Hannah has often told me that I looked like a little angel in my velvet suit. I had long golden curls—'

'This is loathsome,' said the Biscuit austerely. 'Stop it. There are certain subjects which should not be mentioned when gentlemen are present. Get on with the story. Enter rich aunt. So far, so good. What happened then?'

'She did me like a prince. Sent me to school and Cambridge and surrounded me with every circumstance of luxury and refinement, so to speak.'

The Biscuit frowned.

'Obviously,' he said, 'there must be a catch somewhere. But I'm dashed if I can spot it yet. Up to now, you've been making my mouth water.'

'The catch,' said Berry, 'was this. During all those happy, halcyon years, when you and I were throwing inked darts at one another without a care in the world, my aunt, it now appears, had been going through her capital like a drunken sailor. I don't know if she ever endowed a scheme for getting gold out of sea-water, but, if not, that's the only one she missed. Anybody who had anything in the way of a speculation so fishy that nobody else would look at it, used to come frisking up to her, waving prospectuses, and she would fall over her feet to get at her cheque-book.'

'Women,' commented the Biscuit, 'ought never to be allowed cheque-books. I've often said so. Mugs, every one of them.'

'She died two years ago, leaving me everything she possessed. This consisted of about three tons of shares in bogus companies. I was right up against it.'

'From Riches to Rags, what?'

'Yes.'

'Scaly,' said the Biscuit. 'Undeniably scaly.'

'My aunt's lawyer, a man named Attwater, happened by a miracle to be one of those fellows who pop up every now and then just to show that there is a future for the human race, after all. He had an eye like a haddock and a face like teak, and whenever he came to dinner at our place he always snubbed me like a fine old gentleman of the old school if I dared to utter a word; but, my gosh, beneath that rough exterior—! He lent me two hundred pounds to keep me going – two hundred solid quid – and if ever I have a son he is going to be christened Ebenezer Attwater Conway.'

'Better not have a son,' advised the Biscuit.

'That money just saved my life. I managed after running all over London for three months to get a sort of job. And at night I used to sweat away at learning typing and shorthand. Eventually I got taken on as secretary by a man in the Import and Export business. He retired about a month ago, and very decently shoved me off on to this fellow Frisby, who was a friend of his. That's how Frisby comes to own my poor black body now. And that,' concluded Berry, 'is why I am living in the suburbs and have not been mixing much of late with the Biskertons and the rest of the gilded aristocracy. And the really damnable part of it is that at the time when the crash came I was just going to buzz off round the world on a tramp steamer. I had to give that up, of course.'

The Biscuit appeared stupefied.

'You mean to tell me,' he said, 'that you've been avoiding me just because you were hard-up? You were ashamed of your honest poverty? I never heard anything so dashed drivelling in my life.'

Berry flushed.

'It's all very well to talk like that. You can't keep up with people who are much richer than you are.'

'Who can't?'

'Nobody can.'

'Well, I've been doing it all my life,' said Lord Biskerton stoutly, 'and – God willing – I hope to go on doing it till I am old and grey. Do you suppose for a moment, old bag, that I'm any richer than you are? Why, I only know what money is by hearsay.'

'You don't mean that?'

'I certainly do. If you want to see real destitution, old boy, take a look at my family. I'm broke. My guv'nor's broke. My Aunt Vera's broke. It's a ruddy epidemic. I owe every tradesman in London. The guv'nor hasn't tasted meat for weeks. And, as for Aunt Vera, relict of the late Colonel Archibald Mace, C.V.O., she's reduced to writing Glad articles for the evening papers. You know – things on the back page pointing out that there's always sunshine somewhere and that we ought to be bright, like the little birds in the trees. Why, I've known that woman's circumstances to become so embarrassed that she actually made an attempt to borrow money from *me*. Me, old boy! Lazarus in person.'

He laughed again, tickled by the recollection. Then, helping himself to fruit salad, he became grave once more and pointed the moral earnestly.

'The fact of the matter is, laddie, there's nothing in being an Earl nowadays. It's a mug's game. If ever they try to make you one, punch them in the eye and run. And being an Earl's son and heir is one degree worse.'

'But I've always thought of you as rolling in money, Biscuit. You've got that enormous place in Sussex—?'

'That's just what's wrong with it. Too enormous. Eats up all the family revenues, old boy. Oh, I know how you came to be misled. The error is a common one. You see a photograph in *Country Life* of an Earl standing in a negligent attitude outside the north-east piazza of his seat in Loamshire, and you say to yourself, "Lucky devil! I'll make that bird's acquaintance and touch him." Little knowing that even as the camera clicked the poor old deadbeat was wondering where on earth the money was coming from to give the piazza the lick of paint it so badly needed. What with the Land Tax and the Income Tax and the Super Tax and all the rest of the little Taxes, there's not much in the family sock these days, old boy. It all comes down to this,' said the Biscuit, summing up. 'If England wants a happy, well-fed aristocracy, she mustn't have wars. She can't have it both ways.'

He sighed, and fell into a thoughtful silence.

'I wish I could find some way of making a bit of money,' he said, resuming his remarks. 'I don't seem able to do it, racing. And I don't seem able to do it at Bridge. But there must be some method. Look at all the wealthy blighters you see running round. They've managed to find it. I read a book the other day where a bloke goes up to another bloke in the street – perfect stranger with a rich sort of look about him – and whispers in his ear – the first bloke does – "A word with you, sir!" Addressing the second bloke, you understand. "A word with you, sir. I know your secret!" Upon which, the second bloke turns ashy white and supports him in luxury for the rest of his life. I thought there might be something in it.'

'About seven years, I should think.'

'Well, if I try it, I'll let you know. And if they send me to the Bastille, you can come and see me on Visiting Days and hand me tracts through the bars.'

He ate cheese, and returned to an earlier point in the conversation.

'What did you mean about buzzing off round the world on a tramp steamer?' he asked. 'You said, if I remember, that when the fuse blew out that was what you were planning to do. It sounded cuckoo to me. Why buzz round the world in tramp steamers?'

'Well, that's what I wanted to do – get off somewhere and have adventures. You know that thing of Kipling's? "I'd like to roll to 'Rio, roll down, roll down to 'Rio. Oh, I'd like to . . ."'

'Sh!' said the Biscuit, scandalized. 'My dear chap! You can't recite here. Against the club rules. Strong letter from the committee.'

'I was talking to a fellow the other day,' said Berry, with a smouldering eye, 'who had just come back from Arizona. He was telling me about the Mojave Desert. He had been prospecting out there. It made me feel like a caged eagle.'

'A what?'

'Caged eagle.'

'Why?'

'Because I felt that I should never get away from Valley Fields and see anything worth seeing.'

'You've seen me,' said the Biscuit.

'Think of the Grand Canyon!'

Lord Biskerton closed his eyes dutifully.

'I am,' he said. 'What next? Double it?'

'What chance have I of ever seeing the Grand Canyon?'

'Why not?'

Berry writhed.

'Haven't you been listening?' he demanded.

'Certainly I've been listening,' replied the Biscuit, with spirit.

'I haven't missed a word. And your statement seems to me confused and rambling. As I understand you, you wish to roll to 'Rio. And you appear to be beefing because you can't. Why can't you? 'Rio is open for being rolled to at this season, I presume?'

'What about Attwater and that money he lent me? I can't pay him back unless I go on earning money, can I? And how can I earn money if I chuck my job and go tramping round the world?'

'You want to pay him back?' said the Biscuit, startled.

'Of course I do.'

'In that case, there is nothing more to be said. If you intend to go through life deliberately paying back money,' said the Biscuit, a little severely, 'you must be content not to roll.'

There was a silence. Berry's face clouded.

'I get so damned restless sometimes,' he said, 'I don't know what to do with myself. Don't you ever get restless?'

'Never. London's good enough for me.'

'It isn't for me. That man who had come from Arizona was telling me how you prospect in the Mojave.'

'A thing I wouldn't do on a bet.'

'You tramp about under a blazing sun and sleep under the stars and single-jack holes in the solid rock—'

'How perfectly foul. And not a chance of getting a drink anywhere, I take it? Well, if that's the sort of thing you've missed, you're well out of it, my lad. Yes, dashed well out of it. No matter how much you may feel like a prawn in aspic.'

'I didn't say I felt like a prawn in aspic. I said I felt like a caged eagle.'

'It's the same thing.'

'It isn't at all the same thing.'

'All right,' said the Biscuit, pacifically. 'Let it go. Have it your own way. But do you mean to say you can't raise even a couple of hundred quid? Weren't any of these shares your aunt left you any good at all?'

'Just waste paper.'

'What were they?'

'I can't remember them all. There were about five thousand of a thing called Federal Dye, and three thousand of another called the Something Development Company. . . . Oh, and a mine. I'd forgotten the mine.'

'What! You really own a mine? Then you're on velvet.'

'But it's a dud, like everything else my aunt bought.'

'What sort of a mine?'

'I don't know how you would describe it, because it hasn't anything in it. It started out with some idea of being a copper mine, I believe. It's called the Dream Come True, but it sounds to me more like a nightmare.'

'Berry, old boy,' said the Biscuit, 'I repeat, and with all the emphasis at my command, that you are on velvet. Why people want copper, I can't say. If you carry it in your trouser-pocket, it rattles. And if you put it in your waistcoat, you feel as if you had a tumour or something. And what can you buy with it? An evening paper or a packet of butterscotch from a slot-machine. Nevertheless, it is an established fact that people do tumble over themselves to buy copper mines. What you must do – and instantly – is to sell this thing, pay old Attwater his money (if you really are resolved on that mad project), lend me what you may see fit of the remainder, and then you would be free to go anywhere and do what you jolly well liked.'

'But I keep telling you the Dream Come True hasn't any copper in it.'

'Well, there are always mugs in the world, aren't there? It will be a sorry day for old England,' said Lord Biskerton, 'when one can't find some mug to buy a mine, however dud. You say yours hasn't anything in it? What of that? My old guv'nor once bought shares in an oil-well, and not only was there no oil, there wasn't even a well. I venture to say that, if you look about you, you will find a dozen fatheads willing and anxious to give you a few hundred quid for the thing.'

Berry picked at the table-cloth. His was an imagination that never required a great deal of firing.

'Do you really think so?'

'Of course I do.'

Berry's eyes were glowing.

'If I could find somebody who would give me enough to pay back old Attwater's loan I wouldn't stay here a day. I'd get on the first boat to America and push West. I can just picture it, Biscuit. Miles of desert, with mountain ranges that seem to change their shape as you look at them. Wagon tracks. Red porphyry cliffs. People going about in sombreros and blue overalls.'

'Probably fearful bounders, all of them,' said the Biscuit. 'Keep well away, is my advice. You're not leaving me?' he asked, as Berry rose.

'I must, I'm afraid. I've got to get back to work.'

'Already.'

'I'm only supposed to take an hour for lunch, and today isn't a good day for breaking rules. Old Frisby's got dyspepsia again, and is a bit edgy.'

'Well, push off, if you must,' said the Biscuit resignedly. 'And don't forget what I said about that mine. I wish I had had an aunt who had left me something like that. There have only been two aunts in my life. One is Vera, on whom I have already touched.

The other, Caroline, passed on some years ago, respected by all, owing me two-and-sixpence for a cab fare.'

II

At about the moment when Berry Conway, having reluctantly torn himself away from his old school friend, entered the Underground train which was to take him back to the City and the resumption of the daily round of toil, T. Paterson Frisby, his employer, was seated in his office at 6, Pudding Lane, E.C.4, talking to his sister Josephine on the telephone.

T. Paterson Frisby was a little man who looked as if he had been constructed of some leathern material and subsequently pickled in brine. His expression, as he took up the instrument, was one of acute exasperation. His sister always irritated him, especially on the telephone, when her natural tendency to babble became intensified; and he was also suffering severely from those pangs of indigestion to which Berry had alluded in his conversation with Lord Biskerton.

The fact that he had been expecting these pangs did nothing to mitigate them. Indeed, it added to the physical anguish a spiritual remorse which was almost as unpleasant. A whole medical college of doctors had told Mr Frisby to avoid roast duck, and as a rule he was strong enough to do so. But last night the craving had been too much for him. He had wallowed madly and recklessly in roast duck, tucking into the stuffing like a farmhand. Today had come the inevitable retribution. And on top of that Josephine was calling him on the telephone.

''Lo?' said Mr Frisby, and the word was like a cry from the pit.

He took a pepsine tablet from the bottle on the desk and tossed it into his mouth – not in the gay, dashing manner of some debonair monarch flinging largess to the multitude, but sullenly, with the air of one reluctantly compelled to lend money to an importunate cadger. His gastric juices, he knew, would give him no peace till they had had the stuff, so he gave it to them.

In a world so full of beautiful things, it seems a pity that one has got to talk about Mr Frisby's gastric juices, but it is the duty of the historian to see life steadily and see it whole.

''Lo?' said Mr Frisby.

A clear soprano answered him.

'Paterson!'

'Ugh?'

'Is that you?'

'Ugh.'

'Listen.'

'I'm listening.'

'Well, listen, then.'

'I *am* listening, I tell you. Get to the point. And talk quick, darn it. Remember it's costing forty-five bucks every three minutes.'

For Mrs Moon was speaking from her apartment on Park Avenue, New York. And though it was the woman who would pay, waste even of other people's money was agony to Mr Frisby. He possessed twenty million dollars himself, and loved every cent of them.

'Paterson! Listen!'

'What *is* it?'

'Can you hear?'

'Of course I can hear.'

'Well, listen. I'm going to Japan next week with the Henry Bessemers.'

A low moan escaped Mr Frisby. His face, which was rather like that of a horse, twisted in pain. Of the broad principle of his sister going to Japan he approved, Japan being further away than New York. What rived his very soul was that she should be squandering her cash to tell him so. A picture postcard from Tokyo, with a cross and a 'This is my room' against one of the windows of a hotel, would so easily have met the case.

'Is that,' he asked in a strained voice, 'all you called up to say?'

'No. Listen.'

'I AM listening.'

'It's about Ann.'

'Oh, Ann?' said Mr Frisby, grunting to suggest that he found this a little better. His interest in his sister's affairs was tepid, but her daughter he rather liked. He had not seen her for some years, for the shifting of the centre of his business operations had taken him away from his native land, but he remembered her as a pretty girl with a pleasingly vivacious manner.

'Really, Paterson, I am at my wits' end about Ann.'

Mr Frisby grunted again, this time to indicate the opinion that she had not had to travel far.

'Paterson!'

'Well?'

'Listen.'

'I *am*—'

'I said I was at my wits' end about Ann.'

'I heard you.'

'Do you know what she did last week?'

Mr Frisby gave a lifelike imitation of a man who has just discovered that he is sitting on an ants' nest.

'How the devil should I know what she did last week? Do you think I'm a clairvoyant?'

'She refused Clarence Dumphry, the son of Mortimer J. Dumphry. She said he was a stiff. And Clarence is the nicest young fellow. He doesn't drink or smoke, and he will have millions some day. And do you know what she said to the Burwash boy?'

'Who *is* the Burwash boy?'

'Twombley Burwash. *You* know. The Dwight N. Burwashes. She told him she would marry him if he would hit a policeman.'

'Do what?'

'Hit a policeman.'

'What policeman?'

'Any policeman. She said he could choose his policeman. Naturally Twombley refused. He would not do anything like that. And it's that sort of thing all the time. I am in despair about getting her married and settled down, and I'm always in a state of the greatest alarm lest she may run off with someone impossible. She is so appallingly romantic. The ordinary young man isn't good enough for her, it seems. Oh dear, no! I asked her the other day what she did want, and she said something like a mixture of Gene Tunney and T. E. Lawrence and Lindbergh would do if he looked like Ronald Colman. So, as I am going to Japan, it seems an excellent opportunity to send her over to England for the summer. Perhaps if she has a London Season she may meet someone nice.'

Mr Frisby choked.

'Listen!' he said tensely, reckless of plagiarism. 'If you think you're going to plant her on me—'

'Of course not. A bachelor establishment like yours would be most unsuitable. She must have every chance of meeting the right people. I want you to put an advertisement in the papers, asking for a lady of title to chaperon her. Somebody she can live with and go around with.'

'Ah!' said Mr Frisby, relieved.

'And be careful what sort of a title you choose. Mrs Henry Bessemer was telling me about a friend of hers who advertised and got a Lady Something, and she turned out to be merely the widow of a man who had been knighted for being mayor of some town in Lancashire where the King opened a City Hall or something. Remember that the best kind always have a Christian name – Lady Agatha This or Lady Agatha That. That means that they're related to a Duke or an Earl.'

'All right.'

'It's very confusing, of course, but there seems nothing to be done about it. How is your lumbago?'

'I don't get it.'

'Don't be so silly. You know you're a martyr to it.'

'I mean I can't hear what you're talking about. Spell it.'

'How is your L for lizard, U for union, M for mayonnaise, B for . . .'

'My God!' cried Mr Frisby, deeply moved. 'Are you spending solid money to ask after that? It's better.'

'What?'

'Better – better – BETTER! B for blasted, E for extravagance, T for telephone, T for toll, E for extravagance again, and R for ruin. For Heaven's sake, woman, hang up that receiver before you have to go over the hill to the poorhouse.'

For some minutes after the tumult and shouting had died, Mr Frisby sat brooding and inactive. Then he reached out a hand to where a pair of detachable cuffs stood stacked beside the inkpot. A sloppy dresser, who aimed at comfort rather than elegance, he was in the habit of removing these before settling down to the day's work. And, as always happened with him in times of mental stress, their glistening surface invited literary composition. What his tablets are to the poet, his cuffs were to T. Paterson Frisby.

He picked up one of the horrible objects, and in a scrawling hand wrote the following *pensée*:

Josephine is a pest

The contemplation of this seemed to soothe him somewhat. And he was not altogether satisfied. He licked his pencil, and between the words 'a' and 'pest' inserted the addendum

gosh-darned

It made the thing ever so much better. Stronger. More striking. A writer's prose may come from the heart, but it is seldom that he does not need to polish, to touch up, to heighten the colour.

Content at last that he had given of his best, he hitched his chair forward a couple of inches and returned to his work.

He had been working for what seemed to him about a quarter of an hour, when he was informed that New York wanted him on the telephone again. And presently, across three thousand miles of land and water, there floated to his ears the musical voice of a young girl.

'Hello! Uncle Paterson?'

'Ugh.'

'Hello there, Uncle Paterson. This is Ann.'

'I know it.'

'Isn't it funny how distinctly you can hear!' said the voice chattily. ' It's just as if—'

'– You were sitting in the next room,' said Mr Frisby, sighing. 'I know. Get on. What is it?'

'What is what?'

Mr Frisby groaned quietly.

'What is it you want to say?' he asked, casting his eyes up in the direction of a Heaven which, he seemed to be feeling, ought never to have dreamed of allowing a good man to be persecuted like this.

Ann laughed happily.

'Oh, nothing special,' she said. 'I just came for the ride, so to speak. I'm simply talking. This is a treat for me. I've never called anyone up on the trans-Atlantic 'phone before. Isn't it fascinating to think that this is costing Mother about ten dollars a syllable? Uncle Paterson!'

'Ugh?'

'How's your lumbago?'

'Curse my lumbago!'

'I suppose you do,' said his niece sympathetically. 'But how is it?'

'Better.'

'That's fine. Has Mother been speaking to you?'

'Ugh.'

'Golly! What a bill there's going to be! Did she tell you she was sending me over to London?'

'Ugh.'

'I'm sailing on the *Mauretania* on Friday.'

'Ugh.'

'What's it like in London?'

'Punk.'

'Why?'

'Why not?'

'Well, it's going to look to me like my blue heaven,' said Ann decidedly. 'I never seem to meet anyone over here whose father isn't a multi-millionaire, and, I don't know why it is, rich men's sons are always the worst lemons in creation. Stiffs, every one of them. Besides, I've known them all since we were children together. I don't see how you can expect a girl to get warm and confused about somebody she's seen grow up from a sticky-faced kid in a Lord Fauntleroy suit. I want to meet someone different. I want romance. There must be romance somewhere in the world. Don't you think so, Uncle Paterson?'

'No!'

'Well, I do. What I'm looking for is one of those men you read about in books who meet a girl for the first time and gaze into her eyes and cry "My mate!" and fold her in their arms. And I shan't care if he's a stevedore and hasn't a penny in the world. Oh, by the way, Uncle Paterson, Mother says that if I marry anyone unsuitable while I'm in England, she will hold you strictly responsible. I thought you'd like to know.'

'Ring off!' cried Mr Frisby with extraordinary vehemence.

He replaced the receiver with a bang, looked at his cuffs as if contemplating a short character-sketch of his niece, felt unequal to the effort, and took another pepsine tablet instead. He cupped his chin in his hands, and stared before him into a future that was now darker than ever.

He remembered bitterly that when his sister had married he had been glad. He had put on an infernally uncomfortable suit of clothes and a stiff collar and had given her away at the altar. And he had been glad when the child Ann had been born. He had paid ungrudgingly for a silver christening-mug. And now the years had passed, and this had happened!

He knew the interpretation his sister would place on those

words 'strictly responsible' and 'unsuitable'. And he knew how her displeasure would manifest itself, should her daughter, while ostensibly in his charge, contract a matrimonial alliance of which she did not approve. She would rush over to London and cluck at him—

Something went off in his ear like a bomb. The telephone had selected this most unsuitable moment to ring again. Mr Frisby shied like a startled horse, and came up from the depths.

''Lo?' he gasped.

'Are you they-ah?' asked a voice. It was a female voice, and Mr Frisby, with some lingering remnants of chivalry, suppressed his customary answer to this question. Brought up in a land of civilized Hello's, he had never been able to take kindly to being asked if he was there.

'Mr Frisby speaking,' he said curtly.

'Oh?' said the voice. 'Good morning, sir. I wonder if you could tell me if Master Berry is wearing his warm woollies?'

The financier gulped painfully.

'Could I – what did you say?'

'Isn't that Mr Frisby that Mr Conway works for?'

'I have a secretary named Conway.'

'Well, would it be troubling you too much to ask him if he is wearing his warm woollies. You see, there's quite a snap in the air for the time of year, and he was always so delicate as a child.'

If the prophet Job had entered the room at that moment, T. Paterson Frisby would have shaken his hand and said, 'Old man, I know just how you must have felt.' A tortured frown darkened his brow. If there was one thing he disliked more than another in a world full of objectionable happenings, it was having his office staff get telephone calls on his personal wire. And when these calls had to do with the texture of their underclothing, the iron entered pretty deeply into his soul.

'Hold the line,' he said, in a low, strained voice.

He touched a button on the desk. This produced, first, a buzzing sound and, shortly afterwards, his private secretary, who advanced into the room, looking bronzed and fit.

Few people would have taken Berry Conway for anyone's private secretary. He did not look the part. Of course, it is not easy to lay down hard and fast rules as to just what a secretary's appearance should be, but one may at least expect it to be – broadly – secretarial. An air of reserved intellectuality might be anticipated. A touch of pallor and a pair of horn-rimmed glasses would not come amiss.

Berry Conway fell very short of the ideal. He was lean and athletic-looking. He had the appearance of a welterweight boxer who takes a cold bath every morning and sings in it. His face was clean-cut, and his figure slim and muscular. And Mr Frisby, even when not feeling as dyspeptic as he did at the present moment, had always in a nebulous sort of way resented this. It subconsciously offended him that anyone circling in his orbit should look so beastly strong and well. Berry was obviously hard stuff. He could have taken Mr Frisby up in one hand and eaten him at his leisure. And sometimes of an evening, when the day's work was over, he regretted not having done so, for Mr Frisby could make himself unpleasant.

He made himself unpleasant now.

'You!' he snapped. 'What do you mean, having your friends call you up here? Some female lunatic wants you on the 'phone. Answer it.'

The conversation that ensued was not a long one. The unseen lunatic spoke – urgently, if the humming of the wire was any evidence – and Berry, a dusky red in the face, and a more vivid red about the ears, replied: 'Of course I'm not – It's quite a warm day – I'm all right – I'm all *right*, I tell you!' and put down the instrument. He looked at his employer with shame written on every feature.

'I'm very sorry, sir,' he said. 'It was an old nurse of mine.'

'Nurse?'

'She used to be my nurse, and she has never been able to get it into her head that I'm not still a child.'

Mr Frisby gulped.

'She asked me – she asked *me* if you were wearing your warm woollies.'

'I know.' Berry blushed hotly. 'It shan't occur again.'

'Are you?' asked Mr Frisby, with pardonable curiosity.

'No,' said Berry shortly.

'Woof!' said Mr Frisby.

'Sir?'

'It's this darned indigestion,' explained the financier. 'Have you ever had indigestion?'

'No, sir.'

Mr Frisby eyed him malevolently.

'Oh? You haven't, haven't you? Well, I hope you get it – you and your nurse, too. Take a note. Niece. Lady of title. Papers.'

'I beg your pardon, sir?'

'Can't you understand plain English?' said Mr Frisby. 'My niece is coming over from America for the London Season, and her mother wants me to put an advertisement in the papers for a lady of title to chaperon her. Can't see what's hard to grasp about that. Should have thought that would have been intelligible to anyone with an ounce of sense in his head. Put it in *The Times* and *Morning Post* and so on. Word it how you like.'

'Yes, sir.'

'Right. That's all.'

Berry turned to the door. As he reached it, he paused. An idea had occurred to him. He was a kind-hearted young man, and liked, when possible, to do his daily Good Deed. It struck him that the opportunity had presented itself.

'Might I make a suggestion, sir?'

'No,' said Mr Frisby.

Berry was not to be discouraged.

'I only thought that what you require might be somebody like Lady Vera Mace.'

'Who?'

'Lady Vera Mace.'

'Who's she?'

'Lord Hoddesdon's sister. She married a man named Mace in the Coldstream Guards.'

'How do you come to know anything about her?'

'I was at school with her nephew, Lord Biskerton.'

Mr Frisby regarded his employee curiously.

'I don't understand you,' he said. 'You seem to mix with the Four Hundred, go to school with their nephews, and all that, and here you are working in my office on a—'

'Ridiculously small salary, sir? Very true. It's rather a sad story. I was adopted by a rich aunt, and she suddenly turned into a poor aunt.'

'Too bad,' said Mr Frisby, taking a pepsine tablet.

'If,' suggested Berry, 'you would care to make some practical demonstration of your sympathy, a small rise—'

'Changing the subject,' said Mr Frisby. 'Go to the devil.'

'Very good, sir. And about Lady Vera Mace?'

'Do you know her?'

'I met her once. She came down to the school one Saturday and stood us a feed. Coffee, doughnuts, raspberry vinegar, two kinds of jam, two kinds of cake, ice-cream, and sausages and mashed potatoes,' said Berry, in whose memory the episode had never ceased to be green.

It was not so green as Mr Frisby. His sensitive stomach had turned four powerful handsprings and come to rest, quivering.

'Don't talk of such things,' he said, shuddering strongly. 'Don't mention them in my presence.'

'Very good, sir. But shall I tell Lady Vera to apply?'

'If you like. No harm in seeing her.'

'Thank you very much, sir,' said Berry.

He went immediately to the telephone in the passage, and rang up the Drones Club. As he had supposed, Lord Biskerton was still on the premises.

'Hullo?' said the Biscuit.

'This is Berry.'

'Say on, old boy,' said the Biscuit, 'I'm with you. Talk quick, because you're interrupting a rather tense game of snooker. What's the trouble?'

'Biscuit, I think I can put you in the way of making a bit of money.'

The wire hummed emotionally.

'You can!'

'I think so.'

The Biscuit seemed to ponder.

'What do I have to do?' he asked. 'I'm not much good at murder, and I'm not sure if I can forge. I've never tried. But I'll do my best.'

'Old Frisby's niece is coming over from America for the Season. He wants someone to chaperon her.'

'Oh?' said the Biscuit disappointedly. 'And where do I come in? I suppose I apply for the job, cunningly disguised as a Dowager Duchess? I wish you wouldn't interrupt a busy man with this sort of drip, Berry. It isn't fair to raise a bloke's hopes, only to dash—'

'You poor ass, I was thinking that this was just the sort of thing that would suit your aunt.'

'Ah!' The Biscuit's tone changed. 'I begin to follow. I begin to see the idea. A job for Aunt Vera, eh? This sounds good. I take it there's money in this chaperoning, what?'

'Of course there is. Pots of money.'

'And she could do with it, poor, broken blossom!' said Lord Biskerton. 'It'll be like manna in the wilderness.'

'Well, ring her up and tell her about it. If it comes off she may give you a bit of the proceeds.'

'May?' said the Biscuit. 'How do you mean, may? I shall naturally insist on an exceedingly stiff commission, which you and I will, of course, split fifty-fifty – you having provided the commercial opening and I the aunt.'

'Not me,' said Berry. 'I'm not in on this. I'm just Santa Claus.'

Lord Biskerton seemed stunned.

'Berry! This is noble. That's what it is. Noble. It's the sort of thing Boy Scouts do. What a pal! Tell me, how do the chances look of the relative landing this extraordinarily cushy job?'

'Great, if she can apply early and get in ahead of the field.'

'I'll have her panting on the mat in half an hour.'

'Tell her to call at 6, Pudding Lane, and ask for Mr Frisby.'

'I will. And may Heaven reward you, boy, for what you have done this day. It's the first bit of joss that's come the family's way for years and years and years. I shall celebrate this. Eggs for tea tonight, my bucko!'

III

If Mr Frisby had been the sort of man who observes shades of emotion in his employees, he might have noticed in the demeanour of his private secretary at their recent encounter a certain unwonted gaiety, a brightness that was almost effervescent. Berry's was a buoyant temperament, easily stimulated by the passing daydream, and the more he had examined the Biscuit's counsel, the better it looked to him. It amazed him that through all these years he had never once thought of raising a little money on the Dream Come True.

Certainly, the thing had never produced enough copper to make a door-knob, but, as the Biscuit had so wisely pointed out, the world was full of mugs. The daily papers proved their existence every morning. They were all over the place, now purchasing a gold brick from some sympathetic stranger, anon rushing to give another stranger all their available assets to hold so that they might show their confidence in him.

It would not be a bad idea, he reflected, to ask his employer's advice on the matter. T. Paterson was, he knew, mixed up in Copper – he was President of Horned Toad, Inc. – and there were moments, in between his dyspeptic twinges, when he frequently became quite genial. It would be simple for a man of discernment to note the approach of one of these moments and put the necessary questions before the milk of human kindness ebbed again.

When he did find himself in Mr Frisby's presence again, however, it was to announce the arrival of Lady Vera Mace. The Biscuit's aunt was not the woman to dally when there was money in the air. She arrived at three-thirty sharp.

'Lady Vera Mace is here, sir,' said Berry. 'Shall I show her in?'

'Ugh.'

'And might I have a word with you later on a personal matter?'

'Ugh.'

Berry returned to his little room, and resumed his daydreams. From time to time he wondered how the interview was coming along. He hoped that the Biscuit's aunt was clicking. She needed the money, and she had once been kind to him as a schoolboy. Besides, the Biscuit would touch his commission, which would mean happiness all round.

She ought to get the job, he reflected. The passage of time, though it had prevented her recognizing him just now and resuming their ancient friendship, had been in other respects kind to Lady Vera Mace. She was still the rather formidably beautiful woman who had come down to the school years ago and stuffed him with food. Her voice was soft and silvery, her manner compelling. Unless he was greatly mistaken, she would rush T. Paterson off his feet and have him gasping for air in the first minute.

The sound of the buzzer broke in on his meditations. Answering its summons, he found his employer alone. T. Paterson Frisby was leaning back in his swivel-chair, looking, as far as a great financier ever can do, rather fatuous. An unwonted smile was on his lips, and it was a foolish smile. Also, there was a rose in his buttonhole which had not been there before.

'Eh?' he said, starting, as Berry entered.

'Yes, sir.'

'What do you want?'

'What do *you* want, sir? You rang.'

Mr Frisby seemed to come out of a trance.

'Oh! Yes. Take a note.'

'Yes, sir.'

'Pim's, Friday.'

'Sir?'

'I'm giving Lady Vera Mace lunch at Pim's on Friday,' translated Mr Frisby. 'She wants to see the Stock Exchange.'

'Yes, sir.'

'And those advertisements. Don't put 'em in. Not needed.'

'No, sir.'

'I have arranged with Lady Vera that she will chaperon my niece when she arrives.'

'Yes, sir.'

Mr Frisby seemed to return to his trance-like state. His eyes had half closed and he looked, though still pickled, almost human.

'That's a remarkable woman,' he murmured. 'She's done my dyspepsia good.'

'Yes, sir?'

'She said it was mainly mental,' proceeded Mr Frisby. He gave the impression of one soliloquizing with no thought of an audience. 'She said drugs are no use. What one ought to do, she said, is think beautiful thoughts. Let sunshine into the soul, she said. She said, "Imagine that you are a little bird on a tree. What would you do? You would sing. So"—'

He broke off. The shock of imagining himself a little bird on a tree appeared to have roused him to a sense of his position.

'Well, she's a very remarkable woman,' he said, almost defiantly. He blinked at Berry. 'What was that you were saying just now? Something about wanting to see me about something? What is it?'

Berry embarked upon his recital with some confidence. His employer's mood seemed to be admirably attuned to the giving of benevolent advice to his juniors. He had not seen him so gentle and amiable since the day Amalgamated Prunes had jumped twenty points at the opening of the market.

'It's about a mine, sir. A mine in which I am interested.'

'What sort of mine?'

'A copper mine.'

Mr Frisby's geniality became frosted over with a thin covering of ice.

'Have you been taking a flyer in Copper?' he asked dangerously. 'Let me tell you here and now, young man, that I won't have my office staff playing the market.'

Berry hastened to reassure him.

'I haven't been speculating,' he said. 'This mine is mine. A mine of my own. My mine. It belongs to me. I own it.'

'Don't be a damned fool,' said Mr Frisby severely. 'How the devil can you own a mine?'

'My aunt left it to me.'

For the second time that day, Berry sketched out his family history.

'Oh, I see,' said Mr Frisby, enlightened. 'Where is this mine?'

'Somewhere in Arizona.'

'What's it called?'

'The Dream Come True,' said Berry uncomfortably. He was wishing that its original owner, in christening his property, had selected a name less reminiscent of a Theme Song.

'The Dream Come True?'

'Yes.'

Mr Frisby sat forward in his chair and stared at his fountain-pen. He seemed to have fallen into a trance again.

'It has never produced any copper,' Berry went on in a rather apologetic voice. 'But I was talking to a man at lunch, and he said that if one looked round one could always find someone to buy a mine.'

Mr Frisby came to life.

'Eh?'

Berry repeated his remarks.

Mr Frisby nodded.

'So you can,' he said, 'if you pick the right sort of boob. And there's one born every minute.'

'I was wondering if you could advise me as to the best way of setting about—'

'You say this mine has never yielded?'

'No.'

'Well, you can't expect to get much for it, then.'

'I don't,' said Berry.

Mr Frisby took up his fountain-pen, gazed at it, and put it down again.

'Well, I'll tell you,' he said. 'Oddly enough, I know a man – Hoke's his name. J. B. Hoke – he might make you an offer. He does quite a bit in that line. Buys up these derelict properties on the chance of some day striking something good. If you like, I'll get in touch with him.'

'Thank you very much, sir.'

'I believe he's in America just now. I'll have to find out. Of course, he wouldn't look at the thing unless he could get it cheap. Well, anyway, I'll get in touch with him.'

'Thank you very much, sir.'

'You're welcome,' said Mr Frisby.

Berry withdrew. Mr Frisby took up the receiver and called a number.

'Hoke?' he said. 'Frisby speaking.'

'Yes, Mr Frisby?' replied a voice deferentially.

It was a fat and gurgly voice. Hearing it, you would have conjectured that its owner had a red face and weighed a good deal more than he ought to have done.

'Want to see you, Hoke.'

'Yes, Mr Frisby. Shall I come to your office?'

'No. Grosvenor House. About six.'

'Yes, Mr Frisby.'

'Be on time.'

'Yes, Mr Frisby.'

'Right. That's all.'

'Yes, Mr Frisby.'

IV

People summoned by Mr Frisby to interviews in his apartment at Grosvenor House always exhibited a decent humility. They seemed to indicate by their manner how clearly they realized that in this inner shrine they were standing on holy ground. The red-faced man who had entered the sitting-room at six precisely almost grovelled.

J. B. Hoke was one of those needy persons who exist on the fringe of the magic world of Finance and eke out a precarious livelihood by acting as 'Hi, you!' and Yes-men in ordinary to any of the great financiers who may wish to employ them. Willingness to oblige was Mr Hoke's outstanding quality. He would go anywhere you sent him and do anything you told him to do.

'Good evening, Mr Frisby,' said J. B. Hoke. 'How are you?'

'Never mind how I am,' said Mr Frisby. 'Got something I want you to do for me.'

'Yes, Mr Frisby.'

'You know I'm President of the Horned Toad Copper Corporation.'

'Yes, Mr Frisby.'

'Well, next door to it there's a small claim called the Dream Come True. It's been derelict for years.'

'Yes, Mr Frisby.'

'I've had a letter from my directors. They seem to want to take it over for some reason. We're putting in some developments on the Horned Toad and maybe they need the ground for workmen's shacks or something. They didn't say. I want you—'

'To trace the owner, Mr Frisby?'

'Don't interrupt,' said T. Paterson curtly. 'I know the owner. The thing belongs to my secretary, a man named Conway. He was left it by someone, he tells me. I want you to go to him and buy it for me. Cheap.'

'Yes, Mr Frisby.'

'I can't appear in the matter myself. If young Conway thought that Horned Toad Copper was after his property, he'd stick his price up at once.'

'Yes, Mr Frisby.'

'And there's no hurry about buying it. I told him I would mention it to you, and I said you were in America. You don't want to seem too eager. I'll tell you when to shoot.'

'Yes, Mr Frisby.'

'Right. That's all.'

T. Paterson Frisby gave a Napoleonic nod, to indicate that the interview was concluded, and J. B. Hoke, just falling short of knocking his forehead on the floor, retired.

Having left the presence, Mr Hoke went downstairs and turned into the passage leading to the American bar. A man who was sitting on a stool, sipping a cocktail, got up as he entered.

'Well?' he said.

He eyed Mr Hoke woodenly. He was one of those excessively smoothly shaved men of uncertain age and expressionless features whom one associates at sight with the racing world. It was on a racecourse that J. B. Hoke had first made his acquaintance. His name was Kelly, and in the circles in which he moved he was known as Captain Kelly, though in what weird regiment of irregulars he had ever held a commission nobody knew.

He drew Mr Hoke into a corner, and once more inspected him with a wooden stare.

'What did he want?' he asked.

J. B. Hoke's manner had undergone a change for the worse since leaving Mr Frisby's sitting-room. His gentle suavity had disappeared.

'The old devil,' he said disgustedly, 'simply wanted me to act as his agent in buying up some derelict copper mine somewhere.'

He chewed a toothpick morosely, for Mr Frisby's summons had excited him and aroused hopes of large commissions. He had come away a disappointed man.

'What does he want with a derelict mine?' asked Captain Kelly, his fathomless eyes still fixed on his companion's face.

'Says it's next door to his Horned Toad,' grunted Mr Hoke, 'and they want the ground for putting up workmen's shacks.'

'H'm!' said Captain Kelly.

'He didn't need me. An office-boy could have done all he wanted. Wasting my time!' said J. B. Hoke.

Captain Kelly transferred his gaze to a fly which had alighted on his sleeve and was going through those calisthenics which flies perform on these occasions. One could gather nothing from his face, but from the fact that he had ceased to speak Mr Hoke presumed that he was thinking.

'Well?' he said, not without a certain irritation. His friend's inscrutability sometimes irked him.

The Captain dismissed the fly with a jerk of the wrist.

'H'm!' he said again.

'What do you mean?'

'Sounds thin to me,' said the Captain.

'What does?'

'What he says he wants that property for.'

'Seemed all right to me.'

'Ah, but you're a fool,' the Captain pointed out dispassionately. 'If you want to know what I think, I'd say at a guess that a new reef of copper had been discovered.'

'Not on this claim,' said Mr Hoke. 'I happen to know the one he means. I was all over those parts a few years ago. I know this Dream Come True, which is its fool name. A fellow named Higginbottom, a prospector from Burr's Crossing, staked it out a matter of ten years back. And from that day to this no one's ever had an ounce of copper out of it. I shouldn't say it had ever been worked after the first six months.'

'But they've been working the Horned Toad.'

'Of course they've been working the Horned Toad.'

'Suppose they had struck a vein and found that it went on into this property next door?'

'Chee!' said Mr Hoke, his none too active brain stirring for the first time.

'I've heard of cases.'

'*I've* heard of cases,' said Mr Hoke.

He stared at his companion emotionally. Rainbow visions had begun to rise before him.

'I believe you're right,' he said.

'That's the way it looks to me.'

'There may be big money in this!'

'Ah!' said the Captain.

'Now, see here—' said Mr Hoke.

He lowered his voice cautiously and began to talk business. From time to time Captain Kelly nodded wooden approval.

CHAPTER 2

And so in due course, in the blue and apricot twilight of a perfect May evening, Ann Moon arrived in England with a hopeful heart and ten trunks and went to reside with Lady Vera Mace at her cosy little flat in Davies Street, Mayfair. And presently she was busily engaged in the enjoyment of all the numerous amenities which a London Season has to offer.

She lunched at the Berkeley, tea-ed at Claridge's, dined at the Embassy, supped at the Kit-Kat.

She went to the Cambridge May Week, the Buckingham Palace Garden Party, the Aldershot Tattoo, the Derby, and Hawthorn Hill.

She danced at the Mayfair, the Bat, Sovrani's, the Café de Paris, and Bray's on the River.

She spent week-ends at country-houses in Bucks, Berks, Hants, Lincs, Wilts, and Devon.

She represented an Agate at a Jewel Ball, a Calceolaria at a Flower Ball, Mary Queen of Scots at a Ball of Famous Women Through the Ages.

She saw the Tower of London, Westminster Abbey, Madame Tussaud's, Buck's Club, the Cenotaph, Limehouse, Simpson's in the Strand, a series of races between consumptive-looking greyhounds, another series of races between goggled men on motor-cycles, and the penguins in St James's Park.

She met soldiers who talked of horses, sailors who talked of cocktails, poets who talked of publishers, painters who talked of sur-realism, absolute form and the difficulty of deciding whether to be architectural or rhythmical.

She met men who told her the only possible place in London to lunch, to dine, to dance, to buy an umbrella; women who told her the only possible place in London to go for a frock, a hat, a pair of shoes, a manicure and a permanent wave; young men with systems for winning money by backing second favourites; middle-aged men with systems that needed constant toning-up with gin and vermouth; old men who quavered compliments in her ear and wished their granddaughters were more like her.

And at an early point in her visit she met Godfrey, Lord Biskerton, and one Sunday morning was driven down by him in a borrowed two-seater to inspect the ancestral country-seat of his family, Edgeling Court in the County of Sussex.

They took sandwiches and made a day of it.

CHAPTER 3

There are those who maintain that the inhabitants of Great Britain are a cold, impassive race, not readily stirred to emotion, and that to get real sentiment you must cross the Atlantic. These would have solid support for their opinion in the sharply contrasting methods employed by the *Courier-Intelligencer* of Mangusset, Maine, and its older-established contemporary, the *Morning Post* of London, Eng., in announcing – some six weeks after the date on which this story began – the engagement of Ann Moon to Lord Biskerton.

Mangusset was the village where Ann's parents had their summer home, and the editor of the *Courier-Intelligencer*, whose heart was in the right place and who had once seen Ann in a bathing-suit, felt – justly – that something a little in the lyrical vein was called for. This, accordingly, was the way in which he hauled up his slacks – and he did it, which makes it all the more impressive – entirely on buttermilk. For, though the evidence seems all against it, he was a life-long abstainer.

'The bride-to-be' (wrote ye Ed.) 'is a girl of wondrous fascination and remarkable attractiveness, for with manner as enchanting as the wand of a siren and disposition as sweet as the odour of flowers and spirit as joyous as the carolling of birds and mind as brilliant as those glittering tresses that adorn the brow of winter and with heart as pure as dewdrops trembling in a coronet of violets, she will make the home of her husband a Paradise of enchantment like the lovely home of her girlhood, so that the heaven-toned harp of marriage, with its chords of love and devotion and fond endearments, will send forth as sweet strains of felicity as ever thrilled the senses with the rhythmic pulsing of ecstatic rapture.'

The *Morning Post*, in its quiet, hard-boiled way, confined itself to a mere recital of the facts. No fervour. No excitement. Not a tremor in its voice. It gave the thing out as unemotionally as on another page it had stated that the Boys and Girls of Birchington Road School, Crouch End, had won the championship and challenge cup for infant percussion bands at the North London Musical Festival held in Kentish Town.

Thus:

MARRIAGE ANNOUNCEMENTS

'The engagement is announced between Lord Biskerton, son and heir of the Earl of Hoddesdon, and Ann Margaret, only child of Mr and Mrs Thomas L. Moon of New York City.'

Sub-editors get that way in London. After a few years in Fleet Street, they become temperamentally incapable of seeing any difference between a lot of infants tootling on trombones and a man and a maid starting out hand in hand on the long trail together. If you want to excite a sub-editor, you must be a Mystery Fiend and slay six with hatchet.

But if the *Morning Post* was *blasé*, plenty of interest was aroused among the public that supports it. In a hundred beds a hundred young men stopped sipping a hundred cups of tea in order to give that notice their undivided attention. To some of these the paragraph had a sinister and an ominous ring. They concentrated their minds, such as they were, on the frightful predicament of the bridegroom-elect: and, muttering to themselves 'My God!' turned to the Racing Page with an uneasy feeling that nowadays no man was safe.

But there were others – and these formed a majority – who sank back on their pillows and stared wanly at the ceiling – silk pyjama-clad souls in torment. They mused on the rottenness of everything, reflecting how rotten, if you came right down to it, everything was. They pushed aside the thin slice of bread and butter: and when their gentleman's personal gentleman entered babbling of spats, were brusque with them – in eleven cases telling them to go to the devil.

For these were the young men who had danced with Ann and dined with Ann and taken Ann to see the penguins in St James's Park, and who, if they had happened to read the Mangusset *Courier-Intelligencer*, would have considered the editor a writer of bald and uninspired prose who did not even begin to get a grasp of his subject.

Ann Moon, in her progress through the London Season, had undoubtedly made her presence felt. A girl cannot go about the place for a month and a half with a manner as enchanting as the wand of a siren without bruising a heart or two.

In the dining-room of The Nook, Mulberry Grove, Valley Fields, S.E.21, Berry Conway came on the notice while skimming the paper preparatory to the morning dash for London on the 8.45. He was finding some difficulty in reading, owing to the activities of the Old Retainer, who had a habit of drifting in and out of the room during breakfast, issuing the while a sort of running bulletin of matters of local interest.

Mrs Wisdom was plump and comfortable. She gazed at Berry with stolid affection, like a cow inspecting a turnip. To her, he was still the infant he had been when they had first met. Her manner towards him was always that of wise Age assisting helpless Youth through a perplexing world. She omitted no word or act that might smooth the path for him and shield him against life's myriad dangers. In winter, she thrust unwanted hot-water bottles into his bed. In summer, she would speak freely, not mincing her words, of flannel next to the skin and of the wisdom of cooling off slowly when the pores had been opened.

'Major Flood-Smith,' said the Old Retainer, alluding to the retired warrior resident at Castlewood, next door but one, 'was doing Swedish exercises in his garden early this morning.'

'Yes?'

'And the cat at Peacehaven had a sort of fit.'

Berry speculated absently on the mysteries of cause and effect.

'I hear Mr Bolitho's firm are sending him to Manchester. Muriel-at-Peacehaven told me. He wants to let Peacehaven, furnished. I think he ought to put an advertisement in the papers.'

'Not a bad idea. Ingenious.'

Something in the passage attracted Mrs Wisdom's attention. She drifted out, and Berry heard umbrella-stands falling over. Presently she drifted in again.

'After the Major had gone, his niece came out and picked some flowers. A sweetly pretty girl, I always say she is.'

'Yes?'

'And what's funny is, she was looking quite happy.'

'Why was that funny?'

'Why, Master Berry! Surely I told you about her? Her sad story?'

'I don't think so,' said Berry, turning the pages. She probably had, he thought, but she told him so much local gossip – taking, as she did, a ghoulish relish in every disaster that happened to everybody in the suburb – that he had developed a protective deafness.

Mrs Wisdom clasped her hands and threw up her eyes, the better to do justice to the big scoop.

'Well, really, I can't imagine how I came not to tell you. I had it all from Gladys-at-Castlewood, and she got it partly by listening while waiting at table and the rest of it one evening when the young lady came down to the kitchen and wanted to know if the cook could make something she called fudge and then she stayed on herself and made this fudge which seems to be a sort of soft toffee and told them her sad story while stirring up the sugar and butter.'

'Ah!' said Berry.

'The young lady has come over from America. Her mother is the Major's sister, who married an American, and they live in a place near New York which is called, though you can hardly believe it, Great Neck. Well, I mean, what a name to call a place. And Great Neck, it seems, Master Berry, is full of actors and the young lady, her name is Katherine Valentine, was foolish enough to think she had fallen in love with one of them and wanted to marry him and he wasn't anybody really as he only acted small parts and her father, of course, was furious, and he sent her over here to stay with the Major in the hope that she might be cured of her infatuation.'

'Ah?' said Berry. 'Good Lord! Look at this! The Biscuit has gone and jumped off the dock! Biskerton. Fellow I was at school with.'

'Committed suicide?' cried Mrs Wisdom, delightedly. 'How dreadful!'

'Well, not exactly suicide. He's engaged to be married to an

American girl. Ann Margaret, only child of Mr and Mrs Thomas L. Moon of New York.'

'Moon?' Mrs Wisdom wrinkled her forehead. 'Now I wonder if that is the same young lady Gladys-at-Castlewood told me Miss Valentine told her about. Miss Valentine travelled over on the boat with a Miss Moon, and I feel sure Gladys told me that she told her that her name was Ann. They became great friends. Miss Valentine told Gladys that her Miss Moon was a very nice young lady. Very pretty and attractive.'

'The *Morning Post* doesn't mention that. Still, if she's pretty and attractive, I may be wronging the Biscuit in thinking he is selling himself for gold.'

'Why, Master Berry! What a thing to say of a friend of yours.'

'Well, it's a bit of luck for him, anyway. I suppose this girl is rolling in money.'

'I hope you won't ever marry for money, dear.'

'Not me. I'm romantic. I'm one of those fellows who are practically all soul.'

'I often say it's love that makes the world go round.'

'I've never heard it put as well as that before,' said Berry, 'but I shouldn't wonder if you weren't absolutely right. Was that the clock striking? I must rush.'

George, sixth Earl of Hoddesdon, father of the bridegroom-to-be, did not see his *Morning Post* till nearly eleven. He was a late riser and paper-reader. Having scanned the announcement with silent satisfaction, fingering at intervals the becoming grey moustache which adorned his upper lip, he put on a grey top-hat, and went round to see his sister, Lady Vera Mace.

''Morning, Vera.'

'Good morning, George.'

'Well, I see it's in.'

'The announcement? Oh, yes.'

Lord Hoddesdon eyed her reverently.

'How did you work it?' he asked.

'I?' His sister raised her eyebrows. 'Work it?'

'Well, dash it,' said Lord Hoddesdon, who, like so many of England's aristocracy, was prone to be a little unenthusiastic about his offspring. 'Don't tell me that a girl like Ann Moon would accept a boy like Godfrey unless somebody had put in the deuce of a lot of preliminary spadework.'

'Naturally, I did my best to throw them together.'

'You would.'

'I told her as often as I could what a charming boy he was.'

'You said that!' exclaimed Lord Hoddesdon, incredulously.

'Well, so he is, when he likes to be. At any rate, he can be quite amusing.'

'He's never made me so much as smile,' said Lord Hoddesdon. 'Except once,' he corrected himself, 'when he tried to touch me for a tenner at Newmarket. Thank God he has found this girl.'

Once more he inflated the chest beneath his perfectly cut waistcoat. He sighed a sigh of exquisite contentment, and his handsome face glowed.

'It'll be the first time the family has seen the colour of real money,' he said, 'since the reign of Charles the Second.'

There was a pause.

'George,' said Lady Vera.

'Hullo?'

'I want you to attend to me very carefully, George.'

Lord Hoddesdon surveyed his sister almost affectionately. He was seeing everything through rose-coloured spectacles on this morning of mornings: but, even making the necessary allowances for that, he was bound to admit that she looked extraordinarily attractive. Upon his word, felt Lord Hoddesdon, she seemed to get handsomer all the time. He made a mental calculation. Yes, well over forty, and anyone might take her for thirty-two. A thrill of pride passed through him, heightened as he caught sight of his own reflection in the mirror. Whatever you might say about them, the family did keep their looks.

His second thought was that, much as he admired the flawless regularity of his sister's features, he was not at all sure that he liked the expression they were wearing at the moment. An odd expression. Rather hard. She reminded him of a governess who had rapped his knuckles a good deal when he was a child.

'I want you to remember, George, that they are not married yet.'

'Of course. Naturally not. Announcement's only just appeared in the paper.'

'And so will you, please,' proceeded Lady Vera, her beautiful eyes now definitely stony, 'abandon your intention of calling on Mr Frisby and asking him to oblige you with a small loan. It is just the sort of thing that might upset everything.'

Lord Hoddesdon gasped.

'You don't imagine I would be fool enough to go touching Frisby?'

'Wasn't that your idea?'

'Of course not. Certainly not. I was thinking – er – I was wondering – well, to tell you the truth, it crossed my mind that *you* might possibly be willing to part with a trifle.'

'It did, eh?'

'I don't see why you shouldn't,' said Lord Hoddesdon plaintively. 'You must have plenty. There's a lot of money in this chaperoning business. When you took on that Argentine girl three years ago you got a couple of thousand pounds.'

'I got fifteen hundred,' corrected his sister. 'In a moment of weakness – I can't imagine what I was thinking of – I lent you the rest.'

'Er – well, yes,' said Lord Hoddesdon, not unembarrassed. 'That is, in a measure, true. It comes back to me now.'

'It didn't come back to *me* – ever,' said Lady Vera, in a voice that sounded, though not to her brother, like the tinkling of silver bells.

There was another pause.

'Oh, well, if you won't, you won't,' said Lord Hoddesdon gloomily.

'No,' agreed Lady Vera. 'But I'll tell you what I will do. I was going to take Ann to lunch at the Berkeley, but Mr Frisby has rung up to ask me to motor down to Brighton for the day, so I will give you the money and you can look after her.'

Lord Hoddesdon felt a little like a tiger which has hoped for a cut off the joint and has been handed a cheese-straw, but he told himself with the splendid Hoddesdon philosophy that it was better than nothing.

'All right,' he said. 'I'm not doing anything. Hand over the tenner.'

'The what?'

'Well, the fiver or whatever it may be.'

'Lunch at the Berkeley,' said Lady Vera, 'costs eight shillings and sixpence. For two, seventeen shillings. Waiter, two shillings. Possibly Ann may like a lemonade or some water of some kind. Say two shillings again. Your hat-check, sixpence. For coffee and unforeseen emergencies, half a crown. If I give you twenty-five shillings, that will be ample.'

'Ample?' said Lord Hoddesdon.

'Ample,' said Lady Vera.

Lord Hoddesdon fingered his moustache unhappily. He was feeling now as Elijah would have felt in the wilderness if the ravens had suddenly developed cut-throat business methods.

'But suppose the girl wants a cocktail?'

'She doesn't drink cocktails.'

'Well, I do,' said Lord Hoddesdon mutinously.

'No, you don't,' said Lady Vera, her resemblance to the departed governess now quite striking.

Lord Biskerton was not a reader of the *Morning Post*. The first intimation he received that the announcement of his betrothal had appeared in print was when Berry Conway rang him up from Mr Frisby's office to congratulate him. He accepted his friend's good wishes in a becoming spirit and resumed his breakfast in a quiet and orderly manner.

He was busy on the marmalade when his father arrived.

It was not often that Lord Hoddesdon visited his son and heir, but in some mysterious way there had floated into his lordship's mind as he left Lady Vera's flat the extraordinary idea that Biskerton might possibly have a little cash in hand and be willing to part with some of it to the author of his being.

'Er – Godfrey, my boy.'

'Hullo, guv'nor.'

Lord Hoddesdon coughed.

'Er – Godfrey,' he said, 'I wonder – it so happens that I am a little short at the moment – I suppose you could not possibly—'

'Guv'nor,' said the Biscuit, amusedly. 'This is Today's Big Laugh. Don't tell me you've come to make a touch?'

'I thought—'

'What on earth led you to suppose I'd got a bean?'

'I fancied that possibly Mr Frisby might have made you some small present.'

'Why the dickens?'

'In celebration of the – er – happy event. After all, he is the uncle of your future bride. But, of course, if such is not the case—'

'Such,' the Biscuit assured him, 'is decidedly not. The old, moth-eaten fossil to whom you allude, guv'nor, is the one man in this great city who never makes small presents in celebration of any happy event. His family motto is *Nil desperandum* – Never give up.'

'Too bad,' sighed Lord Hoddesdon. 'I was hoping that you would be able to help me out. I am sorely in need of monetary assistance. Your aunt has asked me to take your *fiancée* to lunch at the Berkeley this afternoon, and her idea of expense-money is little short of Aberdonian. Twenty-five shillings!'

'Lavish,' said the Biscuit firmly. 'I wish somebody would give me twenty-five bob. I've just a quid to see me through to the end of the month.'

'As bad as that?'

'One pound, two and twopence, to be exact.'

'Still,' Lord Hoddesdon pointed out, 'you must remember that your prospects are now of the brightest. You have been wiser in your generation than I in mine, my boy.' He stroked his moustache and heaved another regretful sigh. 'As a young man,' he said, 'my great fault was impulsiveness. I should have married money, as you are sensibly doing. How clearly I see that now. And I had my opportunity – opportunity pressed down and running over. For months after I succeeded, wall-eyed heiresses were paraded before me in droves. But I was too romantic, too idealistic. Your poor mother was at that time a humble unit of the Gaiety Theatre company, and after I had been to see the piece in which she was performing sixteen times I suddenly noticed her. She was standing on the extreme O.P. side. Our eyes met – Not that I regret it for a moment, of course,' said Lord Hoddesdon. 'As fine a pal as a man ever had. On the other hand – Yes, you have shown yourself a wiser man than your old father, my boy.'

Several times during this address the Biscuit had given evidence of a desire to interrupt. He now spoke forcefully.

'I wish you wouldn't talk of Ann and wall-eyed heiresses without taking a long breath in between,' he said, justly annoyed. 'When you say I'm marrying money, it makes it sound as if the cash was all I cared about. Let me tell you, guv'nor, that this is love. The real thing. I'm crazy about Ann. In fact, when I think that a girl can be such a ripper and at the same time so dashed rich, it restores my faith in the Providence which looks after good men. She's the sweetest thing on earth, and if I had more than one pound, two and twopence I'd be taking her to lunch today myself.'

'A charming girl,' agreed Lord Hoddesdon. 'How did you ever induce her to accept you?' he asked, a father's natural bewilderment returning.

'It was Edgeling that did it.'

'Edgeling?'

'Edgeling. You may say what you like against our old ancestral seat, guv'nor – it costs a fortune to keep up and it's too big to let and a white elephant generally, but there's one thing about it – it's romantic. I proposed to Ann in the old bowling-green – we had driven down in Bobby Blaythwait's two-seater – and it's my belief there isn't a girl in the world who could have held out in a setting like that. Doves were cooing, bees were buzzing, rooks were cawing, and the setting sun was gilding the ivied walls. No girl could have refused a fellow in such surroundings. Believe me, whatever its faults, Edgeling has done its bit and deserves credit.'

'And, talking of credit,' said Lord Hoddesdon, 'it is pleasant to think that yours will now be excellent.'

The Biscuit laughed bitterly.

'Don't you imagine it for an instant,' he said vehemently. He indicated a pile of papers on the table. 'Look at those.'

'What are they?'

'Judgment summonses. If I hadn't a good, level head, I'd be in the County Court tomorrow.'

Lord Hoddesdon uttered a startled cry.

'You don't mean that!'

'I do. Those fellows are out for blood. Shylock was a beginner compared with them.'

'But, good God! Have you reflected? Do you realize? If you are taken into court, your engagement will be broken off. It is just the sort of thing that would appal a man like Frisby.'

The Biscuit held up a soothing hand.

'Have no fear, guv'nor. I have the situation well taped out. Trust me to take precautions. Look here.'

He went to a drawer, took something out, concealed himself for a swift instant behind the angle of the book-case, and emerged. And as he did so Lord Hoddesdon emitted a strangled cry.

He might well do so. Except for the fact that he possessed his mother's hair Lord Biskerton's appearance had never appealed strongly to the sixth Earl's aesthetic sense. And now with a dark wig covering that hair and a black beard of Imperial cut hiding his chin, he presented a picture so revolting that a father might be excused for making strange noises.

'Bought 'em at Clarkson's yesterday,' said the Biscuit, regarding himself with satisfaction in the mirror. 'On tick, of course. Some eyebrows go with them. How about it?'

'Godfrey – My boy—' Lord Hoddesdon's voice trembled, as a man's will in moments of intense emotion. 'You look terrible. Shocking. Ghastly. Like an international spy or something. Take the beastly things off!'

'But would you recognize me?' persisted his son. 'That's the point. If, say, you were Hawes and Dawes, Shirts, Ties and Linens, twenty-three pounds, four and six, would you imagine for an instant that beneath this shrubbery, Godfrey, Lord Biskerton, lay hid?'

'Of course I should.'

'I'll bet you wouldn't. No, not even if you were Dykes, Dykes and Pinweed, Bespoke Tailors and Breeches-Makers, eighty-eight pounds, five and eleven. And I'll tell you how I'll prove it. You say you and Ann are lunching at the Berkeley. I'll be there, too, at a table as near yours as I can manage. And if Ann lets out so much as a single "Heavens! It is my Godfrey!" I'll call a waiter, give him beard, wig, and eyebrows, instruct him to have them fricasseed, and eat them.'

Lord Hoddesdon uttered a faint moan and shut his eyes.

CHAPTER 4

I

With his usual masterful dash in the last fifty yards Berry Conway had beaten the 8.45 express into Valley Fields station by the split-second margin which was his habit. Alien though he felt the suburbs were to him, he possessed in a notable degree that gift which marks off suburbanites from other men – the uncanny ability always to catch a train and never to catch it by more than three and a quarter seconds. And, as those who race for early expresses to the City have sterner work to do en route than the observing of weather conditions, it was only after he had taken his seat and regained his breath and had leisure to look about him that he realized how particularly pleasant this particular day was.

It was, he perceived, a day for joy and adventure and romance. The sun was shining from a sapphire sky. Under its rays Herne Hill looked quite poetic. So did Brixton. And the river, as he crossed it, positively laughed up at him. By the time he reached Pudding Lane, he had come definitely to the conclusion that this was a morning which it would be a crime to waste cooped up in a stuffy office.

He had frequently felt like this before, but never had Mr Frisby appeared to see eye to eye with him. Hard, prosaic stuff had gone to the making of T. Paterson Frisby. You didn't find him flinging work to the winds and going out and dancing Morris dances in Cornhill just because the sun happened to be shining. As a rule, it was precisely those magic mornings of gold and blue that seemed to stimulate the old buzzard to perfectly horrid orgies of toil. 'C'mon now!' he would say, eyeing a sunbeam as if it wanted to borrow money from him, and on Berry would have to come.

But miracles do happen, if one is patient and prepared to wait for them. Just as Berry had finished sorting as dull a collection of letters as ever offended a young man's sensibilities on a glowing summer day, the door was flung open and there came in something so extraordinarily effulgent that he had to blink twice before he could focus it.

It was not merely that T. Paterson Frisby was wearing a suit of light grey flannel. It was not even the fact that he had a panama hat on his head and a Brigade of Guards tie round his neck that stupefied the observer. The really amazing thing about him was his air of radiant *bonhomie*. The man seemed positively roguish. He had gone gay. As Berry stared at him dumbly, a sort of spasm passed over T. Paterson Frisby's face, causing a hideous distortion. It was a smile.

''Morning, Conway!'

'Good morning, sir,' said Berry blankly.

'Anything in the mail?'

'Nothing of importance, sir.'

'Well, leave it all till tomorrow.'

'Till tomorrow?'

'Yes. I'm off to Brighton.'

'Yes, sir.'

'You can take the day off.'

'Thank you very much, sir,' said Berry.

He was stunned. Such a thing had never happened before. Not once in the whole course of his association with Mr Frisby had there ever been even the suggestion of such a thing. He could hardly believe that it was happening now.

'Got to start right away. Motoring. Shan't be back till this evening. Two things I want you to do. Go to Mellon and Pirbright in Bond Street and get me a couple of aisle seats for some good show tonight. Put them down to my account and have them sent to my apartment.'

'Yes, sir.'

'Tell them I want something good. They know what I've seen. And then go on to the Berkeley and book me a table for supper.'

'Yes, sir.'

'Table for two. Not too near the band.'

'Yes, sir.'

'Right. By the way, I knew there was something. I saw that man Hoke last night. I told him about that mine of yours. He's interested.'

A thrill shot through Berry.

'Is he, sir?'

'Yes. Oddly enough, he happens to know that particular property. Will you be in this evening?'

'Yes, sir.'

'I'll tell him to run down and see you. Between ourselves – don't let him know I told you – he will go to five hundred pounds.'

'He will!'

'He told me so. He was going to have tried for less, but I said that was your lowest figure. So, if you're satisfied, he'll bring down all the papers and you can get the thing settled tonight. And I won't charge you agent's commission,' said Mr Frisby chuckling like a Cheeryble brother.

Berry blinked. Exquisite remorse racked him when he thought that not once but several times in his private reflections he had labelled this golden-hearted man a fish-faced little slave-driver. He saw him now for what he was – an angel in disguise.

'I'm most awfully obliged, sir,' he stammered.

'You're welcome.'

'You really think he will give me five hundred pounds?'

'I know he will. Well, that's all. 'Morning,' said Mr Frisby and took his departure. It was as if both Cheeryble Brothers had left the office arm in arm.

For some moments after he had gone, Berry remained motionless. Motionless, that is to say, as far as his limbs were concerned. His brain was racing tempestuously.

Five hundred pounds! It was the key to life and freedom. Attwater's loan – he could repay that. The Old Retainer – he could fix her up so that she would be all right. And, when these honourable duties were performed, he would still have something in pocket to start him off on the path of Adventure.

He drew a deep breath. In body he was still in his employer's office, but in spirit he was making his way through the streets of a little sun-baked town that lay in the shadow of towering mountains. And as he passed along the natives nudged one another, awed.

'There he goes,' they were saying. 'See that man? Hard-Case Conway! They don't come any tougher.'

It was getting on for lunch-time when Berry, having completed the purchase of the theatre-tickets, sauntered from the emporium of the Messrs Mellon and Pirbright into the rattle and glitter of Bond Street once more.

The day seemed now to have touched new heights of brilliance. There was sunshine above, and sunshine in his heart. A magic ecstasy thrilled the air. He gazed upon Bond Street, fascinated.

To the *blasé* man about town and the jaded *boulevardier*, Bond Street at one o'clock in the afternoon at the height of the London Season is just Bond Street. But to a young man with romance in his soul, an unexpected holiday on his hands, and the prospect of freedom and adventure gleaming before him, it is Main Street, Baghdad. The feeling of being in the centre of things intoxicated Berry.

It was his practice, when walking in London, to look hopefully about him on the chance of exciting things happening. Nothing of the slightest interest had ever happened yet, and he had sometimes felt discouraged. But Bond Street restored his optimism. This, he felt, was a spot where anything might occur at any moment.

Here if anywhere, he said to himself, might beautiful women in slinky clothes sidle up to a man and slip into his hand the long envelope containing the Naval Treaty stolen that morning from a worried Foreign Office, mistaking him – on the strength of the carnation in his buttonhole – for Flash Alec, their accomplice. Whereas in Threadneedle Street or Valley Fields you might hang about all your life without drawing so much as a picture postcard.

Up and down the narrow street expensive automobiles were rolling, and the pavements were full of expensive-looking pedestrians. One of these had just elbowed Berry towards the gutter, when he became aware that a two-seater had stopped beside him. The next moment its occupant was addressing him in a strong foreign accent.

'Pardon me, but is it that you could dee-reck-ut me to Less-ess-ter Skervare?'

Berry looked up. It was not an exotically perfumed woman. It was a rather shocking-looking bounder with prominent eyebrows and a black beard of Imperial cut.

'Leicester Square?' he said. 'You turn to the left and go across Piccadilly Circus.'

'I tank you, sare.'

Berry stood staring after the car. The man had excited him. True, he had said nothing to suggest that he was not a perfectly respectable citizen, but there was something about him that gave one the idea that his pockets were simply bulging with stolen treaties. So Berry stood, gaping, and might have stood indefinitely, had not a hungry pedestrian, hurrying to his lunch, butted him in the small of the back.

Jerked into the world of practical things again by this shock, he made his way to the Berkeley to order Mr Frisby's supper table.

Mr Frisby was evidently a popular customer at the Berkeley. The mention of his name aroused interest and respect. A head-waiter who looked like an Italian poet assured Berry that all would be as desired. A table for two, not too near the band. Correct.

He then inquired with a charming deference if Berry proposed to take luncheon at the restaurant, indicated temptingly a small table at his side. And Berry was about to reply that such luxuries were not for him, when, turning to look wistfully at the table, he saw a sight that struck the words from his lips.

The bearded bounder was sitting not six feet away, tucking into smoked salmon.

Only for an instant did Berry hesitate. For a man of his

straitened means, lunch at a place like this would be a bold, one might almost say, a reckless and devil-may-care adventure. It would hit the privy purse one of the nastiest wallops it had received for many a long day. But Fate had gone out of its way to send him this Man of Mystery, and it would be making a churlish return for Fate's amiability if he were to reject him on the pusillanimous grounds of economy.

The man intrigued him. Obviously, he was a suspicious character. Nobody who wasn't would parade London in a beard like that. Moreover, after being definitely instructed to turn to the left and go across Piccadilly Circus, he had turned to the right and gone to the Berkeley. If that wasn't sinister, what was?

Berry sat down, and a subordinate waiter swooped on him with the bill-of-fare.

The bearded man was now eating some sort of fish with sauce on it. And Berry, watching him intently, became gripped by a suspicion that grew stronger each moment. That beard, he could swear, was a false one. It was so evidently hampering its proprietor. He was pushing bits of fish through it in the cautious manner of an explorer blazing a trail through a strong forest. In short, instead of being a man afflicted by nature with a beard, and as such more to be pitied than censured, he was a deliberate putter-on of beards, a self-bearder, a fellow who, for who knew what dark reasons, carried his own private jungle around with him, so that any moment he could dive into it and defy pursuit. It was childish to suppose that such a man could be up to any good.

And then, as if to confirm this verdict, there suddenly occurred a scene so suggestive that Berry quivered as he watched it.

Into the restaurant there had just strolled a distinguished-looking man of about fifty, stroking a becoming grey moustache. He spoke to the head-waiter, evidently ordering a table. Then, as he turned to go back to the anteroom where hosts at the Berkeley await their guests, his eye fell on the bearded man. He started violently, stared as if he had seen some horrible sight, as indeed he had, and crossed to where the other sat. A short conversation ensued, during which he appeared to be expostulating. Then, plainly shaken, he tottered out.

Berry leaned forward in his seat, thrilled. He had placed the bearded man now. He saw all. Quite obviously this must be The Sniffer, the mysterious head of the great Cocaine Ring which was causing Scotland Yard so much concern. As for the grey-moustached one, he would be an accomplice in high places, a Baronet of good standing, or perhaps a well-thought-of Duke, on whose reputation no suspicion of wrongdoing had ever rested. And his unmistakable agitation must have been caused by the shock of meeting The Sniffer in a place like this, where his beard might come unstuck at any moment and betray him.

'Go back to the underground cellar in Limehouse, where you are known and respected,' he had probably whispered feverishly. And The Sniffer, jeering – Berry had distinctly seen him jeer – had replied that he had already started his lunch and so would have to pay for it, anyway, and, risk or no risk, he was dashed if he intended to leave before he had had his eight bobs' worth.

Upon which, the other, well knowing his chief's stubbornness, had given up the argument and gone out, practically palsied.

The daydream was shaping well, and, had nothing occurred to interrupt it, would probably have continued to shape well. But a moment later all thoughts of The Sniffer had been driven from Berry's mind. The grey-moustached man had re-entered the room, and this time he was not alone.

Walking before him, like a princess making her way through a mob of the proletariat, came a girl. And at the sight of her,

Berry's eyes swelled slowly to the size of golf-balls. His jaw dropped, his heart raced madly, and a potato fell from his trembling fork.

For it was the girl he had been looking for all his life – the girl he had dreamed of on summer evenings when the Western sky was ablaze with the glory of the sunset, or on spring mornings when birds sang their anthems on dewy lawns. He recognized her immediately. For a long time now he had given up all hope of ever meeting her, and here she was, exactly as he had always pictured her on moon-light nights when fiddles played soft music in the distance.

He sat staring: and when the waiter broke in upon this holy moment to ask him if he would like a little cheese to follow, he found some difficulty in maintaining the Conways' high standard for courtesy.

II

In staring at Ann Margaret, only child of Mr and Mrs Thomas L. Moon of New York City, Berry Conway had no doubt been guilty of a breach of decorum. But it was a breach of which many, many young men in restaurants had been guilty before him. Ann Moon was the sort of girl at whom young men in restaurants have to summon all their iron will to keep from staring.

We have seen what the knowledgeable editor of the Mangusset *Courier-Intelligencer* thought of Ann, and it may be stated now officially that his description erred, if at all, on the side of restraint and understatement. Possibly through pressure of space, he had omitted one or two points on which he might well have touched and on which, to present the perfect portrait, he should have touched. The dimple in her chin, for instance, and the funny way in which that chin wiggled when she laughed. Still, in the matter of the wondrous fascination and the remarkable attractiveness and the disposition as sweet as the odour of flowers, he was absolutely right. Berry had noticed these at once.

Lord Hoddesdon had noticed them, too, and once again there crossed his mind a feeling of dazed astonishment that a girl like this, even under the influence of Edgeling Court in the gloaming, could ever have accepted that son of his who was now sitting two tables away crouched behind his zareba of beard.

However, the main thing on which he was concentrating his mind at the moment was the problem of how to keep Ann's share of the luncheon down to a reasonable sum. If he could only head her off any girlish excesses in the way of drinks and coffee the exchequer, as he figured it out, would just run to a cigar and a liqueur, for both of which he had a strong man's silent yearning.

'Something to drink, my dear?' he said, as the waiter approached and hovered.

Ann withdrew her gaze from the middle distance.

'No, thanks. Nothing.'

'Nothing,' said Lord Hoddesdon to the waiter, trying not to sing the word.

'Vichy?' said the waiter.

'Nothing, nothing.'

'St Galmier? Tonic Water? Evian?'

'No, thank you. Nothing.'

'Lemonade?' said the waiter, who was one of those men who never know when to stop.

'Yes, I think I would like a lemonade,' said Ann.

'I wouldn't,' advised Lord Hoddesdon earnestly. 'I wouldn't, honestly. Bad stuff. Full of acidity.'

'All right,' said Ann. 'Just some plain water, then.'

'Just,' said Lord Hoddesdon, looking the waiter dangerously in the eye, 'some plain water.'

He bestowed upon his future daughter-in-law the affectionate smile of a man who is two shillings ahead of the game. Charming, he felt, to find a girl nowadays who did not ruin her complexion and digestion with cocktails and wines and what not.

The smile was wasted on Ann. She did not observe it. She was looking out across the room again. The noise of music and chattering came to her as from a distance. Her father-in-law-to-be on the other side of the table seemed very far away. Once more she had become occupied with the train of thought which this discussion of beverages had interrupted. Ever since she had read in her paper that morning the plain, blunt statement that she was engaged to be married, she had been feeling oddly pensive.

There is about the printed word a peculiar quality which often causes it to exercise a rather disquieting effect on the human mind. It chills. It was only after seeing that announcement set forth in cold type that Ann had come to a full realization of the extreme importance of the step she was about to take and the extreme slightness of her acquaintance with the man with whom she was going to take it.

A sudden thirst for information seized her. She leaned towards her host.

'Tell me about Godfrey,' she said abruptly.

'Eh?' said Lord Hoddesdon, blinking. He, too, had been busy with his thoughts. He had been speculating as to the odds on and against the girl wanting coffee and wondering how a well-judged word about it being bad for the nerves would go. 'What about him?'

It was a question which Ann found difficult to answer. 'What sort of man is he?' she would have liked to say. But when you have agreed to marry a man, it seems silly to ask what sort of a man he is.

'Well, what was he like as a little boy?' she said, feeling that that was safe. Indeed, the words had a rather pleasantly naïve and *fiancée*-like ring.

Lord Hoddesdon endeavoured to waft his memory over scenes which he had always preferred to forget.

'Oh, the usual grubby little brute,' he said. 'I mean of course,' he added hastily, 'very charming, and lively and – er – boyish.'

He perceived that he had been within an ace of allowing his heart to rule his head, of permitting candour to overcome diplomacy. Greatly as he would have liked to pour a trenchant character-sketch of the young Biskerton into a sympathetic ear, he saw how madly rash such a course would be. Old grievances about jam on the chairs would have to remain unventilated. As his sister had pointed out, this girl and Biskerton were not married yet. It would be insanity to say anything to put her off. Knowing Biskerton as he did, it seemed to him that what she must be needing was encouragement.

'Boyish and vivacious,' he proceeded. 'Full of spirits. But always,' he said impressively, 'good.'

'Good?' said Ann with a slight shiver.

'Always the soul of honour,' said Lord Hoddesdon solemnly.

Ann shivered again. Clarence Dumphry had been the soul of honour. She had often caught him at it.

'Neither during his boyhood nor since,' went on Lord Hoddesdon, warming to his work and finding the going less sticky as he got into his stride, 'has he ever given me a moment's anxiety.' He glanced over his shoulder with a sudden nervous movement, as if expecting to see the Recording Angel standing there with pen and note-book. Relieved at discovering only a waiter, he resumed. 'He was never one of those young men who go about dancing half the night with chorus girls and so forth,' he said. 'I don't think he ever gambled, either.'

'You don't know that,' said Ann, refusing to abandon hope.

'Yes, I do,' replied Lord Hoddesdon glibly. 'Now I come to think of it, I asked him once, and he told me he didn't. If he had been in the habit of gambling, he would have said, "Yes, dad." That has always been his way – frank and manly. Whatever I asked him, it would be "Yes, dad" or "No, dad," looking me straight in the face. I remember once,' said Lord Hoddesdon, going off the rails a little, 'he smeared jam all over my chair in the library.'

'He did?' said Ann, brightening.

'Yes,' said Lord Hoddesdon. 'But,' he went on, recovering himself, 'he came straight to me and looked me in the face and said, "Dad, it was I who put that jam on your chair in the library. I'm sorry. I felt I had to tell you because otherwise somebody else might have been suspected."'

'How old was he then?'

'About ten.'

'And he really said that?'

'He really did.'

'And he's like that now?'

'Just like that,' said Lord Hoddesdon doggedly. 'A real, true-blue English gentleman, honourable to the core.'

Ann winced slightly, and returned to her reflections. She was thinking now about Edgeling Court, and not too cordially.

In attributing to the glamour of the family's ancestral seat his *fiancée*'s acceptance of his proposal of marriage, Lord Biskerton had shown penetration. Edgeling Court had had quite a good deal to do with it. Its old-world charm, Ann was thinking, had undoubtedly weakened that cool, clear judgment on which she had always prided herself – that Heaven-sent gift of level-headed criticism which enables girls to pass unscathed among the Clarence Dumphrys of this world. Those bees and doves and rooks, she realized, had conspired together to sap her defences, and here she was, engaged to be married to a true-blue English gentleman.

Ann pulled herself together. She told herself that she must not believe everything she heard. Quite likely Lord Biskerton had never really been a true-blue English gentleman. She had only his father's word for it. And, if he had been, it was quite possible that he had got over it. She liked him, she assured herself. He amused her. He made her laugh. They would be very happy together – very, very, very happy.

All the same, she wished that he was not quite such a total stranger. And, while it would be too much to say that she actually regretted the step she had taken, she could not help the thought that a girl who had become engaged so recently as she had done, ought to be feeling a little more comfortable in her mind. There was no denying that she was not conscious of that complete happiness and content which would have been fitting. She felt doubtful and disturbed – rather like a young author who has just put his signature to a theatrical manager's contract, and is wondering if all is quite well concerning that clause about the motion-picture rights.

'You're very quiet, my dear,' said Lord Hoddesdon.

Ann started.

'I'm so sorry. I was thinking.'

Lord Hoddesdon wavered on the brink of something about lovers' reveries, but decided not to risk it.

'This chicken's good,' he said, choosing a safer subject.

'Yes,' said Ann.

'A few more potatoes?'

'No, thank you.'

'You will have a sweet after this?'

'Yes, please.'

'And about coffee,' said Lord Hoddesdon. A grave look came into his clean-cut face. 'I don't know how you feel about coffee, but I always maintain that, containing, as it does, an appreciable quantity of the drug caffeine, it is a thing best avoided. Bad for the nerves. All the doctors say so.'

'I don't think I will have any coffee. As a matter of fact, I would like to go directly I have finished the sweet. If you don't mind my leaving you?'

'My dear girl, of course not. Not at all. I will just sit here and listen to the music. I may possibly have a cigar and a liqueur. Got some shopping to do?'

'No – but it's such a lovely day, I rather wanted to go for a run in my car. I've got it outside. I thought I would go down to the river somewhere.'

'Streatley is a charming spot. Or Sonning.'

'I somehow feel as if I want to get away and think today.'

'I understand,' said Lord Hoddesdon paternally. 'Naturally. Well, don't you bother about me. I'll just sit. I like sitting.'

Ann smiled, and looking out across the room again, immediately found her eye colliding with that of the young man in brown at the table by the wall – the seventh time this had happened since her arrival.

There were two reasons why Ann Moon, sitting where she did, should have caught Berry Conway's eye so frequently. One was that when she looked up she had to look in his direction, because in the only other possible direction there was seated a bearded man of such sinister and revolting aspect that, whenever her gaze met his, she recoiled as if she had touched something hot. And he was not only most unpleasant to look at, but in an odd way he reminded her the tiniest little bit of her betrothed, Lord Biskerton, and she found this disturbing.

The other reason was that, rebuke herself for the weakness though she might, she liked catching Berry's eye. The process definitely gave her pleasure. His eye seemed to her an interesting eye. It had, she noted, a kind of odd, smouldering, hungry sort of gleam in it – a gleam that might have been described as yearning. It was novel to her. None of the men she had met had ever had yearning gleams in their eyes. Clarence Dumphry, the well-known stiff, hadn't. Nor had the Burwash boy. Nor, for that matter, had Lord Biskerton. And it was a gleam she liked.

He intrigued her, this lean, slim young man with his keen face and fine shoulders. He had the air, she thought, of one who did things. He somehow suggested brave adventures. She could picture herself, for instance, trapped in a burning house and this young man leaping gallantly to the rescue. She could see herself assailed by thugs and this young man felling them with a series of single blows. That was the sort of man he seemed to her.

She wished she knew him.

Berry, at his table, was wishing even more heartily that he knew her. If his eye gleamed yearningly, it had every reason to do so. He was regretting passionately that Fate, having planned that he should feel about a girl the extraordinary flood of mixed emotions which were now making him dizzy, had not arranged that he should feel them about some girl with whom he might conceivably at some time become acquainted.

It was quite evident to him by now that he had happened upon the one member of the opposite sex who might have been constructed from his own specifications. If all the arrangements had been in his personal charge, there was not the smallest alteration which he would have made. Those eyes; that small, provocative nose; those teeth; that hair; those hands – they were all exactly right.

And for all the chance he had of ever getting to know her they might be on different planets.

Ships that pass in the night.

She was leaving now. So, as a matter of fact, was the bearded man. But Berry had ceased to waste thought on him. The bearded man had been eliminated by the pressure of competition. By this time, he was to Berry just a bearded man, if that.

It seemed to Berry that he might as well be leaving too. He called for his bill, and tried not to wince at the sight of it.

Out in the sunshine, Ann walked pensively towards her two-seater. She had parked it up near the Square. The bearded man had parked his somewhere up there, too, it appeared, for he now passed her, giving her, as he went, a swift, strange, sinister look. The resemblance to Lord Biskerton was even more striking than it had been at a distance in the restaurant. Seen close to, he might have been Lord Biskerton's brother who had gone to the bad and taken to growing beards.

The sight of him gave Ann a guilty feeling. In thought, she realized, she had not been altogether true to her Godfrey. She found, examining her soul, that she had been comparing him to his disadvantage with that strong, romantic-looking young man in brown, whose eye had seemed so yearning and who now, as she settled down at the wheel of her two-seater, jumped abruptly in beside her and in a voice that electrified every vertebra in her spine, whispered hoarsely:

'Follow that car!'

III

In addition to galvanizing her spine, this polite request had had the effect of causing Ann to bite her tongue. It was with tear-filled eyes that she turned, and in a voice thickened with anguish that she replied.

'Wock car?' asked Ann.

Berry did not reply immediately. His emotions at the moment were those of one who has just jumped into a pool of icy water and is trying to get used to it. He was still endeavouring to convince himself that it was really he who had behaved in this remarkable manner. Such is often the effect of acting upon impulse.

'Wock car?' said Ann.

Berry pulled himself together. He had started something, and he must go on with it.

'That one,' he said, pointing.

He would have been amazed, had he known that his companion was thinking what an attractive voice he had. To his ears, the words had sounded like the croak of an aged frog.

'The one with the bearded man in it?' said Ann.

'Yes,' said Berry. 'Follow him wherever he goes.'

'Why?' said Ann.

It is proof that she was no ordinary girl that she had not begun by asking this question.

Berry had not spent much of his valuable time in brooding on the bearded man for nothing. His answer came readily.

'He's wanted.'

'Who by?'

'The police.'

'Are you a policeman?'

'Secret Service,' said Berry.

Ann stepped on the accelerator. The sun was shining. The birds were singing. She had never felt so happy and excited in her life.

It charmed her to think that her long-range estimate of this young man had not been at fault. She had classed him on sight as one who lived dangerously and dashingly, and she had been right.

She quivered from head to foot, and her chin wiggled. At last, felt Ann Moon, she had met somebody different.

IV

Godfrey, Lord Biskerton, was also feeling in the pink.

'Tra-la!' he carolled as he steered his car into Piccadilly, and 'Tum tum ti-umty-tum,' he chanted, turning southwards at Hyde Park Corner. He was filled with the justifiable exhilaration which comes to a man who has made a great and momentous experiment and has seen that experiment not only come off but prove an absolute riot from start to finish.

In risking the trial trip of his beard and eyebrows (by Clarkson) at such a familiar haunt of his as the Berkeley, the Biscuit had known that he was applying the acid test. If nobody recognized him there, nobody would recognize him anywhere. Apart from the fact that he would be sitting in the midst of a platoon of his intimates, most of the waiters knew him well. In fact, the head-waiter had always treated him more like a younger brother than a customer.

And what had happened? Neither Ferraro nor any of his assistants had shown in his manner the slightest suggestion of Auld Lang Syne. They might have been saying to themselves 'Ha! A distinguished, bearded stranger!' They had certainly not been saying to themselves 'Well, well! What a peculiar appearance jolly old Biskerton has today!' Not one of them had spotted him. He had passed the scrutiny with honours.

And Ann. He had given her every opportunity. He had stared meaningly at her in the restaurant, and he had passed within a foot of her when going to depark his car. But she, too, had failed to penetrate his disguise.

And old Berry. That, he reflected complacently, had been his greatest triumph. 'Is it that you can dee-reck-ut me to Less-ess-ter Skervare?' Right in the open, face to face. And not a tumble out of the man.

To sum up, then. If all these old friends and acquaintances had been utterly unable to recognize him, what hope was there for the bloodsuckers with their judgment summonses – for Jones Bros, Florists, twenty-seven pounds, nine and six, or for Galliwell and Gooch, Shoes and Bootings, thirty-four, ten, eight?

A great relief stole over Lord Biskerton. Thanks to this A1 beard and these tried and tested eyebrows, he would be able to remain in London and go freely and without fear about his lawful occasions. Until this afternoon he had doubted whether this were possible. There had been pessimistic moments when he had seen himself having to fly to Bexhill or take cover in Wigan.

For the rest, it was a lovely day: the car was running sweetly:

and if he stepped on the gas a bit he would just be able to get to Sandown Park in time for the three o'clock race. He knew something pretty juicy for the three o'clock at Sandown and, thank Heaven, there were still a brace or so of bookies on the list who, though noticeably short on Norman blood, fully made up for the deficiency by that simple faith which the poet esteems so much more highly.

By the time he reached Esher, the Biscuit was trolling a gay stave. And it was as he approached the Jolly Harvesters, licensed to sell wines, spirits and tobacco, that there floated into his mind the thought that what the situation called for was a beaker of the best.

He braked the two-seater and went in.

V

In the car which was following him there had at first reigned a silence broken only by the whirring of the engine as Ann's shapely foot bore down on the accelerator. It was not until the Kingston by-pass had been reached that its two occupants substituted talk for meditation. Each had begun the journey borne down by weight of thought, and each had good reason to think.

Ann was a conscientious girl. Indeed, her conscience, the legacy of a long line of New England ancestors, had always had an unpleasant habit of spoiling for her many of the more attractive happenings of life. It had clawed her in the restaurant. It now bit her. It was a conscience that seemed to possess all the least likeable qualities of a wild-cat.

She could not deceive herself. Hers was essentially an honest nature, and she was well aware that, having pledged herself to marry Lord Biskerton, she had limited the scope of her actions. There are certain things which an engaged girl has not the right to do. Or, if she does them, she must not like doing them. As, for instance, catching the eye of strange young men in restaurants. As, for further instance, thinking long and earnestly about a strange young man whose eye she has caught in a restaurant and wishing she could get to know him. And, for a final instance, allowing such a young man to leap into her car and initiate what, despite its grim, official, Secret Service nature, Conscience persisted in describing as a joy-ride.

'Don't talk to me about the call of duty,' said Conscience, in its worst New England manner. 'You're liking it.'

And Ann had to admit that she was. Reluctantly, she was obliged to confess to herself that she had never felt happier since, at the age of fourteen, she had received a signed photograph from John Barrymore.

If the possession of parents with a great deal of money and a high social position has a defect, it is that it involves on a girl a rather sheltered and conventional life. Ann's, ever since she was old enough to remember, had been lived in a luxurious and somewhat narrow groove. A finishing-school in Paris, a series of seasons in New York, winters at Palm Beach or Aiken, summers in Maine or at Southampton . . . A cramping existence for a romantic soul.

The men she knew were well-groomed, handsome, polite, but – well, ordinary. Of a pattern. Sometimes she had to collect herself to remember which was which. This one beside her was something new.

Nevertheless, it was quite wrong of her – and she knew that it was quite wrong – to feel this extraordinary fluttering sensation. She should either have refused his extraordinary request, or if an excusable desire to assist the Secret Service of Great Britain had led her to comply with it, should have preserved a detached and impersonal attitude, as if she had been a taxi-driver.

So Ann drove on, and her conscience clawed her abominably.

As for Berry, it would be too much to say that anything in the nature of a real reaction had set in from the mood of rash impulsiveness which had spurred him on to take that sudden leap into this car. He still felt he had done the right thing. Looking back, he could find nothing in his conduct to deplore. Behaviour which in other circumstances might possibly have lain open to the charge of being slightly eccentric, became on a day like this normal and prudent. Had he not acted as he had done, this wonderful girl would have passed out of his life for ever. To prevent a tragedy so unthinkable, no course of action could be called injudicious.

Nevertheless, he was sufficiently restored to sanity to realize that his position might be described as one of some slight embarrassment. Like an enthusiastic but ill-advised sportsman in the jungles of India who has caught a tiger by the tail, he was feeling that he was all right so far, but that his next move would require a certain amount of careful thought.

And so, wrapped in silence, the car turned into the Kingston by-pass. The other car was bowling rapidly ahead over the smooth concrete. Where its occupant was going it was impossible to guess, but he was certainly on his way.

Berry was the first to break the silence.

'This is most awfully good of you,' he said.

'Oh, no,' said Ann.

'Oh, yes.'

'Oh, no.'

'Oh, but it is,' said Berry.

'Oh, but it isn't,' said Ann.

'Well, all I can say,' said Berry, 'is that I think it's most awfully good of you.'

These polite exchanges seemed to diminish the tension. Berry began to breathe again, and Ann went so far as to take an excited eye off the road and flash it at his face. Seen in profile, that face appealed to her strongly. Strenuous exercise and a sober life had given Berry rather a good profile, lean and hard-looking. There were little muscles over his cheekbones and a small white scar in front of the ear which had an attractive and exciting aspect. A bullet graze, Ann knew, would cause a scar just like that.

'Most girls would have been scared stiff,' said Berry.

'Well, I was.'

'Yes,' said Berry with rising enthusiasm. 'But you didn't hesitate. You didn't falter. You took in the situation in a second, and were off like a flash.'

'Who is he?' asked Ann breathlessly, peering through the wind-screen at the flying two-seater. 'Or,' she added, 'mustn't you say?'

Berry would have preferred not to say, but there was plainly nothing else to be done. The owner of a commandeered car has certain rights. He felt that it was fortunate that in his meditations in the restaurant he had gone so deeply into this question of the identity of the bearded bird.

'I think,' he said, 'he is The Sniffer.'

'The Sniffer?' Ann's voice was a squeak. 'What Sniffer? How do you mean, The Sniffer? Who is The Sniffer? Why The Sniffer?'

'The head of the great cocaine ring. They call him The Sniffer. If, that is to say, he is the man I suppose. He may be a perfectly innocent person—'

'Oh, I hope not.'

'– Who has the misfortune to resemble one of the most dangerous criminals at present in the country. But I feel sure it's the man himself. You have probably heard how the drug traffic has been increasing of late?'

'No, I haven't.'

'Well, it has. And it is this man who is responsible.'

'The Sniffer?'

'The Sniffer.'

There was silence for a moment. Then Ann drew a deep breath.

'I suppose all this seems very ordinary to you,' she said. 'But I'm just quivering like an aspen. You take it just as a matter of course, I suppose?'

Young men in Old England do not possess New England consciences. There is the Nonconformist conscience, but Berry was not subject even to that. He replied not only steadily, but with a quiet smile.

'Well, of course, it is all in the day's work,' he said.

'You mean this sort of thing is happening to you all the time?'

'More or less.'

'Well!' said Ann.

It was a personal question, she felt, but she could keep it in no longer.

'How did you get that scar?' she asked breathlessly.

'Scar?'

'There's a little white scar just in front of your ear. Was that caused by a bullet that grazed you?'

Berry swallowed painfully. Girls bring these things on themselves, he felt. Look at Othello and Desdemona. Othello hadn't dreamed of saying all that stuff about moving accidents by blood and field, of hair-breadth 'scapes i' the imminent deadly breach, until that girl dragged it out of him with her questions. Othello knew perfectly well that when he talked of the Cannibals that each other eat and the men whose heads grow beneath their shoulders he was piling it on. But what could he do?

And what, in a similar situation, could Berry Conway do?

'It was,' he said, and felt that from now on nothing mattered.

'Coo!' said Ann. 'It must have come pretty close.'

'It would have come closer,' said Berry, his better self now definitely dead, 'if I had fired a second later.'

'You fired?'

'Well, I had to.'

'Oh, I'm not blaming you,' said Ann.

'I saw his hand go to his pocket....'

'Whose hand?'

'Jack Malloy's. It was when I was rounding up the Malloy gang.'

'Who were they?'

'A gang of men who went in for arson.'

'Fire-bugs?'

'That's it,' said Berry, wishing he had thought of the word himself. 'They had a headquarters in Deptford. The Chief sent me there to spy out the ground, but my beard came off.'

'Were you wearing a beard?'

'Yes.'

'I don't think I should like you in a beard,' said Ann critically.

'I never wear one,' Berry hastened to explain, 'unless I'm rounding up a gang.'

'How many gangs have you rounded up?'

'I forget.'

'It must be very interesting work, rounding up gangs.'

'Oh, it is.'

'Look!' said Ann. 'The Sniffer's gone into that inn.'

Berry followed her gaze.

'So he has.'

'What are you going to do?'

This was a point which was perplexing Berry, also. In the exhilaration of this ride, he had rather overlooked the fact that sooner or later it would be necessary to do something.

'Well. . .' he said.

Inspiration came to him, as it had come to Lord Biskerton. The afternoon was of a warmth that turned the thoughts in that direction. He would go in and have a drink.

'Would you mind waiting here?' he said.

'Waiting?'

She saw a cold, stern look come into his face.

'I'm going in after him.'

'Well, can't I come in, too?'

'No. There may be unpleasantness.'

'I like unpleasantness.'

'No,' said Berry firmly. 'Please.'

Ann sighed.

'Oh, very well. Have you got your gun?'

'Yes.'

'Well, have it ready,' said Ann, 'and don't fire till you see the whites of his eyes.'

Berry disappeared. He walked, Ann thought, just like a blood-hound. Leaning back against the warm leather, she gave herself up to delicious meditation. It was the first time anything of this kind had happened to Ann Moon. Never before had she been even in so much as a night-club raid. The only occasion on which she had ever touched lawlessness and crime had been once on the road between New York and Piping Rock, when a motorcycle policeman had handed her a ticket for exceeding the speed-limit.

And then suddenly in the midst of her ecstasy something hard and sharp dug into the roots of her soul.

'Hey!' said Conscience unpleasantly, resuming work at the old stand. 'Just a moment!'

VI

The saloon-bar of the Jolly Harvesters at the moment of Lord Biskerton's entry was unoccupied save by a robust lady in black satin with the sunlight, or something similar, in her hair, and a large brooch athwart her bosom with the word 'Baby' written across it in silver letters. She stood behind the counter, waiting, like some St Bernard dog on an Alpine pass, to give aid and comfort to the thirsty. She smiled genially at the Biscuit and favoured him with a summary of the weather.

'Nice day,' she said.

'Of the best,' agreed the Biscuit cordially.

A foaming mug changed hands, and they fell into that pleasant, desultory chat which is customary on these occasions.

The art of exchanging small-talk across the counters of saloon-bars is not given to everybody. Many of the world's finest minds have lacked the knack. The late Herbert Spencer is a case in point. But the Biscuit was in his element. He was at his best with barmaids. He had just the right manner and said just the right things. He was, moreover, a good listener. And as every barmaid has a long, complicated tale of grievances against her employer to tell, this gift is almost more valuable than that of easy speech.

By the time he had quaffed a quarter of a pint of Surrey ale, relations of cordial intimacy had been established between his hostess and himself. So much so that the former at last felt justified in giving the conversation a more personal turn. Right from the start she had had a critical eye on the beard, but until now her natural breeding had kept her from anything in the shape of verbal comment.

'Why ever do you wear that beard?' she asked.

'It's the only one I've got,' said the Biscuit.

'It looks funny.'

'Don't you like it?

'Oh, I've nothing against it. It looks funny, though.'

'It would look a lot funnier,' argued the Biscuit, 'if it was half green and half pink.'

The barmaid considered this and was inclined to agree.

'Well, it does look funny,' she said.

'Do you know how I got this beard?' asked the Biscuit.

'Grew it, I suppose.'

'Not at all. Far from it. Very much otherwise. It's a long story and reflects a good deal of discredit on some of the parties concerned. When I was a baby, you must know, I was a beautiful little girl. But one day my nurse took me out in my perambulator and stopped to talk to a soldier, as nurses will, and when her back was turned a wicked gipsy sneaked out of the bushes, carrying in her arms an ugly little boy with a beard. And do you know what she did? She stole me out of my perambulator and put that ugly little boy with a beard in my place. And ever since then I've been an ugly little boy with a beard.'

'Pity she didn't leave a razor, too.'

'Razors are no use,' said the Biscuit. 'They just fall back blunted and discouraged. So do barbed-wire clippers. One doctor I consulted advised me to set fire to the thing. I pointed out that this might possibly destroy the growth but that I also must inevitably perish in the conflagration. He seemed impressed and said he never thought of that. The whole affair is most unpleasant and constitutes a very difficult problem.'

'Well, do you know what I'd have done, if you had come in here a few years ago when everybody was doing it?'

'What?'

'I'd have said "Beaver" and gone like this.'

She reached out and gave the beard a hearty tweak. As she did so she chuckled merrily.

It was the last chuckle she was to utter for days and days. Indeed, many people say she was never quite herself again. Berry, turning the door handle at that moment, stood transfixed as a piercing scream smote his ears. It sounded like part of a murder. He snatched the door open, and once more stood transfixed. In fact, he was now, if anything, a trifle more transfixed than he had been before.

The spectacle he beheld was enough to transfix anyone. Behind the counter, holding a beard of Imperial cut in her hand, stood a barmaid. She seemed upset about something. In front of the counter, also ill at ease, stood his old school friend, Lord Biskerton. Berry stared. Many a time had he had nightmares much less weird than this.

The next moment, the picture in still life had dissolved. Snatching the beard from the barmaid, the Biscuit replaced it hurriedly on his face. And the barmaid, uttering a long, whistling sigh, fell over sideways in what appeared to be a ladylike swoon.

The Biscuit, though kindly disposed to the barmaid and ranking her among those whose conversation he enjoyed, was not feeling fond enough of her to remain and apply first aid. He wished to be elsewhere, and that right speedily. He turned, bounded towards the door, saw Berry and stopped in mid-stride.

'Biscuit!' cried Berry.

'Oh, my God!' said Lord Biskerton.

With no further comment for the moment, he seized Berry by the arm and hurried him along the passage. Only when they were in the privacy of the stable-yard, concealed from view by a stone wall, did he pause for speech.

'What on earth are you doing here, Berry?'

'What are you?'

'I was on my way to Sandown. What brought you here?'

'I followed you to see what you were up to.'

'How do you mean, up to?'

'Well, dash it,' said Berry, 'when you go charging about all over London and the home counties in a long beard...'

The Biscuit was registering deep concern.

'Do you mean to say,' he faltered, shaken, 'that you recognized me all along?'

It was not for Berry to dispel this idea. A swift thinker, he saw that he had been given the choice of appearing in the light of a shrewd and lynx-eyed observer and of a gullible chump. He chose the former.

'Of course I recognized you,' he said stoutly.

'Not in Bond Street?' pleaded the Biscuit.

'Certainly.'

'You mean, right from the start, directly I spoke to you?'

'Of course.'

'Well, why didn't you say so?'

'I was humouring you, you old ass.'

'Humouring me?'

'Yes. I thought you would be disappointed if you didn't imagine you had fooled me.'

'Gosh!' said the Biscuit, in the depths.

'What was the idea?'

'Berry,' said the Biscuit, his voice shaking. 'Do you suppose that Ferraro and everybody at the Berkeley knew who I was?'

'I suppose so.'

'Well, all I can say is,' said the Biscuit, 'this opens up a new line of thought.'

He followed this line of thought for a while in silence.

'I bought that beard to deceive my creditors,' he explained at length. 'There's a whole pack of them baying on my trail, and I thought that if I could assume some impenetrable disguise I could go about London undetected. But you say you saw through the thing at once?'

'In a flash.'

'Then what it comes to,' said Lord Biskerton despondently, 'is that I shall have to leave the metropolis after all. I daren't risk being jerked before a tribunal and having my financial condition X-rayed in the County Court. I must lie low somewhere. Bexhill, perhaps. Southend, possibly. But, good Lord! How am I to explain?'

'Explain?'

'Well, dash it, I shall have to give some explanation of why I've suddenly disappeared. I've just got engaged to be married. My *fiancée* will be a little surprised, won't she, if I vanish off the map without a word.'

'I never thought of that,' said Berry.

'I only just thought of it myself,' admitted the Biscuit handsomely. 'How would it be to write and tell her I've broken my leg and am confined to bed? No. She would come and see me, complete with flowers and grapes. Of course she would. Silly of me. Dash it, this is complex.'

'I know,' said Berry. 'Mumps.'

'What?'

'Say you've got mumps. She won't come near you then.'

The Biscuit patted his shoulder with a trembling hand.

'Genius,' he said. 'Absolute genius, probably inherited from male grandparent. You've solved it, old boy. The only thing to decide now is where shall I go? I must go somewhere. I shall sell a few trinkets to obtain a bit of the ready for necessary expenses, and then fly at dead of night to – well, where? It must be somewhere in the wilds. No good a place like Brighton, for instance. Dykes, Dykes and Pinweed probably spend their week-ends in Brighton. Bexhill? I don't know. Hawes and Dawes have most likely got bungalows there. I believe Wigan would be safest, after all.'

The history of this summer day has shown already that Berry Conway's brain was at its nimblest. Ever since Mr Frisby had breezed into the office and given him the freedom of the city, he had been in a highly stimulated cerebral condition. To this must be attributed the inspiration which seized him now.

'Biscuit,' he said, 'I've got it. The fellow who lives next door to me – Bolitho, his name is, not that it matters – has had to leave suddenly for Manchester...'

'He been having unpleasantness with his creditors, too?' asked Lord Biskerton sympathetically.

'He wants to let his house, furnished. You could walk right in. I'll see him this evening, if you like. Or he may have gone already. Anyway, I could fix things through the house agent. That's the thing for you to do. Nobody would ever find you in

Mulberry Grove. You could lie low there for the rest of your life. And we should be next door to one another.'

'Prattle across the fence of an evening?' cried the Biscuit enthusiastically.

'That's it.'

'Gossip about the neighbours! Borrow each other's garden roller!'

'Exactly.'

'Berry, old boy,' said Lord Biskerton, 'you've hit it. That male grandparent of yours must have been a perfect mass of brain cells. I expect they ran excursion trains to see him. Fix up the details and drop me a line at my flat. Drop it dashed soon, mark you, because it's only a matter of days before I shall feel the hot breath of Dykes, Dykes and Pinweed on the back of my neck. I'm going to enjoy life in the suburbs. Get a nice rest.'

'I'll have everything settled tonight.'

'God bless you! A true friend, if ever man had one. And now,' said the Biscuit, 'I suppose I had better be getting back to that unfortunate female and explaining that I'm on my way to a fancy-dress garden-party or something. She had a severe shock, poor child, when the fungus came away in her hands. But no doubt I shall be able to smooth things over. How did you get down here, by the way?'

'In a car,' said Berry guardedly.

'Your own?'

'No.'

'Hired, eh? Well, I think I will remain lurking here till you've proceeded a parasang or two. Common prudence suggests the course. I owe a bit here and there at various garages, and your bloke may quite possibly be attached to one of them. So forgive me if I don't come to see you off.'

'I will.'

'What's the name of this desirable residence I'm renting?'

'Peacehaven.'

'Peacehaven!' said the Biscuit. 'The very sound of the word is balm. In passing, old boy, the fine old crusted title will have to go, I'm afraid. No mention of the Sieur de Biskerton if you don't mind. Tell this bird Bolitho that a Mr Smith wishes to take his shack, with use of bath. One of the Smithfield Smiths. Right. And now to trickle back and comfort Baby. When I left her, poor lamb, she was snorting like a steam-engine and turning blue round the nostrils.'

VII

Berry came out of the Jolly Harvesters, smiling contentedly. He had his plan of action perfectly shaped. He would tell the girl that the suspect had cleared himself, had proved not to be The Sniffer after all. And then he and she would drive off into Fairy-land together and talk together of all those things which suit a perfect summer day.

A good programme, he felt. Even an admirable programme.

But programmes are notoriously subject to alteration without warning. Suddenly, abruptly, as if he had received some deadly stroke, the smile faded from his face, and he stared about him with a fallen jaw.

The car had disappeared.

CHAPTER 5

About the entry of Lord Biskerton into the suburb which was to be his temporary home there was nothing that savoured even remotely of the ostentatious or the spectacular, no suggestion whatever of a conquering king taking seisin of subject territory. He behaved from the start like one desirous of attracting as little attention to himself as possible. A purist might even have considered him furtive.

Having partaken of an early lunch at his club, he stole out on to the front steps, looked keenly up and down the street with his hat well over his eyes, and then, leaping into a passing taxi, drove to Victoria, where he caught the one-fifty-nine. Only when the train rolled out of the station did he allow himself to relax. Unless Dykes, Dykes and Pinweed were hiding under the seat, he was now safe.

Valley Fields, when he reached it a short while later, came as an agreeable surprise. Essentially urban in his prejudices, the Biscuit had always thought of the Surrey-side suburbs, when he thought of them at all, as grim and desolate spots where the foot of white man had not trod nor the Gospel been preached. Valley Fields, sunlit and picturesque, struck him as distinctly jolly. With its pleasant gardens and leafy trees, it had something of the air of a village, and he was puzzled to see what there was about the place to arouse his friend Berry Conway's dislike.

The very station had the look of a country station. Grass banks sloped away from it, gaily decorated with cabbages, beets, and even roses. Not to mention four distinct beehives. The Biscuit came to the conclusion that Berry did not know a good thing when he saw it. Why, Valley Fields, as far as a cursory inspection would allow him to judge, appeared to be the sort of place an American song-writer would have wanted to go back, back, back to. It was in excellent humour that he called at the offices of Messrs Matters and Cornelius, House Agents, for the keys of his new domain.

Mr Cornelius welcomed him paternally. He was an old gentleman of Druidical aspect with a long, white beard at which the Biscuit, that connoisseur of beards, looked with respectful envy. Full of patriotic spirit where Valley Fields was concerned, Mr Cornelius approved of those who wished to come and live there.

'A most desirable property,' he assured the Biscuit. 'A bijou bower of verdure. The house is a beautifully appointed modern residence, fitted with every up-to-date convenience and in perfect order.'

'Company's own water?' asked the Biscuit, keenly.

'Certainly.'

'Both H and C?'

'Quite.'

'The usual domestic offices?'

'Of course.'

'And how about the estate?'

'Peacehaven,' said Mr Cornelius, 'has park-like grounds extending to upwards of an eighth of an acre.'

'What happens if you get lost?' asked the Biscuit, interested. 'I suppose they send St Bernard dogs in after you.'

He proceeded on his way, and came presently to his journey's end, Mulberry Grove. And his contentment deepened. For his eye, as he approached, was caught by what appeared to be a most admirable pub just round the corner. He went in and tested the beer. It was superb. Every explorer knows that the most important thing in a strange country is the locating of the drink supply: and the Biscuit, satisfied that this problem had been adequately solved, came out of the hostlery with a buoyant step, and a moment later the full beauties of Mulberry Grove were displayed before him.

In the course of a letter to the *South London Argus* exposing the hellhounds of the local Gas Light and Water Company, Major Flood-Smith of Castlewood had once referred to Mulberry Grove as a 'fragrant backwater'. He gave the letter to his parlour-maid to post, and she forgot it and found it three weeks later in a drawer and burned it, and the editor would never have printed it, anyway, as it was diametrically opposed to the policy for which the *Argus* had always fearlessly stood, but – and this is the point we would stress – in describing Mulberry Grove as a fragrant backwater the Major was dead right.

Mulberry Grove was a tiny *cul-de-sac*, bright with lilac, almond, thorn, rowan and laburnum trees. There were only two houses in it – Castlewood (detached) and a building of the same proportions next door which some years earlier had been converted into two semi-detached residences, The Nook and Peacehaven. The other side of the road was occupied by a strip of ornamental water, with two swans on it – reading from left to right, Egbert and Percy. And the general effect of rural seclusion was completed by the fact that the back-gardens of the houses terminated in the verdant premises of the Valley Field Lawn Tennis Club. There was, in short, a pastoral charm about the place which – to quote Major Flood-Smith once again – made it absolutely damned impossible for you to believe that you were only seven miles from Hyde Park Corner – or if a crow, only five.

Nothing marred the quiet peace of Mulberry Grove. No policeman ever came near it. Tradesmen's boys, when they entered it on tricycles, hushed their whistling. And even stray dogs, looking in with the idea of having a bark at the swans, checked themselves with an apologetic cough on seeing where they were and backed out respectfully.

The Biscuit was well pleased with the place.

'O. jolly K.,' he said to himself.

And, pausing for an instant to throw a banana skin at the swan Percy, who had stretched out his neck and was making a noise like an escape of steam and appeared generally to be getting a bit above himself, he passed on and came to a gate on which was painted in faded letters the word:

PEACEHAVEN

Peacehaven was a two-storey edifice in the Neo-Suburbo-Gothic style of architecture, constructed of bricks which appeared to be making a slow recovery from a recent attack of jaundice. Like so many of the houses in Valley Fields, it showed what Montgomery Perkins, the local architect, could do when he put his mind to it. It was he, undoubtedly, who was responsible for the two stucco Sphinxes on either side of the steps leading to the front door.

Where Nature had collaborated with Mr Perkins, the result was more pleasing. A merciful rash of ivy had broken out over one half of the building, and a nice box hedge ran along the front fence. Substantial laurel-bushes stood here and there, and there were flowers bordering the short snail-walk which Mr

Cornelius would most certainly have described as a sweeping carriage-drive.

To the right, shaded by a rowan tree, was a latticed door, leading apparently to the back premises. And the Biscuit, with a nature-lover's eagerness to set his eye roaming over the park-like grounds, made for it immediately.

He passed through and, having passed, paused, not exactly spellbound but certainly surprised. Digging energetically in one of the borders with a spade not so very much smaller than herself was a girl.

Nothing in Mr Cornelius's conversation had prepared the Biscuit for girls in the park-like.

'Hullo!' he said.

The digger ceased to dig. She looked up, and straightened herself.

'Hello!' she replied.

A man who has so recently become engaged to be married as Lord Biskerton has, of course, no right to stare appreciatively at strange girls. But this is what the Biscuit found himself doing. The fact that Ann Moon had accepted his hand had done nothing to impair his eyesight, and he could not fail to note that this girl was an exceptionally pretty girl. Her blue eyes were resting on his: and what the Biscuit felt was, as far as he was concerned, let the thing go on.

Something – perhaps the fact that she was a blonde and he a gentleman – seemed to draw him strangely to this intruder.

'Are you anybody special?' he asked. 'I mean, do you go with the place?'

'Are you Mr Smith?'

'Yes,' said the Biscuit.

'Pleased to meet you,' said the girl.

Her voice had that agreeable intonation which he had noticed in a slighter degree in the voice of his betrothed.

'You're American, aren't you?' asked the Biscuit.

She nodded, and a bell of gold hair danced about her face. Very attractive, the Biscuit – quite improperly – thought it. At the same time she made an observation which was neither 'Yep,' 'Yup,' nor 'Yop,' but a musical blend of all three.

'I've just come over from America,' she said.

This was undoubtedly the moment at which the Biscuit should have been frank and candid. 'Ah!' he should most certainly have remarked in a casual tone. 'An odd coincidence. My *fiancée* is also American.'

Instead of which, he said:

'Oh? And how were they all?'

'I'm visiting with my uncle at Castlewood,' said the girl. 'Over there,' she indicated with a sideways shake of the golden bell. 'I came over the fence. Your garden looked awful. It hadn't had a thing done to it in weeks, I should think. If there's one thing that gives me the megrims, it's a neglected garden. I've been trying to get it straight.'

'Frightfully good of you,' said the Biscuit. 'The real Girl Guide spirit. I'm glad you like gardening. I fancy it's going to be one of my hobbies. We must do a bit of spade and trowel work together.'

'You're just moving in, aren't you?'

'Yes. My things came down the day before yesterday. I expect old Berry has fixed them all up neatly by now. He said he would.'

'Berry?'

'Squire Conway of the Nook. His property marches with mine.'

'Oh? I haven't met Mr Conway.'

'Well, you've met me,' said the Biscuit. 'Isn't that enough of a treat for a small girl about half the size of a peanut?'

He paused. He perceived that he was allowing his tongue to run away with him. A newly engaged man, conversing with blue-eyed girls, should be austerer, more aloof.

'Nice day,' he said, primly.

'Fine.'

'Making a long stay over here?'

'I shouldn't wonder.'

'Capital!' said the Biscuit. 'And what might the name be?'

'What name?'

'Yours, of course, fathead. Whose did you think I meant?'

'My name is Valentine.'

'And the Christian name, for purposes of informal chat?'

'Kitchie.'

'Caught cold?' asked the Biscuit.

'I was telling you my name. It's Kitchie.'

Something of sternness crept into the Biscuit's gaze.

'You needn't think that just because I've got one of those engaging, open faces you can kid me,' he said. 'I'm pretty intelligent, let me tell you, and I know the difference between a name and a sneeze. Nobody could possibly be called Kitchie.'

'Well, I am. It's short for Katherine. What's your first name?'

'Godfrey. Short for William.'

'Well,' said the girl, who during these conversational exchanges had been eyeing his upper lip with some intentness, 'let me just tell you one thing. You ought to do something about that moustache of yours – either let it grow or cut it off. At present it makes you look like Charlie Chaplin. If you'll excuse me being personal.'

'Replying to your remarks in the reverse order,' said the

Biscuit, 'be as personal as you desire. If two old buddies like us can't be frank with one another, who can? In the second place, I see no harm in resembling Charlie Chaplin, a man of many sterling qualities whom I respect. Thirdly, I *am* letting it grow – in moderation and within due bounds. And, finally, the object under discussion is not a moustash, you poor Yank, it is a moustarsh. These points settled tell me how you like England. Enjoying your visit, are you? Glad you came?'

'I like it all right. I wish I was back home, though.'

'Oh? Where's that?'

'Great Neck, New York.'

'And you wish you were there?'

'I certainly do.'

'Why "certainly"?' asked the Biscuit, nettled. 'What an extraordinary girl you must be. Here you are, having an absorbing conversation with one of the best minds in Valley Fields – and that best mind, mark you, wearing a new suit made by the finest bespoke tailor in London, and you say you wish you were elsewhere. Inexplicable! What is there so wonderfully attractive about Great Neck?'

Kitchie's blue eyes clouded.

'Mer's there,' she said.

'Ma? Your mother, you mean?'

'I didn't say Ma. I said Mer. Merwyn Flock. The boy I'm engaged to. Dad got sore because Mer's an actor, and he sent me over to England to get me away from him. Now do you understand?'

The Biscuit understood. Yet, oddly, he was not pleased. To an engaged man the news that a golden-haired, blue-eyed girl he has just met is an engaged girl ought to be splendid news. It ought to make him feel that he and she belonged to a great fellowship. He ought to feel like a brother hearing joyful tidings about a sister. Lord Biskerton felt none of these things. Utterly immersed though he was in a wholehearted worship of his *fiancée*, the information that this girl before him was also betrothed made him feel absolutely sick.

'Merwyn Flock!' he said, and clenched his teeth to say it.

'You ought to hear Mer play the uke!'

'I don't want to hear Mer play the uke,' said Lord Biskerton vehemently. 'I wouldn't listen to him playing the uke if you paid me. Merwyn! Ha!'

'That's all right, you standing there saying "Merwyn",' said Miss Valentine with equal warmth. 'It's a darned sight better name than Godfrey.'

It struck the Biscuit that he was allowing the tone of conversation to become acrimonious.

'I'm sorry,' he said. 'Don't let's quarrel. Cheer up, half-portion, and let us speak of other things. Tell me your impressions of England. What's it like living at Castlewood? Jolly? Festive?'

'Not so very. And I expected it would be a bigger place. When I was told I had an uncle living in a house called Castlewood, I thought it was going to be a sort of palace.'

'Well, so it is. It's got a summer-house, and a bird-bath. What more do you want? And, if you're disappointed, what about me? What's become of the civic welcome I was entitled to expect? Where are the villagers?'

'What villagers?'

'I always understood that a chorus of villagers turned out on these occasions to welcome the new Squire with dance and song. It won't be long before I find myself believing that I have no seigneurial rights at all. How about that, by the way?'

'What about it?'

'Well, for one thing, as I came along here I noticed a sort of lake or mere across the road. Do I own the fishing? And the swanning, what of that? I shall most certainly want to have a pop at those swans with my bow and arrow very shortly.'

The girl was looking at him earnestly.

'You know,' she said, 'when you talk quick, you remind me of Mer. His nose twitches like that.'

It was on the tip of Lord Biskerton's tongue to say something so scathing and devastating about Mer that the friendship ripening between this girl and himself would have withered like a juvenile crocus in an early blizzard. At this moment, however, he perceived out of the corner of his eye that strange things were going on in Castlewood.

'I say,' he said, directing his companion's attention to these phenomena. 'there's an extraordinarily ugly little devil in an eyeglass next door, glaring and waving his hands at one of the windows.'

'That's my uncle.'

'Oh? I'm sorry.'

'It isn't your fault,' said the girl kindly.

The Biscuit surveyed the human semaphore with interest.

'What is it? Swedish exercises?'

'I expect he wants me to come in. Now I remember, when I said I was thinking of coming over into your garden, he told me that I wasn't on any account to stir a step till he had called on you and seen what you were like. I suppose I'd better go.'

'But I was just going to ask you to come in and see my little home. I expect there are all sorts of things in it that call for the feminine touch.'

'Some other day. Anyway, I've some letters to write. A girl I met on the boat has just got engaged, I see in the paper. I must write and congratulate her.'

'Engaged!' said the Biscuit gloomily. 'It seems to me that the whole bally world is engaged.'

'Are you?'

'Me!' said the Biscuit, starting. 'I say, I think you had better rush. Uncle seems to be hotting up.'

He stood where he was for a moment, admiring the nimble grace with which his small friend shinned over the fence. Then, pondering deeply, he made his way into the house to ascertain what sort of a dump this was into which Fate and his creditors had thrust him.

That night, smoking a friendly cigarette with his next-door neighbour, John Beresford Conway of the Nook, Lord Biskerton, somewhat to his companion's surprise, spoke with warm approbation, rising at times to the height of enthusiasm, of the home-life of the Mormon elder.

A Mormon elder, said the Biscuit, had the right idea. His, he considered, was the jolliest life on earth. He also stated that in his opinion bigamy, being, as it was, merely the normal result of a generous nature striving to fulfil itself, ought not to be punishable at law.

'And what you've got against Valley Fields, old boy,' he said, 'is more than I can see. I don't know when I've struck a place I liked more. I consider it practically a Garden of Eden, and you may give that statement to the Press, if you wish, as coming from me.'

He then relapsed into a long and thoughtful silence, from which he emerged to utter a single word.

It was the word 'Merwyn!'

CHAPTER 6

I

It was hardly to be expected that Lord Biskerton's dis-
appearance from his customary haunts should have gone un-
noticed and unmourned by the inhabitants of his little world.
Hawes and Dawes felt it deeply. So did Dykes, Dykes and
Pinweed and the rest of his creditors. They or their representatives called daily at the empty nest, only to be informed by
Venner, the Biscuit's trusted manservant, that his lordship had
left Town and that it was impossible to say when he would
return. Upon which they took their departure droopingly, feeling, as so many poets have felt, that there is no tragedy like the
tragedy of the vanished face.

The Earl of Hoddesdon was another of those whom the young
man's flight distressed. He went round to see his sister about it.

'Er – Vera.'

Lady Vera Mace raised a shapely hand.

'No, George,' she said, 'not another penny!'

Lord Hoddesdon's aristocratic calm was shaken by a spasm of
justifiable irritation.

'Don't sit there making Stop and Go signals at me,' he snapped.
'You aren't a traffic policeman.'

'Nor am I a moneylender.'

'I didn't *come* to borrow money,' cried his lordship, passionately. 'I came to discuss this lunacy of Godfrey's.'

'It is annoying that Godfrey should have got mumps,' said Lady Vera, who was a fair-minded woman, 'but I fail to see...'

Lord Hoddesdon ground the teeth behind his grey moustache. In their nursery days he would have found vent for his emotion by hitting his sister on the side of the head or pulling her pigtail. Deprived of this means of solace by the spirit of *Noblesse oblige* and the fact that the well-coiffured woman does not wear a pigtail, he kicked a chair. The leg came off, and he felt better.

'Never mind the dashed chair,' he said, as Lady Vera fell to lamentation over the wreck. 'This business is much more important than chairs. I've been round to Godfrey's flat and I've got the truth out of that man of his, that fellow Venner. The boy hasn't got mumps. He's living down in the suburbs.'

'Living down in the suburbs?'

'Living down in the suburbs. Under the name of Smith. At Peacehaven, Mulberry Grove, Valley Fields. Venner told me so. He's forwarding letters there.'

Lady Vera forgot the chair.

'Is he mad?' she cried.

'No,' Lord Hoddesdon was forced to admit. 'He's doing it to keep from being County-Courted by, as far as I can make out, about a hundred tradesmen. As far as that goes, his conduct is sensible. At any rate, it's a lot better than going about London in a false beard, which was what he wanted to do. What is the behaviour of a lunatic is this telling the girl he's got mumps.'

'I don't understand what you mean.'

'Why, use your intelligence, dash it. She must have accepted him from some sort of passing whim, and it was vital that he refrained from doing anything to make her think it over and regret. And he goes and tells her he's got mumps. Mumps! Of all infernal, loathsome things. How long do you think that girl is going to cherish her dream of a knightly lover, when every time she thinks of him it is to picture a hideous object with a face like a football, probably with flannel wrapped round it? I shouldn't wonder if she isn't weakening already.'

'George!'

'It's maddening. When there are a dozen things he could have told her. That's what makes my blood boil. If he had consulted me, I could have suggested a hundred alternatives. He could have said that he thought of going into Parliament and that he had to go and live in this beastly suburb to nurse the constituency. She would never have seen through that. Or he could have invented a dying relative in Ireland or Mentone or Madeira. But, no! He has to go and say that he's swelling horribly in bed at his flat. I shouldn't wonder if the girl hasn't changed her mind already. You've been seeing her every day. How is she? Thoughtful? Have you caught her musing lately? Meditating? Like a girl who's been turning things over in her mind and has come to the conclusion that she has made a grave mistake?'

Lady Vera started.

'It's odd that you should say that, George!'

'It isn't at all odd,' retorted Lord Hoddesdon. 'It's what any sensible, far-seeing man would say. What makes you call it odd?'

'She *has* been thoughtful lately. Very thoughtful.'

'Good God!'

'Yes. I have noticed it. Several times lately, when we have been dining quietly at home, I have seen a curious, pensive expression come into her face. I've seen just the same look in my dear Sham-Poo's eyes when he has heard the coffee-cups rattle outside. He is so devoted to coffee sugar, the darling.'

'Don't talk to me about Sham-Poo,' said Lord Hoddesdon vehemently. He was not an admirer of his sister's Pekingese. 'If you have anything to say about Sham-Poo, tell it to the vet. For the moment oblige me by concentrating upon this girl Ann Moon.'

'I am simply telling you,' replied his sister with spirit, 'that there was the same look in her eyes as there is in Sham-Poo's when he thinks of coffee sugar. As if she were dreaming some beautiful dream.'

'But, dash it, that's all right, then. I mean, if all she is doing is dreaming beautiful dreams . . .'

Lady Vera crushed his rising hopes. Her face was very grave.

'But, George, consider. Would a girl who was thinking of Godfrey look as if she were dreaming a beautiful dream?'

'Good Lord, no. That's right. You mean . . . ?' exclaimed his lordship, quivering from head to foot as the frightful significance of his sister's words came home to him. 'You don't mean . . . ?'

Lady Vera nodded sombrely.

'Yes, I do. I think Ann has met somebody else.'

'Don't say such awful things, Vera!'

'Well, I really do believe that is what has happened. She gave me the impression of a girl who was wondering about something. And what would she have to wonder about except whether she had made a mistake in accepting Godfrey and wouldn't be doing better to break the engagement and leave herself free to marry this new man?'

Lord Hoddesdon fought stoutly against a sea of fears.

'Don't talk of "this new man", as if he really existed. You can't know. You're only guessing.'

'I have a woman's intuition, George. Besides . . .'

'But who could it be? Where would she have met him? I know she goes out to lunches and dinners and dances every day and meets a thousand men, but they're all exactly like Godfrey. I can't tell these modern young fellows apart. Nobody can. They all look alike and think alike and talk alike. It's absurd to suppose that any one of them could suddenly exercise an overwhelming spell over her. If she had been to a prize-fight or something and had conceived a sudden passion for some truck-horse of a chap just because his muscles bulged, I could understand it. But why should a girl want to change one Biskerton for another Biskerton? When I said just now she might be thinking of breaking the engagement, it never occurred to me that she could be planning to marry anybody else. I simply feared that she might give Godfrey his *congé* and go back to America.'

'Well, let me tell you a very curious thing, George. You remember the day you took Ann to lunch at the Berkeley?'

'What about it?'

'I happened to meet Lady Venables that night, and she asked me who the young man was that she saw driving along Piccadilly with Ann in her car. She said it was nobody she knew, and she knows every young man in London.'

'What!'

'A very good-looking man, she said, with a strong, handsome face. She was certain he wasn't anybody she had ever met. And, as I say, Lady Venables gives so many parties, trying to get Harriet off, poor dear, that by this time in the Season there isn't a single young man anywhere in Mayfair that she doesn't at least know by sight. She takes a regular census and works through it. So, if she really did see Ann with anyone, it must have been somebody no one knows anything about – this prize-fighter of yours, for instance.'

Lord Hoddesdon had been pacing the floor. He sat down abruptly.

'You're making my flesh creep, Vera!'

'I'm sorry. I'm simply telling you.'

'And Godfrey supposed to be in bed with mumps! What are we to do?'

'The first thing is obviously to see Godfrey and tell him of the risk he is running by staying away of losing Ann altogether. I think that, tradesmen or no tradesmen, he ought to come back.'

'How can he come back? The girl thinks he's ill in bed.'

'He could say that the doctor found he had made a mistake. Lots of things look like mumps at first. Toothache makes your face swell.'

'A chill in the facial muscles,' said Lord Hoddesdon, inspired.

'Yes, that would do.'

'But what about all these fellows who want to County-Court him?'

'Something could be arranged about that. Surely, now that they know that he is engaged to the daughter of a millionaire . . .'

'Yes, that's true.'

'Well, he must at least get in touch with Ann again, and immediately. So that he can at any rate write to her. Perhaps if she kept getting letters from him it would help. I think he ought to tell her that he has had to go to Paris. Perhaps he might really go to Paris, and then she could go to Paris, too.'

'Where's the money to come from?'

'I could manage that.'

'You could?' said Lord Hoddesdon, eagerly. 'Then, while we are on the subject . . .'

'No,' said Lady Vera firmly. 'I said I could manage enough to send Godfrey to Paris, but I refuse to subsidize you, George.'

'I only want twenty pounds.'

'When you leave this flat, you will still be wanting it.'

'It isn't much,' said Lord Hoddesdon wistfully. 'Twenty pounds.'

'It is twenty pounds more than you are going to get out of me,' replied his sister.

'All right,' said his lordship. 'All right. No harm in asking, was there?'

'I am always delighted to have you ask, George,' said Lady Vera. 'At any time. Whenever you want money, I hope you will always ask me. You won't get it, of course.'

Lord Hoddesdon took a pull at his moustache.

'Then, shelving that for the moment,' he said, 'you think I ought to go and see Godfrey?'

'I consider it essential. Ann is a very impulsive girl, and even now it may be too late.'

'I wish you wouldn't talk like that, Vera,' said Lord Hoddesdon irritably. 'You seem to take a joy in looking on the dark side. Very well, then. I will go down to this infernal suburb. Or shall I write him a letter?'

'No. You express yourself so badly in letters. He would never understand how vital the thing was. Go down to Valley Fields at once and see him personally.'

'And the money for the taxi?'

'What taxi?' said Lady Vera.

She found a railway time-table and began to turn its pages briskly. Lord Hoddesdon watched her with a growing dislike. He had his own rigid, old-fashioned ideas of how a sister should behave to a brother, and Lady Vera outraged them. He was just letting his mind drift off into a reverie in which there figured a wonderful dream-sister whose leading qualities were a big bank-balance, a cheque-book, an intense fondness for her brother and scribbling-itch, when he was called back to the sternly practical by the sound of her voice.

'"Frequent trains from Victoria,"' read Lady Vera. 'So you had better start at once. And do contrive, if you can possibly manage it, not to bungle the thing. The fare, first class, is one and a penny.'

'Oh? You're sure,' said Lord Hoddesdon bitterly, 'you wouldn't rather I went third class?'

'You must please yourself entirely, George,' said Lady Vera equably. 'You will be paying for the ticket.'

II

The manifold beauties of Valley Fields, which had so impressed his son and heir on his first introduction to them, made a weaker appeal to the sixth Earl of Hoddesdon. Lord Hoddesdon's outlook on life, from the very start of his expedition, had been a jaundiced one, and Valley Fields did nothing to change it. Indeed, his first move on alighting from the train was to give Valley Fields an extremely nasty look. Then, having inquired of the porter at the station the way to Mulberry Grove, he set out thither, thinking dark thoughts.

Berry Conway, when at the peak of his form, could do the distance from Mulberry Grove to Valley Fields station in about eighty-three seconds. Lord Hoddesdon, a slower mover, took longer. However, pausing at frequent intervals to remove his grey top-hat and dab his forehead with a handkerchief, for the day was warm, he eventually reached Benjafield Road, at the corner of which stands the public-house which had exercised so powerful an attraction for Lord Biskerton on the day of his arrival. Here, having by now completely forgotten the instructions given to him at the station, he came to a halt, feeling lost.

From the spot where Lord Hoddesdon was standing to the gates of Peacehaven was, as it happened, a matter of a few dozen yards. Unaware of this, he looked about him for guidance and observed, his powerful shoulders shoring up the wall of the public-house, a man in a cloth cap. He was sucking thoughtfully at an empty pipe, and he regarded Lord Hoddesdon, as he approached, with a rather unpleasant expression. The fact was, he had taken an instant dislike to his social superior's grey top-hat.

Nothing in the life of a great city is more complex than the rules that govern the selection of the correct headgear for use in the various divisions of that city. In Bond Street, or Piccadilly, a grey top-hat is *chic*, *de rigueur*, and *le dernier cri*. In Valley Fields, less than seven miles distant, it is *outré* and, one might almost say, *farouche*. The Royal Enclosure at Ascot would have admired Lord Hoddesdon's hat. The cloth-capped man, in a muzzy, beery sort of way, took it almost as a personal affront. It was as if he felt that his manhood and self-respect had been outraged by this grey topper.

Between Lord Hoddesdon and the cloth-capped man, therefore, there may be said to have existed an imperfect sympathy from the very start.

'I want to go to Mulberry Grove,' said Lord Hoddesdon.

The man, without shifting his position, rolled an inflamed eye at him. He stared in silence for a while. Then he gave a curt nod.

'Awright,' he said. 'Don't be long.'

Lord Hoddesdon endeavoured to make himself clearer.

'Can you – ah – direct me to Mulberry Grove?'

The eye rolled round once more. It travelled over Lord Hoddesdon's person searchingly, from head to foot and back again. Reaching the head, it paused.

'What sort of a hat do you call that you've got on?' asked the man coldly. 'A nice sort of hat, I don't think.'

Lord Hoddesdon was in no mood to chat of hats. In spite of the sunshine, the world was still looking loathsome to him. He had been fermenting steadily from the moment of leaving his sister Vera's door.

'Never mind my hat!' he said austerely.

The man, however, continued to toy with the theme. Indeed, he harped on it.

'The way you City clurks get yourselves up nowadays,' he said with evident disapproval, ''s enough to make a man sick. They wouldn't 'ave none of that in Moscow. No, *nor* in Leningrad. The Burjoisy, that's what you are, for all your top-'ats. Do you know what would happen to you in Moscow? Somebody – as it might be Stayling – would come along and 'e'd look at that 'at and 'e'd say "What are you doing, you Burjoise, swanking round in a 'at like that?", and he'd . . .'

Lord Hoddesdon moved away. He lost thereby some probably very valuable and interesting information about the manners and customs of Moscow, but he gained release from the society of one on whom he could never look as a friend. There was a small boy standing by the horse-trough in front of the public-house, and to him he now addressed his questioning.

'Which is the way to Mulberry Grove, my little fellow?' he asked, quite amiably for a man with murder in his heart and a blood-pressure well above the normal. 'I should be much obliged if you would inform me.'

Civility met with civility. His little fellow stopped dabbling his fingers in the water and pointed.

'Dahn there, sir, and first to the left,' he said politely.

'Thank you,' said Lord Hoddesdon. 'Thank you. Thank you.'

He moved off in the direction indicated, casting at the cloth-capped man as he went a look of censure. It is not easy to express very much in a look, but what Lord Hoddesdon wished to convey was that he hoped the cloth-capped man had been listening in on this scene and had been properly impressed by the exemplary attitude of one who, though so many years his junior, might well be taken by him as a model of deportment. A vague idea of returning and giving the suave lad a penny passed through his mind, to be abandoned immediately in favour of the far more sensible and businesslike step of going on and doing nothing of the kind. However, he had almost decided to look back and smile at the little fellow, when something exceptionally hard struck him suddenly between the shoulder blades. It was a flint. And, spinning round, he perceived the youthful Chesterfield in full flight up the road.

Lord Hoddesdon was dumbfounded. What had occurred seemed to him for an instant incredible. If he had been aware that the polite stripling and the man in the cloth cap were son and father, he would have divined that the same hatred of grey top-hats which animated the father ran also in the blood of the son. It was a simple case of hereditary instinct. But he did not know this. All he thought about the blood of the son was that he wanted to have it, and with this end in view he got smartly off the mark and, though he had not run for years, was soon pelting up the road at an excellent pace – a pace far too gruelling for the little fellow, whom he overtook in the first ten yards.

There are two schools of thought concerning the correct

method of dealing with small boys who throw stones at their elders and betters in the public street. Some say they should be kicked, others that they should be smacked on the head. Lord Hoddesdon, no bigot, did both. And for a man who had not smacked head or kicked trouser-seat since his early days at Eton he acquitted himself remarkably well. For the space of about half a minute he worked vigorously; then, turning, somewhat out of breath, he retraced his steps and resumed the trek to Mulberry Grove.

He felt strangely elated. It was as if some healing balm had been applied to his bruised soul. For the first time that afternoon he was conscious of being quietly happy. As the result of this burst of exercise, venom had gone out of him. An urge came upon him to whistle, and he was just pursing his lips to do so, when a voice spoke at his side.

''Oy!' said the voice.

It was the cloth-capped man. He had put his pipe away, and was walking by Lord Hoddesdon's side, smelling strongly of mixed ales. His eyes were bulging and had in them a red gleam, like fire seen through smoke. From the recent battlefield there came shrilly the wailings of the wounded.

'What did you want to hit the nipper for?' asked the cloth-capped man.

Lord Hoddesdon made no reply. It was not that the conundrum baffled him, for he had an excellent answer. But he disliked the idea of making this person a confidant. He walked on in silence.

'What did you want to hit my young 'Erbert for?'

Lord Hoddesdon started a little uneasily. *My* young 'Erbert? This was the first intimation he had received that ties of relationship linked these two. What had seemed at first merely the inquisitiveness of a stranger took on a more sinister significance when it became the muttered outpourings of a father's heart. From the corner of his eye he flashed a glance at his companion, and wished that it had not been so easy to see him. There was, he perceived, a great deal of this man.

He quickened his steps. He had become now uneasily aware of the deserted nature of the ground he was covering. There was not a policeman in sight. In a place like this, he reflected bitterly, there would probably be only one policeman and he would probably be asleep somewhere instead of doing his duty and busying himself in the interests of the public weal. For a moment, in his shrinking mind, Lord Hoddesdon became rather mordant about the police force of the suburbs.

But he was not able to think long about anything except this unpleasant-looking man who continued to walk step by step with him. Incoherent mutterings had now begun to proceed from this person. His lordship caught the words 'City clurk' and 'Burjoisy', repeated far too often for his peace of mind. In any circumstances, for he was a man of haughty spirit, he would have resented being taken for a City clerk: but the misapprehension was particularly disquieting now, for his companion was only too obviously a man who entertained a strong dislike for City clerks. This became sickeningly manifest when he began to speak with a sort of gloating note in his voice of knocking their heads off and stamping them into the mud, even if – or, perhaps, even more strongly because – they went swanking about in grey top-hats. That, as far as Lord Hoddesdon was able to follow his remarks, was, it appeared, the way Stayling would have behaved in Moscow, and what was good enough for Stayling was, the cloth-capped man frankly admitted, good enough for him.

It was at the point where the other, struck with a new idea, had begun to waver between stamping him into the mud and impaling him on the railings which decorated the further side of the pavement that Lord Hoddesdon, who for some little time had been covering the ground in a style which would certainly have led to his disqualification in a walking-race, definitely and undisguisedly broke into a run. They had turned the corner now, and had come in sight of houses: and it seemed to him that inside one of those houses sanctuary might be obtained.

With a sudden, swift movement Lord Hoddesdon's rapid walk turned into a gallop.

It is curious to reflect how often in life Fate chooses the same object as a means toward two quite opposite ends. It was Lord Hoddesdon's grey top-hat which had placed him in this very delicate situation, and it was this same top-hat which now for the moment extricated him from it. For, even as he started to run, it leaped from his head and rolled across the road, and his companion, sternly set though his mind was on the Holy War before him, was humanly frail enough not to be able to resist the lure. The hat went bouncing away, and the cloth-capped man, after but a second's hesitation, charged in pursuit.

He cornered the hat in the gutter and kicked it. He followed it to where it lay and kicked it again. Finally, he jumped upon it with both feet and then kicked it for the third time. This done, he looked round and was aware of its owner's coat-tails vanishing at a considerable speed through the gate of the last house down the road. Following swiftly, he passed through the gate, which bore upon it the word 'Castlewood', and, finding nothing of interest in the front garden, hastened round to the back.

Here, too, he found only empty space. He paused awhile in thought.

In moments of extreme peril the mind moves rapidly. In the beginning, Lord Hoddesdon had planned to walk with as great a dignity as he could achieve to one of these front doors, to ring the bell, to ask to see the master of the house, to inform the master of the house that he was being followed in a threatening manner by a ruffian who appeared to be worse for drink, to be invited into the drawing-room, and to remain there in a comfortable chair while his host telephoned for aid to the police-station. And the entire programme had had to be scrapped at a moment's notice.

Obviously, there was no time for leisurely ringing of bells. An alternative scheme had to be planned out. This alternative scheme Lord Hoddesdon had not been able to shape at the moment of his entry into the garden of Castlewood, but it came to him as he rounded the angle of the house and perceived on the ground floor an open window. Through this window he dived with an adroitness which would have given a rabbit, had one been an eye-witness, an idea or two for the brushing-up of its technique: and, when his pursuer also entered the garden, he was lurking on all fours inside the room.

And there for a moment the matter rested.

How long it would have gone on resting, it is difficult to say. The cloth-capped man was a slow thinker, and it might have been some little while before he would have been able to observe and deduce. As it happened, however, an irresistible urge came over Lord Hoddesdon at this moment to raise his head and peer out of the window, to see what was happening in the great world outside. The first thing he saw was his pursuer, and his pursuer most unfortunately chanced to be looking in that very direction.

The next instant, the peaceful stillness of Mulberry Grove was shattered by a stern View Halloo, and the instant after that Lord Hoddesdon had banged the window down and bolted it. And then for a space these two representatives of Labour and the Old Regime stood staring at one another through the glass, like rare fishes in adjoining compartments of an aquarium.

Lord Hoddesdon was the first to weary of the spectacle. He had seen a good deal of the cloth-capped man in the last quarter of an hour, and he was feeling surfeited. Even observed through glass, the other's inflamed eyes had so hideous a menace that he wished to be as far away from them as possible. Hastily withdrawing, therefore, he backed out of the room and found himself in a passage. At the end of this passage was the front door, and beside the front door a hat-stand, from which protruded, like heads of the Burjoicy neatly skewered on pikes after the Social Revolution, divers hats. And at the sight of these his lordship's mind began working along new lines.

The loss of his grey topper had not until now affected Lord Hoddesdon very deeply. Subconsciously, no doubt, he had been aware of it, but it was only at this moment that the full shock of bereavement really smote him. Seeing these hats, he realized for the first time his own lidless condition, and for the first time appreciated the vital necessity of remedying it. It was his ambition, if he ever got out of this ghastly suburb alive, to return to London. And at the thought of accomplishing that return bareheaded every blue drop of Hoddesdon blood in his veins froze. To go through London's streets without a hat was unthinkable.

Nevertheless, as he stood scanning the hat-stand with the eyes of a shipwrecked mariner sighting a sail, his heart distinctly sank. Whoever owned this house appeared to have a perfectly astonishing taste in hats. On the three pegs were a cap with purple checks (a thing of pure nightmare); an almost unbelievable something constructed of black straw; and a bowler. It was at the bowler that his lordship directed his gaze. The other two, he saw at a glance, were out of the question.

Even the bowler was not ideal. It was of a type not often met with nowadays, being almost square in shape and flattened down at the top. But it was so distinctly better than the cap and the straw that Lord Hoddesdon did not hesitate. Bounding swiftly forward, he snatched it from its peg. And, as he did so, there came from behind him a roar like that of a more than usually irritable lioness witnessing the theft of one of her cubs.

'Hi!'

Lord Hoddesdon turned as if the word had been a red-hot poker pressed against his form-fitting trousers. He beheld, hurrying swiftly down the stairs, a little man with a mauve face and a monocle.

It was the practice of Major Flood-Smith, of Castlewood, to take a *siesta* in his bedroom on these warm afternoons. Today, he had been looking forward to uninterrupted repose. His niece Katherine had gone off with that young fellow, Smith, from next-door, to a *matinée* performance at the Brixton Astoria, and he had the house to himself. Well content, he was just dozing off, when that View Halloo from the garden had jerked him off the bed like a hooked minnow: and a glance out of the window had shown him a revolting-looking individual in a cloth cap, standing with his nose glued against the window of the morning-room. Pausing only to snatch his Service revolver out of its drawer, Major Flood-Smith had charged downstairs, and he would be damned if here wasn't another blasted fellow strolling about the hall pinching his hats.

All the householder in Major Flood-Smith was roused.

'You!' he thundered. 'What the devil are you doing?'

The whole trend of Lord Hoddesdon's education and up-bringing had gone, from his earliest years, towards the instilment in him of a deep love of Good Form. There were things, he had been taught at Eton, at Oxford, and subsequently during his brief career as a member of His Majesty's Household Brigade, which were not done. And one of these things, he felt instinctively, was the stealing of square-topped bowler hats from men to whom he had never been introduced.

It was not unnatural, therefore, that the suave calm with which he usually met life's happenings should now have deserted him. Unable to speak, he remained standing where he was, holding the bowler.

'Who are you? How did you get in? What are you doing with that hat?' proceeded the Major, decorating the bald questions with a few of the rich expletives which a soldier inevitably picks up in his years of service. Major Flood-Smith had spent seven years with the Loyal Royal Worcestershires, who are celebrated for their plain speech.

Lord Hoddesdon was still unable to utter, but he was capable of the graceful gesture. With something of old-world courtesy, he replaced the bowler on its peg.

The Major, however, appeared dissatisfied.

'Breaking and entering! In broad daylight! Stealing my hats under my very nose! Well, I'll be . . .'

He mentioned some of the things he would be. Most of them were spiritual, a few merely physical.

Lord Hoddesdon at last found words. But, when they came, it would have been better if he had remained silent.

'It's quite all right,' he said.

He could scarcely have selected a more unfortunate remark.

Major Flood-Smith's ripe complexion deepened to a still more impressive purple. He jumped about.

'Quite all right?' he cried. 'Quite all right? Quite all right? Quite all right? I catch you in my hall, sneaking my ensanguined hats, and you have the hæmorrhagic insolence to stand there and tell me it's quite all right. I'll show you how all right it is. I'll...'

He stopped abruptly. This was not because he had finished his observations, for he had not. If ever there was a retired Major of the Line who had all his music still within him, he was that Major. But at this moment there came from the rear of the house the dreadful sound of splintering glass. It rang out like an explosion, and it spoke straight to the deeps in Major Flood-Smith's soul.

He quivered from head to foot, and said something sharply in one of the lesser-known dialects of the Hindu Khoosh.

Lord Hoddesdon, though he was not feeling himself, was capable of understanding what had happened. There is a certain point past which you cannot push the freemen of Valley Fields. That point, he now realized, had been reached when he had closed the morning-room window, leaving the cloth-capped man standing outside like a Peri at the gates of Paradise. It is ever the instinct of the proletariat, when excluded from any goal by a sheet of glass, to throw bricks. This the cloth-capped man had now done, and it surprised Lord Hoddesdon that he had not done it sooner. No doubt what had occasioned the delay was the selection of a suitable brick.

Major Flood-Smith was torn between two conflicting desires. On the one hand, he yearned to remain and thresh out with his present companion the whole question of hats. On the other, his windows were being broken.

The good man loved his hat. But he also loved his windows.

Another crash swayed the balance. The windows had it. Barking like a seal, Major Flood-Smith disappeared down the passage, and Lord Hoddesdon, saved at the eleventh hour, snatched at the hat-stand, wrenched the front door open, banged it behind him, leaped into the street, and raced madly out of Mulberry Grove in the direction of the railway-station

It was only when he had come in sight of it that he discovered that what he had taken from the stand was the cap with the purple checks.

III

'I knew you would bungle it,' said Lady Vera.

CHAPTER 7

I

Berry Conway came round the corner into Mulberry Grove and paused outside the gate of The Nook to fumble in his pocket for his latch-key. In the fading sunlight of the summer evening, Mulberry Grove was looking its best and most pastoral. A gentle breeze whispered through the trees: and in the ornamental water, which shone like an opal, one of the swans was standing on its head, while the other moved to and fro in a slow, thoughtful sort of way like a man hunting for a lost collar-stud. It would seem, in short, almost incredible that anyone could have seen the place at this particular moment without instantly being reminded of the Island Valley of Avilion, where falls not hail, nor rain nor any snow, nor ever wind blows loudly.

But if this comparison presented itself to the mind of Berry Conway, he gave no sign of it. He eyed Mulberry Grove with dislike. He frowned at the trim little house. At the two swans, Egbert and Percy, he glowered. And when from the premises of the Valley Fields Lawn Tennis Club there was borne to his ears the happy yapping of eager flappers, he groaned slightly, and winced, like Prometheus watching his vulture dropping in for lunch.

The inexplicable removal from his life of the only girl he had ever loved or could love had made existence a weary affair for Berry these days.

Having found his key, he entered the house and went to his bedroom. There he removed his clothes and, putting on a dressing-gown, proceeded to the bathroom. He splashed about in cold water for a while: then, returning to the bedroom, began to don the costume of the English gentleman about to dine. For tonight was the night of the annual banquet of the Old Boys of his school; and, though since his entry into the ranks of the wage-slaves he had preferred to lead a hermit existence and avoid, as far as was possible, the companions of his opulent days, some lingering sentimentality still caused him to turn out for these functions.

He had just completed his toilet when a knock sounded on the door. He had expected it sooner. He opened the door, congratulating himself, as he did so, that he had finished tying his tie. Otherwise, the faithful Old Retainer would have insisted on doing it for him.

'I didn't hear you come in, Master Berry,' said the Old Retainer, beaming. 'How nice you look. Would you like me just to straighten your tie?'

'Go ahead,' said Berry resignedly.

'I always think a tie looks so different when you straighten it.'

'I know what you mean,' said Berry. 'Straighter.'

'That's it. Straighter. Gladys-at-Castlewood tells me,' said the Old Retainer, beginning the *News Bulletin*, 'that they had burglars there this afternoon. She says she's never seen the Major look so purple. It was her afternoon out, she says, and when she came home he was walking round and round the garden with a pistol in his hand, muttering to himself. He was very cross,

Gladys tells me. Well, I mean, enough to make any gentleman cross having men break into his house and steal his caps.'

'Did somebody steal that cap of the Major's?' asked Berry, brightening. He had disliked the thing for eighteen months.

'They did, Master Berry. And somebody else broke two of the back windows with a stone.'

'Mulberry Grove is looking up.'

'But it's all right,' said Mrs Wisdom soothingly. 'I've had a word with Mr Finbow, and he's promised to keep an eye on us.'

'Who's Mr Finbow?'

'He's a gentleman in the police, and though Mulberry Grove, he says, isn't strictly speaking on his beat, he will make a point, he says, of looking in every now and then to see that we are all right. I thought it very civil of him and gave him a slice of cake. Isn't it odd, it seems that Mr Finbow comes from the very same part of the country where I used to live when I was a slip of a girl. I always say it's a small world, after all. Well, I mean, when I say the very same part of the country, my dear father and mother had a cottage in Herefordshire and Mr Finbow lived in Birmingham, but it does seem odd, all the same. We had a nice talk. Would you like me to get a brush and give you a good brushing, Master Berry?'

'No, thanks,' said Berry hastily. 'I haven't time. I must hurry. If I miss the six-fifty, I shall be late for my dinner.'

'Be careful not to overheat yourself, dear.'

'Don't worry. I'm not as hungry as all that.'

'I mean to say, it's so dangerous to sit in a draughty railway carriage with the pores open.'

'I'll shut them,' said Berry. 'Good-bye.'

He charged out of the house, causing his next-door neighbour, Lord Biskerton, to utter a startled cry of admiration. The Biscuit at the moment was engaged in weeding his front garden, a pursuit which, like a good householder, he had taken up with energy.

'Golly!' said the Biscuit, eyeing his friend's splendour open-mouthed. 'Giving the populace a thorough treat, are you not? What is it? Meat tea at Buckingham Palace?'

'O.B. dinner,' explained Berry briefly. 'And if you weren't a slacker you would be coming, too.'

The Biscuit shook his head.

'Never again for me,' he said. 'Not any more of those binges for me. I know them too well. The Committee of Management either stick you in among a drove of dotards who talk across you about the time they were given a half-holiday because of the Battle of Crécy, or else you get dumped down with a lot of kids whose heads you want to smack. And it is a very moot point which of the two situations is the fouler. I was with the kids last time. I'll swear some of them had come in prams. Have you noticed, Berry, old man, how extraordinarily young everybody seems to be nowadays? That's because we're getting on. Silver threads among the gold, laddie. How old are you?'

'Twenty-six next birthday.'

'Pretty senile,' said the Biscuit, clicking his tongue and jabbing at a weed. 'Pretty senile. And the year after that you'll be twenty-seven, and then, if I have got my figures correct, twenty-eight. Just waiting for the end, you might say. It's no use kidding ourselves, old friend, we're ageing rapidly, and our place is by the hearth.'

'You won't come, then?'

'No. I shall remain here and stroll in my garden. Quite possibly little Kitchie Valentine will be strolling in here, and we will exchange ideas across the fence. I maintain that in the suburbs it is a duty to cultivate one's neighbours. There is in English life too much of this ridiculous keeping of oneself to oneself. I deprecate it.'

It did not take Berry long, once the company had seated itself in the Oriental Banquet-Room of the Hotel Mazarin in Piccadilly, to realize which of the two alternatives mentioned by the Biscuit was to be his fate tonight. Dotards in considerable force had attended this Old Boys' dinner, but they were sitting at distant tables. His own was the very heart and centre of the younger set. Boisterous striplings, who all seemed to know one another intimately and to have no desire to know him at all, encompassed him on every side. And gradually, as he watched them, his mood of sombre sadness deepened.

He knew now that he had made a mistake in exposing himself to this ordeal. He was in no frame of mind to suffer gladly beardless juveniles like these. Swollen with soup, they had now begun to rollick and frolic in a manner infinitely distressing to a heart-broken elder. Their infantile frivolity afflicted him more and more every moment with a sense of the passage of the years.

Once, he reflected – how long ago! – he, too, had had spirits like that. Once he, also, had lived in Arcady and thrown bread at Old Boys' dinners. How far in the distant past all that sort of thing lay now.

Twenty-six next birthday! That was what he was. Twenty-bally-six, and no getting away from it.

And what had he done with his life? Nothing. Apart from being the sort of chump who, when he has the luck to meet the only girl in the world, lets her slip away from him like a dream at daybreak, what had he achieved? Nothing. If he were to pass away tonight – poisoned, let us say, by this peculiar-looking fish which, having died of some unknown complaint, had just been placed before him by an asthmatic waiter – what sort of gap would he leave? An almost invisible one. Scarcely a dimple.

Would that girl regret him? Most unlikely. Would she even remember that she had ever met him? Probably not. A wonderful girl like that met so many men. Why should she have continued to bear in mind so notably inferior a specimen as himself? Such a girl could take her pick of all that was best and brightest of England's masculinity. Hers was a life spent in the centre of a whirling maelstrom of handsome, dashing devils with racing Bentleys and all the money in the world. What earthly reason had he to suppose that she had ever given him another thought? A doddering wreck like him – twenty-six next birthday. In a flash of morbid intuition he realized now why she had driven off that day and left him flat. It was because she was bored with him and had jumped at the chance of getting away while his back was turned.

He had reached this depth of self-torment and was preparing to go still deeper, when half a roll, propelled by a vigorous young hand, struck him smartly on the left ear. He leaped convulsively and for an instant forgot all about the girl. In similar circumstances, Dante would have forgotten Beatrice. The roll was one of those hard, jagged rolls, and the effect of its impact was not unlike that of a direct hit from a shell. He looked up wrathfully. And, as he did so, a child at the other end of the table, smirking apologetically, applied the last straw.

'Oh, sorry, sir!' cried this babe and suckling. 'Frightfully sorry, sir. Most awfully sorry, sir. I was aiming at young Dogsbody.'

Berry contrived to smirk back, but with an infinite wryness, for his heart was as lead. This, he felt, was the end.

The young germ had called him 'Sir'.

'*Sir!*'

It was what he himself called T. Paterson Frisby, that genuine museum-piece who could not be a day less than fifty.

Now he saw everything. Now he understood. That girl had been civil to him at first because she was a sweet, kind-hearted girl who had been taught always to be polite to Age. What he had mistaken for *camaraderie* had been merely the tolerance demanded by his white hairs. Right from the start, no doubt, she had been saying to herself 'At the very earliest opportunity I must shake this old buster!' and at the very earliest opportunity she had done so. 'Sir!' indeed! How right the Biscuit had been. He should never have been such a fool as to come to this blasted *crèche*. And the best thing he could do, having come, was to repair his blunder by oiling out immediately.

To leave a public dinner at the height of its fever is not easy, and it is to be doubted whether mere senile gloom, however profound, would have been enough to nerve Berry to the task. But at this moment his eye fell on the table at the top of the room, along which, on either side of the President, were seated some twenty of the elect: and it now flashed upon him that of these at least eight must almost certainly be intending to make speeches. And right in the middle of them, with a nasty, vicious look in his eye, sat a Bishop.

Anybody who has ever attended Old Boys' dinners knows that Bishops are tough stuff. They take their time, these prelates. They mouth their words and shape their periods. They roam with frightful deliberation from the grave to the gay, from the manly straightforward to the whimsically jocular. Not one of them but is good for at least twenty-five minutes.

Berry hesitated no longer. The Banquet had reached the Petrified Quail stage now, which meant that there was only the Hair-Oil Ice-cream, the Embalmed Sardines on Toast and the Arsenical Coffee to go before the dam of oratory would burst. There was not an instant to be lost. He pushed his chair back and sidled furtively to the door. He reached the door and pulled it open. He slid through and closed it behind him.

He was standing now in the main lobby of the hotel. Festive-looking men and women were passing through, some to the dining-room, whence strains of music proceeded, others to the lifts. There seemed to be a dance or some other sort of entertainment in progress upstairs somewhere, for traffic on the lifts was heavy. Revellers were being taken up in dozens, and Berry watched them with a growing feeling of desolation and disapproval. Their light-heartedness irked him as the exuber-ance of his recent companions in the Oriental Banquet-Room had irked him. It is not pleasant, when one is face to face with one's soul, to see a lot of fatheads enjoying themselves. Berry had achieved by this time a frame of mind which would have qualified him to walk straight into a Tchekov play and no ques-tions asked: and he resented all this idiotic gaiety. As the crack-ling of thorns under a pot, he felt, so is the laughter of a fool.

An unusually large consignment was on the point of starting now. The lift was crammed with perishers of both sexes – the girls giggling and the men what-whating in a carefree manner that made him feel sick. So full was it that it scarcely seemed as if there would be room for the girl in the green opera-cloak who was hurrying with her escort across the lobby. But the man at the wheel contrived to squeeze them in somehow, and as the car started on its journey the girl turned to her companion and said something with a smile. And for the first time Berry saw her face.

And, as he saw it, the lobby rocked about him. A wordless

exclamation burst from his lips. Reeling, he clutched at a passing waiter.

'Sir?' said the waiter, courteously ceasing to pass.

Berry smiled radiantly at the man. He could only see him through a sort of mist, but he was able to realize that this was by a considerable margin the nicest-looking waiter he had ever set eyes on. And all those people in the lifts – how wrong he had been, he now saw, in thinking of them as perishers. They were in reality a most extraordinarily jolly crowd. And how capital it was to think that they were enjoying themselves so much.

'What's going on up there?' he asked.

The waiter informed him that Sir Herbert and Lady Bassinger were giving a ball in the Crystal Room on the first floor.

'Ah!' said Berry thoughtfully. 'A ball, eh?'

He handed the man half a crown, and stood for a moment gazing wistfully across the lobby. How splendid, he was thinking, it would have been if only he had been acquainted with these Bassingers. Then they might have invited him. . . .

Berry pulled himself up with a start. He was shocked to find that for an instant he had been allowing himself to fall so far from the standard of a man of enterprise, dash, and resource as to look on a card of invitation as an essential preliminary to the enjoyment of the hospitality of Sir Herbert and Lady Bassinger. But it had been merely a passing weakness. He was himself again now, and what he felt was that any ballroom, Bassinger or non-Bassinger, where that girl was to be found, was Liberty Hall for him.

The lift had just descended, and was standing on the ground floor once more, waiting for custom. Berry pulled down his waistcoat and walked towards it with resolute steps.

II

Lady Bassinger's ball at the Hotel Mazarin was an entertainment to which Ann Moon had been looking forward with pleasurable anticipation. Toddy Malling, the young man who, in the unfortunate absence of her *fiancé*, Lord Biskerton, was acting as her escort, had been almost lyrical about it in the car. It promised, said Toddy, to be the jamboree of the season. Champagne, he assured her, always flowed like water where the Bassingers set up their banner.

'Old B.,' said Toddy, 'is not the sort of fellow I'd care to go on a walking-tour with, but at providing refreshment for man and beast he has few equals. He made about ten million quid in the clove market. And God bless cloves, say I,' he added devoutly.

On Toddy's suggestion, they had made straight for the supper-room. He held the view, for which there was much to be said, that it was silly to think of doing any hoof-shaking till they had stoked up. Having deposited Ann at a table for two, he had gone off to forage. And now she was sitting waiting for him to come back. And, as she watched the crowd, she wished that she could achieve something of the hearty party-spirit which so obviously animated Sir Herbert and Lady Bassinger's other guests. She was conscious of a feeling of flatness ill-attuned to the rollicking note of the festivities.

It was strange, she reflected. Her conscience assured her that the most sensible thing she had ever done in her life was to drive off in her car and leave that attractive young man to catch his Sniffers for himself. She was engaged, Conscience pointed out, and girls who have plighted their troth must not hob-nob with handsome Secret Service men. And yet, so far from experiencing the glow of satisfaction which good girls are entitled to expect, she was feeling as if she had deliberately thrown away something wonderful and precious.

In torturing himself with the thought that this girl had forgotten him, Berry Conway had tortured himself unnecessarily.

'Bollinger, one bot.,' said Toddy Malling, appearing suddenly at her side. 'I snaffled it off another table. Stick to it like glue and guard it with your life.'

The supper-room was looking now like a popular store during a bargain-sale. The idea of taking refreshment before dancing had not occurred to Toddy alone. On every side, thrustful cavaliers, like knights jousting for their ladies, were hurling themselves into the dense throng that masked the table where food and drink were being doled out. Supper at a Bassinger ball was always a test of manhood, and the lucky ones were those who had played Rugby football at school.

'Somewhere in the heart of that mob,' said Toddy, laying his precious burden on the table, 'there is provender of sorts. I'll try to get you something. I can't guarantee what it will be, but are you more or less prepared for whatever I can snitch?'

'Anything,' said Ann. She came out of her thoughts with a little jump. 'I'm not hungry.'

'You're not?' said her escort incredulously. 'Gosh! I could eat old Bassinger in person, if a spot of chutney went with him. I'll try to hook a chicken. Amuse yourself somehow while I'm gone. And if I don't come back, you'll know I died game.'

He disappeared again, and Ann returned to her thoughts.

Yes, something wonderful and precious. And she had thrown it away. And its going had left life flat and monotonous.

And that was odd, too, because she had never supposed that anything could make life seem monotonous. She had always had the enviable gift of being able to enjoy. Even when in the midst of the Clarence Dumphrys and surrounded by the Twombley Burwashes, she had never really been bored. But now, beyond a doubt, she was. And it seemed to her that, except during that short summer afternoon's ride, she always had been. That ride stood out in her memory like an oasis in a desert, the solitary break in a dull and unprofitable existence.

The crowd was surging to and fro. Sharp, anguished cries rang through the room, as men balancing plates of salmon mayonnaise perceived men with plates of chicken salad backing into them. The heat and the noise combined to induce in Ann a distant dreaminess. Dimly she became aware that somebody was sitting down in the chair opposite her, and she roused herself to protect the rights of the absent Toddy.

'I'm sorry. That chair is . . .'

She broke off. She was not dreaming now. Her whole body was tingling as though fire had touched it.

'Oh!' said Ann breathlessly.

And that, for a while, was all she was able to say. Her heart was racing, and already Conscience was beginning to comment on the deplorable way in which her lips had begun to tremble.

'All wrong!' said Conscience rebukingly. 'This man is nothing but a casual acquaintance. Treat him as such. Bow stiffly.'

Ann did not bow stiffly. She went on staring. And across the table the intruder went on staring.

A young man in spectacles, bearing treasure trove on a plate, tripped over somebody's foot and bumped heavily into the table. Something fell squashily between them.

'My cutlet, I think,' said the young man, retrieving it. 'Awfully sorry.'

He passed on, and Ann found herself able to smile a tremulous smile.

'Good evening!' she said.

'Good evening.'

'You do keep popping up, don't you!' said Ann. 'You always seem to appear from nowhere, out of a trap.'

Her companion did not smile. There was something forceful and urgent about him. He conveyed the impression of one who is in a hurry and in no mood for light conversation.

'Where did you get to that day?' he asked abruptly, and frowned, as if at an unpleasant memory.

Ann braced herself to be cool and quelling. She told herself that she resented his tone. He had spoken as if he supposed that he had some claim on her, regarding her as something belonging to him. This, she told herself, offended her, and rightly.

'I went home,' she said.

'Why?'

'Isn't a woman's place the home?'

'It was an awful shock when I came out and found you gone.'

'I'm sorry.'

'I couldn't think where you had got to.'

'Really?'

('The right tone?' asked Ann of her Conscience.

'Quite right,' replied Conscience. 'Admirable. Keep it up.')

'By the way,' said Ann, 'was that man The Sniffer?'

Her companion started. For the first time, the forcefulness of his manner was tempered by something that seemed almost embarrassment. A flush had come into his face, and his eyes, instead of gazing piercingly into hers, wandered away to one side.

'Look here,' he said awkwardly, 'I want to tell you something. You see . . .'

He paused.

'Yes?' said Ann.

'I feel I ought to . . .'

He appeared to be hovering on the brink of a revelation of some kind.

'Well?' said Ann.

Another young man, this time without spectacles, charged breezily into the table, rocking it to its foundations.

'Frightfully sorry,' he said. 'There's an awful storm going on out here. Heaven help the poor sailors.'

He paused to scoop up a portion of chicken salad, and went out of their lives for ever.

'What were you saying?' asked Ann.

Her companion seemed to have been reflecting during the recent diversion. It had sounded to Ann as though he were about to make some sort of confession, but now he appeared to have thought better of it.

'Nothing,' he said.

'You began to say something about telling me—?'

'No, it was nothing. I was going to say something, but I think I won't.'

'You must have your secrets, I suppose. Well, was it The Sniffer?'

'No. It wasn't.'

'I'm glad.'

'Why?'

A sudden and startling change came over Ann's manner. Until now she had won her Conscience's complete approval by the distant coolness of her attitude. At this question she slipped lamentably. From distant coolness she lapsed into a deplorable sincerity.

'I thought you were going into the most terrible danger,' she said breathlessly. 'I thought he might kill you.'

'You were worried about – *me*?'

'Well, it's not very nice for a respectable young girl,' said Ann, recovering, 'to be mixed up in shooting affrays. Think of the papers!'

The eager light died out of her companion's eyes.

'Was that all you cared about?' he asked, hollowly.

'What else would there be?'

'Nothing personal in your alarm, eh?'

'Personal?' said Ann, raising her eyebrows.

'Well, I'm glad you did the prudent, sensible thing,' said her companion, speaking, however, without noticeable elation, 'and got away before there was trouble.'

'But there wasn't,' Ann pointed out.

'No,' said her companion. And there was another silence.

Between Ann and her Conscience there now existed a wide cleavage of opinion. Her Conscience kept telling her that she had borne herself under trying conditions in an exemplary manner. She told herself that she was behaving like an idiot. A little more of this sort of thing, and this man would get up and go away for ever.

('And a very good thing, too,' said Conscience. 'A most excellent termination to a very unfortunate entanglement.'

'Says you!' said Ann. And her lips tightened.)

Her companion had taken up the bottle of champagne and was shaking it in an overwrought sort of way – a proceeding which would have shocked and horrified Toddy Malling, had he been present, to the core. But Toddy was still far away, battling nobly where the fray was thickest.

'Of course I was worried about you,' said Ann impulsively. 'I only said that about the papers because— Of course I was worried about you!'

A gleam like sunshine through cloud-wrack illuminated the brooding face opposite her.

'You were?'

'Of course.'

'You mean, you were?'

'Certainly.'

'You really were?'

'Of course I was.'

He leaned forward.

'Shall I tell you something?'

'What?'

'Just this,' said her companion. 'I've—'

He broke off with a sharp exclamation. Something warm and wet had fallen on the back of his head.

'The fault,' said a cheerful voice behind him, 'is entirely mine. I ought never to have attempted to carry soup through a mob like this. Well, all I can say is, I'm sorry. There's just one bright spot – it's jolly good soup.'

Berry turned savagely. A man in love can stand just so much.

'Let's get out of this,' he said between his teeth. 'There's something I want to tell you. We can't talk here.'

'But Mr Malling will be back in a moment,' said Ann. She had a sense of slipping, of struggling for a foothold.

'Who's he?'

'The man I'm with. He's gone to get me something to eat. If I go away, what will he think?'

'If he's anything like the rest of the men here,' said Berry, 'I don't suppose he's capable of thinking.'

He urged her towards the door. They passed out and were in a small anteroom. From somewhere beyond came the sound of music.

Berry slammed the door behind him and turned to her.

'I've something I want to tell you,' he said.

He seemed to Ann to be swelling before her eyes. He looked huge and intimidating. She became conscious of feeling very small and fragile.

'You'll think me mad, of course.'

He was very close to her now, and Conscience, clucking like a hen, was urging her to draw back. She did not draw back.

He took her hand, and as he did so she saw him start, like one who has observed a snake in his path. It was her left hand that he had taken, and what he was staring at was the ring on the third finger. It was a nice ring, of diamonds and platinum, and Lord Biskerton owed a considerable sum for it, but there was no admiration in the young man's gaze.

'You're engaged!' he said.

The words were hardly a question. They resembled more nearly an accusation. Ann had a fleeting, but none the less disintegrating, sensation of having been detected in some act unspeakably low and base. She felt that she wanted to explain, and it seemed so impossible to explain.

'Yes,' she said, in a small, meek, penitent voice.

'My God!' said the young man.

'Yes,' said Ann.

'Engaged!'

'Yes.'

The young man breathed heavily.

'I don't care!' he said. 'I just want to tell you—'

The lobby between the supper-room and the Crystal Ballroom of the Hotel Mazarin on the night of a Bassinger dance is perhaps, with the exception of the supper-room, the least suitable spot in the whole of London for the conduct of a *tête-à-tête*. Even as he spoke, the young man became aware of something male and intrusive at his elbow. This person seemed to be desirous of speech with him. He was tapping him on the arm.

'Excuse me,' he was saying.

And almost at the same instant the door of the supper-room flew open, and Ann, in her turn, found herself forced to recognize that there were more than two people in the world. The whole place had begun to take on a congested air.

'Oh, there you are!' said Toddy Malling.

Toddy was flushed and dishevelled. He seemed at some point in his recent activities to have run his right eye up against something hard, for it was watery and half closed. In his left eye, which was working under its normal power, there was the light of reproach.

'Oh, *there* you are!' said Toddy Malling. 'I couldn't think where you had got to. I've been looking for you everywhere.'

A sense of being torn in half came upon Ann. She felt as she had sometimes felt when wrenched from some beautiful dream by the ringing of the telephone at her bedside. She looked over her shoulder. The young man who had something which he just wanted to tell her was standing with a dazed expression on his face, gazing down absently at someone whom she recognized as her host, Sir Herbert Bassinger. Sir Herbert appeared to be asking him some question, and the young man was plainly having a little difficulty in giving his mind to it.

'I've snaffled an excellent chicken,' proceeded Toddy, with the modest pride of a Crusader who has done big things among the Paynim. 'Also some salad of sorts. Come along.'

Ann was a kind-hearted girl, and one who hated hurting people's feelings. Well aware of the perils to which Toddy had exposed himself in order that she might sup, she appreciated the justice of his claim on her society. For her sake he had fought and, practically, bled. She could not rebuff him now, in the very hour of his triumph. To do so would be to destroy all young Mr Malling's faith in Woman.

Besides, there would be plenty of opportunity for resuming that interrupted talk later on – in some more secluded spot. From the solicitous way in which Sir Herbert was patting his arm, it was plain that her mysterious friend must be a favoured guest. She would find him in the Crystal Ballroom when she had contrived to shake off the insistent Toddy.

'All right, Toddy,' she said. 'You're a hero. Lead on.'

'You don't mind if young Bertie Winch puts on the nosebag with us, do you?' said Toddy anxiously, as they passed through the door. 'I had to rope him in as an ally. It was imperative. I stationed him by the table and told him to look after that chicken like a baby sister. Otherwise, some of these bally pirates would infallibly have pinched it.'

Berry, meanwhile, had at last had it forced upon his senses that this Voice which was babbling in his immediate neighbourhood was addressing its remarks to him; and, though still distrait, he answered civilly.

'Quite,' he said. 'Absolutely. No doubt.'

The Voice appeared dissatisfied. And, more than dissatisfied, indignant. It rose querulously.

'I'm asking you,' it said, now undisguisedly peevish, 'who the devil you are and where the devil you came from and what the devil you think you're doing here. I don't know you from Adam, and I'd like to see your card of invitation, if you please.'

Berry came out of his reverie. There is a time for dreaming and a time for facing the issues of life in a practical spirit. This seemed to be one of the latter occasions. Peering through the golden mists which float about a lover, he perceived a rubicund little man of middle age with a walrus moustache and two chins. The moustache was twitching, and both chins waggled in an unpleasant and hostile manner.

'I beg your pardon?' he said.

'Never mind about begging my pardon,' replied his new acquaintance. 'Show me your invitation-card.'

In gazing at Berry as if he were an escape of sewer-gas and addressing him in a tone which a bilious warder in a prison might have used toward a convict whom he did not like very much, Sir Herbert Bassinger, Bart, undoubtedly had justice on his side. There had been this season at Society functions quite an epidemic of what is technically known as gate-crashing. At a great number of balls, that is to say, a great number of London's bright young men had put in an appearance, drunk as much champagne as they could hold without spilling over the brim, and danced till their ankles gave out, all without the formality of an invitation. Hosts had come to dislike this practice, and Sir Herbert Bassinger, who had suffered much from it at his last big affair, given earlier in the year, had sworn a dark oath that there was going to be none of that this time. It had, accordingly, been enjoined upon the guests at the dance in the Crystal Ballroom of the Mazarin Hotel that they should bring their invitation-cards with them and be prepared to show them on demand.

'Invitation-card!' said Berry musingly, as if the word was new to him.

'Invitation-card.'

'Well, the fact is . . .' said Berry.

It was a conversational gambit which told Sir Herbert all he wanted to know. Only the sinful and black of heart, he was aware, begin their remarks with that phrase. Comfortably sure now that he was not ejecting from his dance some scion of a noble house whose face he had chanced to forget – or, worse, a gossip-writer from one of the daily papers – he unmasked his batteries.

'I must request you to leave immediately.'

'But—'

'Get out!' said Sir Herbert, becoming terser.

'But I must speak to—'

The walrus moustache quivered like a corn-field in the evening breeze.

'Are you going, or shall I call a policeman?'

Berry perceived that he must be polite and winning. He was still unaware of the name and address of his goddess of the car, and this man could supply them. He forced an ingratiating smile.

It did not go well.

'Don't grin at me!' thundered Sir Herbert Bassinger.

Even filtered through the moustache, his voice made Berry leap a couple of inches. He removed the ingratiating smile. His companion's wish was law. Besides, it was hurting his face.

'I'll go,' he said reassuringly. 'Oh, I'll *go*. Of course I'll go. I quite understand that I have no business here. I'll go all right. I only came because I saw somebody I wanted to speak to going up in the lift. If you will just let me go into the supper-room and have a word with—'

Sir Herbert Bassinger was a man who, when stirred, was accustomed to fall back on a vocabulary of his own invention. He employed it now.

'Stop this tish-tosh!'

Berry continued to be polite and winning.

'Perhaps if you would just tell me her name?'

'Enough of this bubble-and-squeak!'

'Her name?' said Berry urgently. 'I must know her name. If you'll just be kind enough to tell me her name—'

'Will you kindly cease this tingle-tangle and get out of here!' said Sir Herbert Bassinger.

Several attendants in gay uniform had manifested themselves by now and were dotted about the room, eyeing Berry in that cold, severe way in which barmen eye the obstreperous in bars. Reluctantly, he realized that he could do no more. He had shot his bolt. A brawl, agreeable though it would have been to his ruffled feelings, was out of the question.

'Very well,' he said.

With no more tingle-tangle or tish-tosh, he turned and walked in silence to the stairs. His bearing was not exactly dignified, but it was as dignified as a man's can be who is undergoing a spiritual frog's march.

III

A light in the sitting-room of Peacehaven informed Berry on his return to Mulberry Grove that Lord Biskerton was still up and, no doubt, eager for a chat. He rapped on the window. It was opened hospitably, and he climbed through.

'Well?' said the Biscuit. 'What sort of a time did you have?'

He eyed Berry narrowly. There seemed to him in his friend's demeanour something strange – an unwonted sparkle in the eye, a suppressed elation as of one who on honey-dew has fed and drunk the milk of Paradise. This, the Biscuit felt, was scarcely to be accounted for by attendance at an Old Boys' dinner, and he sought elsewhere for the cause.

'What's the matter with you, reptile?' he asked. 'You're fizzing visibly. Come into money, or something?'

Berry sat down, got up, sat down, got up, sat down again, and got up once more. His manner was feverish, and his host disapproved of it.

'Roost!' commanded the Biscuit. 'Park yourself, confound you. You're making me giddy.'

Berry balanced himself on the edge of the horse-hair sofa. He did it as one not committing himself definitely to a sitting position but holding himself in readiness at any moment, should he see fit, to soar up to the ceiling.

'Now then,' said the Biscuit. 'Tell me all.'

'Biscuit,' said Berry, 'the most extraordinary thing has happened. There's a girl . . .'

'A girl, eh?' said the Biscuit, interested. He began to see daylight. 'Who is she?'

'What?' asked Berry, whose attention had wandered.

'I said, who is she?'

'I don't know.'

'What's her name?'

'I don't know.'

'Where does she live?'

'I don't know.'

'You aren't an Encyclopædia, old boy, are you?' said the Biscuit. 'Where did you meet her?'

'I saw her first across a restaurant.'

'Well?'

'We looked at one another a good deal.'

'And then?'

'Then we went on looking at one another. It was that day you were wearing that beard, Biscuit. You remember?'

'I remember.'

'I felt absolutely desperate. I knew, just by looking at her, that I had found the only girl I should ever love...'

'You boys!' interjected the Biscuit tolerantly.

'And how on earth was I to get to know her? That was the problem.'

'It always is. I wish I had a quid for every time....'

'When I came out into the street, I saw her getting into her car. And suddenly I had an inspiration. I jumped in after her, and told her to follow you.'

'Follow me? How do you mean, me? How do I come into it?'

'You were in your car just ahead.'

The Biscuit's interest deepened.

'Do you mean all this happened the day you lunched at the Berkeley, when I was giving the old fungus a trial trip?'

'Of course. I'm telling you.'

'Then who was the girl, I wonder,' mused the Biscuit. 'I don't remember seeing anything very special in the way of girls that time. However, don't let's wander from the point. You jumped into her car. What happened then?'

'You drove off, and we drove after you.'

'You mean she just said, "Yes, sir!" and trod on the self-starter? I should have thought she would have called a cop and two loony-doctors and had you put where you belonged.'

Berry hesitated. They had reached the only point in this romance of his on which he did not like to let his mind dwell. No lover enjoys feeling that he is deceiving the girl he loves. There had been an instant during that scene in the supper-room at the Mazarin when he had braced himself for a full confession. He had thought better of it, but, none the less, his conscience irked him.

'Well, as a matter of fact, Biscuit,' he said, 'I lied to her.'

'Starting early, what?'

'I told her I was a Secret Service man,' said Berry.

The Biscuit gaped.

'You – what?'

'I said I was a Secret Service man. You see, that explained why I wanted her to follow you.'

'Why? Who did you say I was?'

'I told her you were the head of a great Cocaine Ring.'

The Biscuit thanked him.

'I had to give some reason for jumping into her car like that.'

'And what happened when you told her that you had been fooling her?'

'I didn't.'

'You let her go on thinking you were a Secret Service man?'

'Yes.'

'God bless you, laddie! This is the best bed-time story I've heard for months and months and months. So she still thinks you're a Secret Service man? You didn't explain later?'

'No. What happened was this, you see. When I came out of the inn, she had gone. Her car wasn't there. She had driven off. But tonight I met her again. There was a dance going on at the Mazarin, and I had come out from the dinner, and I saw her going up in the lift. So I went up after her, and found her in the supper-room. And we were just starting to talk, when the man who was giving the dance came along and chucked me out.'

The Biscuit uttered appreciative cries.

'But before that happened I had had time to see . . . I mean,' said Berry, becoming incoherent, 'there was something in her eyes . . . The way she looked . . . I believe if only I had had a minute longer ... It was the way she looked, if you know what I mean.'

'You clicked?' said the Biscuit, who liked his bed-time stories crisp.

Berry shuddered. The hideous phrase revolted him.

'I wish you wouldn't ...'

'Either a man clicks or he does not click,' said the Biscuit firmly. 'There are no half measures. You did?'

'I think she was – pleased to see me.'

'Ah! Well, then, of course you proceeded to ask her name?'

'No.'

'You didn't?'

'I hadn't time.'

'Did you ask her where she lived?'

'No.'

'Did she ask you your name?'

'No.'

'Did she ask you where you lived?'

'No.'

'What the dickens *did* you talk about?' asked the Biscuit, curiously. 'The situation in Russia?'

Berry clenched his hands emotionally. Then a black recollection came to him, and his face clouded.

'I found out one thing about her,' he said. 'She's engaged.'

'Engaged?'

'Yes. I'm not worrying about finding her again. I know I shall find her. But if she's engaged ...'

He broke off dejectedly, staring at the carpet.

'You feel that a Conway should refrain from butting in and coming between this girl and some bloke unknown, who no doubt loves her devotedly?' said the Biscuit.

'Yes. All the same . . .'

'All the same, you jolly well mean to do it?'

'Yes.'

'Quite right, too.'

'Do you really think so?'

'Certainly,' said the Biscuit firmly. 'All's fair in love and war, isn't it? I seem to see this other bloke. A weedy bird with a receding chin and an eyeglass. I shouldn't give him another thought. Good heavens! One can't stop to consider the feelings of some unknown wart at a time like this. He's probably someone like Merwyn Flock.'

'Who's Merwyn Flock?'

'Oh, just a fellow,' said the Biscuit. 'Just a blister who happens to be a sort of acquaintance of a friend of mine. From all accounts, one of the less attractive types of human gumboil. Don't you worry, old boy. You take my tip and charge right ahead. There are enough difficulties confronting you already without your having to bother about any vague lizard in the background.'

Berry bestowed upon his friend a look of the utmost gratitude and esteem. He had drawn much comfort from his words.

'I'm glad you feel like that about it,' he said.

'I'm glad you're glad,' said the Biscuit courteously.

CHAPTER 8

Mr Frisby buzzed the buzzer, and his private secretary came gambolling into the room like a lamb in springtime. The remarkable happenings of the previous night had the effect of raising Berry Conway's spirits to the loftiest heights. He felt as if he were walking on pink clouds above a smiling world.

'You rang, sir?' he said affectionately.

'Of course I rang. You heard me, didn't you? Don't ask dam'-fool questions. Get Mr Robbins on the 'phone.'

'Mr Who, sir?' asked Berry. There was nothing he desired more than to assist and oblige his employer, to smooth his employer's path and gratify his lightest whim, but the name was strange to him. Mr Frisby had a habit, which Berry deplored, of being obscure. His construction was bad. He would suddenly introduce into his remarks something like this Robbins motive – vital, apparently, to the narrative – without any preliminary planting or preparation. 'Mr Who, sir?' asked Berry.

'Mr gosh – darn – it – are – you – deaf – I – should – have – thought – I – spoke – plainly – enough – why – don't – you – buy – an – ear – trumpet. *Robbins*. My lawyer. Chancery 09632. Get him at once.'

'Certainly, sir,' said Berry soothingly.

He was concerned about his employer. It was plain that

nothing jolly had been happening to him overnight. He was sitting bunched up in his swivel chair as if he had received a shock of some kind. His equine face was drawn, and the lines about his mouth had deepened. Berry would have liked to ask what was the matter, how bad the pain was and where it caught him. A long, sympathetic discussion of Mr Frisby's symptoms would just have suited his mood of loving-kindness.

Prudence, however, whispered that it would be wiser to refrain. He contented himself with getting the number, and presently found himself in communication with Mr Frisby's legal adviser.

'Mr Robbins is on the wire, sir,' he said in his best bedside manner, handing the instrument to the sufferer.

'Right,' said Mr Frisby. 'Get out.'

Berry did so, casting, as he went, a languishing glance at his overlord. It was meant to convey to Mr Frisby the message that, no matter how black the skies might be, John Beresford Conway was near him, to help and encourage, and it was extremely fortunate that Mr Frisby did not see it.

'Robbins!' he was barking into the telephone, as the door shut.

A low, grave voice replied – a voice suggestive of foreclosed mortgages and lovers parting in the twilight.

'Yes, Mr Frisby?'

'Robbins, come round here at once. Immediately.'

'Is something the matter, Mr Frisby?'

'Oh, no!' The financier yapped bitterly. 'Nothing's the matter. Everything's fine. I've only been swindled and double-crossed by a hell-hound.'

'Tut!' said the twilight voice.

'I can't tell you over the wire. Come round. Hurry.'

'I will start immediately, Mr Frisby.'

Mr Frisby replaced the receiver and, rising, began to pace the room. He returned to the desk, picked up a letter, read it once more (making the tenth time), uttered a stifled howl (his fifteenth), threw it down, and resumed his pacing. He was plainly overwrought, and Berry Conway, if he had been present, would have laid a brotherly hand on his shoulder and patted him on the back and said 'Come, old man, what is it?' It was lucky, therefore, that instead of being present he was in his own little room, dreaming happy dreams.

These were interrupted almost immediately by the sound of the buzzer.

Mr Frisby, when Berry answered the summons, was waltzing about his office. He looked like one of those millionaires who are found stabbed with paper-knives in libraries.

'Sir?' said Berry tenderly.

'Hasn't Mr Robbins come yet?'

'Not yet, sir,' sighed Berry.

'Hell's bells!'

'Very good, sir.'

Mr Frisby resumed his waltzing. He had just paused to give the letter on the desk an eleventh perusal when the door opened again.

This time it was the office-boy.

'Mr Robbins, sir,' said the office-boy.

Mr Robbins, of Robbins, Robbins, Robbins and Robbins, Solicitors and Commissioners for Oaths, was just the sort of man you would have expected him to be after hearing his voice on the telephone. He looked and behaved as if he were a mute at some particularly distinguished funeral. He laid his top-hat on the desk as if it had been a wreath.

'Good morning, Mr Frisby,' he said, and you could see the mortgages foreclosing and the lovers parting all over the place.

'Robbins,' cried the financier, 'I've been hornswoggled.'

The lawyer tightened his lips another fraction of an inch, as if to say that something of this kind was only to be expected in a world in which all flesh was as grass, and where at any moment the most harmless and innocent person might suddenly find himself legally debarred from being a feofee of any fee, fiduciary or in fee-simple.

'What are the facts, Mr Frisby?'

Mr Frisby made a noise extraordinarily like a sea-lion at the Zoo asking for fish.

'I'll tell you what the facts are. Listen. You know I'm interested in copper. I practically own the Horned Toad mine.'

'Quite.'

'Well, the other day they struck a new vein on the Horned Toad. One of the richest on record, it looked like.'

'Excellent.'

'Not so darned excellent,' corrected Mr Frisby. 'It was on the edge of the Horned Toad, and it suddenly disappeared into the claim next door – a damned, derelict dusthole called the Dream Come True, which nobody had bothered to pay any attention to for years. It had just been lying there. That's where the vein went.'

'Most disappointing.'

'Yes,' said Mr Frisby, eyeing this word-painter strangely. 'I *was* a little cross about it.'

'This would, of course,' said Mr Robbins, who had a good head and could figure things out, 'considerably enhance the value of this neighbouring property.'

'You've guessed it,' said Mr Frisby. 'And naturally I wanted to buy it quietly. I made inquiries, and found that the original owner had sold it to a woman named Mrs Jervis.'

'And you approached her?'

'She was dead. But one morning, out of a blue sky, I'm darned if my secretary didn't come in and inform me that he was her nephew and had been left this mine.'

'Your secretary? Young Parkinson?'

'No. Parkinson's gone. This is a new one. A fellow named Conway. You've never seen him. He came in and asked my advice about selling the mine. He said it had never produced any copper, and did I think there was any chance of getting rid of it for a few hundred pounds. I tell you, when I heard him say those words, Robbins, I believed in miracles – a thing I haven't done since I quit attending Sunday School at Carcassone, Illinois, thirty-nine years ago. Can you tie it? A fellow right in my office, and without a notion that the thing was of any value. I nearly broke my fountain-pen.'

'Remarkable.'

Mr Frisby took a turn about the room.

'Well, I hadn't much time to think, and I see now that I did the wrong thing. The way it seemed to me was that if I made a bid for the mine myself he might suspect something. So I told him I knew of a man named J. B. Hoke who sometimes speculated in derelict mines and I would mention the matter to him. This Hoke is a hydrophobia skunk who has been useful to me once or twice in affairs where I didn't care to appear myself. A red-faced crook who makes a living by hanging around on the edge of the financial world and yess-ing everybody. He's yessed me for years. I never liked him, but he was a man I thought you could rely on. So I told him to go to Conway and offer him five hundred pounds.'

'For a property worth millions?' said Mr Robbins, drily.

'Business is business,' said Mr Frisby.

'Quite,' said Mr Robbins. 'And did the young man accept the offer?'

'He jumped at it.'

'Then surely . . .'

'Wait!' said Mr Frisby. 'Do you know what happened? I'll tell you. That double-crossing scoundrel Hoke bought the mine for himself. I might have guessed, if I'd had any sense, that he would suspect something when I told him to go around buying up no-good mines. Maybe he has had private information from somewhere. He's a man with friends in Arizona. Probably there was a leak. Anyway, he went to Conway, gave him his cheque, got his receipt, and now he claims to own the Dream Come True.'

'Tut,' said Mr Robbins.

Mr Frisby performed a few more waltz steps, rather pretty to watch. Finding himself pirouetting in the neighbourhood of the desk, he picked up the letter and handed it to the lawyer.

'Read that,' he said.

Mr Robbins did so, and emitted two 'H'm's' and a 'Tchk'. Mr Frisby watched him anxiously.

'Can he get away with it?' he asked pleadingly. 'He can't get away with it, can he? Don't tell me he can get away with it. Raw work like that. Why, it's highway robbery.'

Mr Robbins shook his head. His manner was not encouraging.

'Have you anything in writing – any letter – or document – to prove that this man was acting as your agent?'

'Of course I haven't. It never occurred to me . . .'

'Then I fear, Mr Frisby, I greatly fear . . .'

'He *can* get away with it?'

'I fear so.'

'Hell!' said Mr Frisby.

A thoughtful expression came into the lawyer's face. He seemed to be testing this oath, assaying it, to see if it was one of the variety for which he was supposed to be a commissioner.

'But it's murder in the first degree!' cried Mr Frisby.

'I note that in his letter,' said Mr Robbins, 'this Mr Hoke says that he is calling here this morning with his lawyer, Mr Bellamy. I know Bellamy well. I am afraid that if Bellamy has endorsed the legality of his action we have little to hope. A very shrewd man. I have the greatest respect for Bellamy.'

'But look what he says on the second page. Look how he proposes to hold me up.'

'I see. He suggests that the Dream Come True be merged or amalgamated with your property, the Horned Toad, the whole hereinafter to be called Horned Toad Copper, Incorporated. . . .'

'And he wants a half-interest in the combination!'

'If Bellamy is behind him, Mr Frisby, a half-interest is, I fear, precisely what he will get.'

'But it's a gold mine!'

'A copper mine, I understood.'

'I mean, I'm parting with a fortune.'

'Most annoying,' said Mr Robbins.

'What did you say?' asked Mr Frisby in a low voice.

'I said it was most annoying.'

'So it is,' said Mr Frisby. 'So it is. You're a great describer.'

Mr Robbins regarded his hat sadly but affectionately.

'If it is necessary for your purposes to acquire this Dream Come True property,' he said, 'I can see no other course but to accept Mr Hoke's proposals. He undoubtedly owns and controls the property in question. If you would care for me to be present at the conference, I shall be delighted to attend, but I fear there is nothing that I can do.'

'Yes, there is,' said Mr Frisby. 'You can stop me beating the fellow with a chair and getting hung for murder.'

The door opened. The office-boy appeared. He was a lad whose voice was passing through the breaking-stage.

'Mr Hoke,' he announced in a rumbling bass.

And then, in a penetrating treble like a squeaking slate-pencil: 'And Mr Bellamy.'

The Hoke–Bellamy combination then entered, both breezy. A very different person now, this J. B. Hoke, from the respectful underling who had yessed Mr Frisby for so many years.

''Morning, Pat,' said Mr Hoke.

'Good morning, Mr Frisby,' said his companion.

'Well, well, well, well, well,' said Mr Hoke. 'You're looking fine.'

'How are you, Bellamy?' said Mr Robbins.

'Fine. And you?'

'In capital health, thank you.'

'Splendid,' said Mr Bellamy.

He took a chair. J. B. Hoke took a chair. Mr Robbins took a chair. Mr Frisby had a chair already.

The conference was on.

When the public reads in its morning paper that a merger has been formed between two financial enterprises, it is probably a little vague as to what exactly are the preliminaries that have to be gone through in order to bring this union about. A description of what took place on the present occasion, therefore, can scarcely fail to be of interest.

J. B. Hoke began by asking Mr Frisby how his golf was coming along. Mr Frisby's only reply being to bare his teeth like a trapped jackal. Mr Hoke went on to say that he himself, while noticeably improved off the tee, still found a difficulty in laying his short mashie approaches up to the pin. Whether it was too much right hand or too little left hand, Mr Hoke could not say, but he doubted if he put one shot in seven just where he meant to. He was also dissatisfied with his putting.

'Well, take the other day for instance, at Oxhey,' said Mr Hoke.

Business men learn to marshal their thoughts clearly. J. B. Hoke left his hearers in no doubt at all as to what had happened the other day at Oxhey. They might have been there in person.

When he had finished, Mr Bellamy mentioned a similar experience he himself had had the Sunday before last down at Chislehurst.

'It's a funny game,' said Mr Bellamy.

'You bet it's a funny game,' said Mr Hoke.

'You never can tell about golf,' said Mr Bellamy.

'That's right,' said Mr Hoke. 'It's funny. It's a game you never can tell about.'

At this point Mr Frisby said something under his breath and broke his pencil in half.

There followed a short pause.

Mr Hoke, resuming, asked the meeting to stop him if they had heard it before, but did they know the story of the two Irishmen?

He proceeded to relate their adventures at considerable length, supplying dialogue, where the narrative called for it, in a strong Swedish accent. He then laughed heartily and left the floor for the next speaker.

This was Mr Bellamy again. Mr Bellamy, overcoming with some difficulty the mirth which his friend's anecdote had stirred in him, said that that reminded him of another, of which the protagonists were a couple of Scotsmen, Donald and Sandy. He apologized for not being able to do the dialect, and then did it, revealing these North Britons as a pair of eccentrics who conversed in a *patois* which was not exactly Cockney and yet not wholly negroid. It made him chuckle a good deal, and it made J. B. Hoke chuckle a good deal. Mr Frisby thought J. B. Hoke looked particularly offensive when he chuckled. Absolutely at his worst.

Mr Frisby did not chuckle. Nor did Mr Robbins. Mr Robbins took up his top-hat, brushed it, eyed it expectantly for a moment, as if weighing the chances of a rabbit coming out of it, and then put it back on the desk again – reverently, as one feeling that there is a home beyond the skies. Mr Frisby, after directing at Mr Hoke a look of extraordinary sourness, picked up one of his cuffs and inscribed on it the words:

J. B. Hoke is a red-faced thug.

The two story-tellers, meanwhile, were fawning on each other in rather a sickening way.

Hoke said, 'That's a hot one, Max.'

Bellamy said, 'Yours was a scream, J. B.'

Hoke said, ' I heard a good one yesterday about two Jews.'

Bellamy said, 'What was that, J. B.?'

Hoke said, 'Well, stop me if you've heard it before.'

It was at this point that Mr Robbins, of Robbins, Robbins, Robbins and Robbins, removed his gaze reluctantly from the hat, coughed in a suggestive sort of way like a distant sheep clearing its throat, and said, 'Er – gentlemen.'

'Yes,' said J. B. Hoke with alacrity, realizing that the second stage in the formalities had now been reached, 'let's get down to brass tacks.'

There was a silence for some moments.

Mr Frisby was the first to break it.

'I've been wondering,' said Mr Frisby in a meditative voice.

'Yeah?' said J. B. Hoke. 'What about?'

'Oh, nothing,' said Mr Frisby. 'Just your initials. I was wondering what the B. stood for.'

'Bernard,' said Mr Hoke, a little proudly.

'Oh?' said Mr Frisby. 'I thought it might be Barabbas.'

'Hey!' said Mr Hoke.

'Gentlemen, gentlemen!' said Mr Robbins.

'Really, really!' said Mr Bellamy.

'Is that actionable?' inquired Mr Hoke of his legal adviser.

Mr Bellamy shook his head.

'To constitute a tort, the words should have been accompanied by a blow or buffet.'

'Is that so?' said Mr Frisby, rising. 'I didn't know. Well, here she comes.'

'Gentlemen, gentlemen, gentlemen, gentlemen!' said Mr Robbins, as if he were all four Robbinses speaking simultaneously.

There was another silence.

'This sort of thing isn't going to get you anywhere,' said Mr Hoke reprovingly.

'Quite,' said Mr Robbins, gazing at his principal as at a favourite, but erring, son.

'Do please, gentlemen,' said Mr Bellamy, 'let us try and endeavour and – er – attempt to steer clear of what you might call – er—'

'Cracks,' said Mr Hoke.

'Snacks,' amended Mr Bellamy.

'Verbal attacks,' said Mr Robbins. 'Personal animadversions. Vituperation, as Mr Hoke has remarked, will get us nowhere.'

'Not that we're trying to get anywhere,' said Mr Hoke, speaking now with a return of his former cheeriness. 'Mean-to-say, we're here already. See what I mean? I mean there's nothing to chew the rag about. The thing's clear. I own the Dream Come True, don't I? Well, say, don't I? What I mean, if any poor fish present wants to argue otherwise, let him explain why. Let him tell this meeting what he thinks is eating him. Let him inform this meeting just where he imagines . . . Well, say, listen,' he said, directing his fire immediately upon Mr Frisby, 'I take it you aren't disputing my title? Of course you aren't. Well then, let's get down to it. Let's talk turkey.'

'Turkey?' said Mr Robbins, in an undertone.

'An American colloquialism,' said Mr Bellamy, 'meaning – let us concentrate on the – ah – *res*.'

'Characteristically quaint,' said Mr Robbins.

Mr Frisby, gallant in defeat, put a point.

'You may own the Dream Come True,' he said, 'just the same as Captain Kidd and Jesse James . . .'

'Please!' said Mr Robbins.

'You may own the Dream Come True, but you can't get the stuff out of it. Not without using my spur-line. You'll have to carry the stuff over the mountains on the backs of mules.'

'My principal,' said Mr Bellamy, 'is cognisant of that fact. Fully cognisant. It is for that reason that he has suggested this merger.'

'Amalgamation,' said Mr Robbins.

'This amalgamation or merger,' said Mr Bellamy.

'And I think I may as well say frankly, my dear Frisby,' said Mr Robbins, 'that in my opinion, my carefully considered opinion, there seems to be no other alternative before you but to accept the proposition on the lines laid down by Mr Hoke.'

A sharp sound broke the silence which followed this observation. It was Mr Frisby snorting. And with that snort ended what may be called the picturesque part of the proceedings. After that, they became dull and technical, with the two lawyers taking matters in hand and doing all the talking. And, as no historian wants to spoil white paper recording the sort of thing lawyers say on these occasions, a further description may be omitted.

Mr Bellamy jotted down a rough memorandum, and handed it to Mr Robbins, saying he hoped it covered everything. Mr Robbins, producing a special pair of spectacles in honour of the importance of the moment, scanned it and said it seemed to cover everything. Mr Bellamy then read it aloud, and Mr Hoke said Yes, that covered everything. Mr Frisby just sat and suffered.

The two lawyers then left, chatting amiably about double burgage, heirs taken in socage, and the other subjects which always crop up when lawyers get together: and Mr Hoke, having seen that the door was closed, approached Mr Frisby's desk in a cautious and conspiratorial manner.

'Hey!' said Mr Hoke.

Mr Frisby looked up wanly. He had been sitting with his head in his hands.

'Haven't you gone?' he asked.

'No,' said Mr Hoke.

'Why not?' said Mr Frisby inhospitably.

Mr Hoke leaned over the desk.

'Say, listen,' he said. 'Now that those two have left, you and I can have a little friendly pow-wow.'

Mr Frisby's reply to this was to inform Mr Hoke that in his opinion he, Mr Hoke, was a robber, a despicable thief, a pickpocket and a body-snatcher. Once, said Mr Frisby, when out in Mexico, he had seen a rattlesnake. He had not liked the rattlesnake – indeed, he had formed a very low opinion of its charm and integrity – but, nevertheless, if it came to friendly pow-wows, he would choose the serpent every time in preference to Mr Hoke. Rather than pow with Mr Hoke, he would wow with a hundred rattlesnakes. This, he explained, was because he considered Mr Hoke a hound, a worm, a skunk, a ghoul, and a low-down, black-hearted hi-jacker.

'Yes, but all kidding aside,' said Mr Hoke amiably, 'listen. Now that we're partners, you and me, here's something we got to make our minds up about. How do you feel about the shareholders? What I mean, what's your reaction to the idea of the shareholders getting money that we could both of us use quite nicely ourselves? What I mean, when do we spill the news of this new reef on the Dream Come True? Before we've bought in all the stock, or after?'

Mr Frisby said nothing.

'It's going to mean a difference of fifty points on the share when the thing comes out. Fifty? It might be a hundred. You never can tell where she'll stop, once they start buying. And if you say you'd like to be loaded up with Horned Toad at four and watch her shooting into the eighties and nineties, you'll only be saying the same as me.'

Mr Frisby chewed his fountain-pen reflectively.

'You know what copper's like,' urged Mr Hoke. 'It's one thing or the other with copper. Either it's down in the cellar, or else it's up singing with the angels. One of the first stocks I ever bought was Green Cananea at twenty-five. I sold at fifty, and kicked myself every morning till it hit two hundred. Today you could buy up all the Horned Toad shares you wanted and still have plenty over for a good meal and a couple of cigars. And a week after this information about the Dream Come True gets out, the National City Bank'll have to hock its undervest if it wants to blow itself to more than about half a dozen. That's how good that stock is going to be. I'm telling you. What we want to do, you and me, is to get together and have a little gentlemen's agreement.'

'Who are the gentlemen?' asked Mr Frisby, interested.

'You and me.'

'Ah!' said Mr Frisby.

Mr Hoke proceeded.

'It wouldn't take us long to corner that stock at rock-bottom prices. It would be pie. What I mean, it isn't as if the Horned Toad was a Kennecott or an Anaconda. It's always been half-way between a may-be and a never-waser. If you start selling shares a couple of thousand at a time, folks'll soon begin to sit up and take notice.'

Mr Frisby bridled a little. He shifted irritably in his chair. It offended his *amour propre* that his companion should imagine it necessary to instruct him in the A.B.C. of market-rigging.

'You go to your broker and start selling,' proceeded Mr Hoke, not observing these signs of impatience, 'and you can bet he'll do something about it. He'll notify his clients that the President of Horned Toad is getting out from under and that things look fishy. They'll tumble over themselves to unload.'

'Naturally,' said Mr Frisby.

'You go to him on 'Change and whisper in his ear that you want him to sell a couple of blocks of two or three thousand...'

'I know,' said Mr Frisby. 'I know, I know.'

'And all the while we'll be buying the stuff up in Paris or Amsterdam. Well, what about it?'

Mr Frisby brooded darkly. On moral grounds he had no objection to the scheme whatever. He heartily approved of it. What was distressing him was the fact that, in enriching himself, he would be compelled also to enrich Mr Hoke.

'Is it a go?' asked that gentleman.

'Yes,' said Mr Frisby.

'Oke,' said Hoke. 'Then that's settled.' A pretty enthusiasm lighted up his face. 'I knew it was a lucky day for me when I went into partnership with you, Pat,' he said, handsomely.

'Don't call me Pat,' said Mr Frisby morosely.

'Well, what's your first name?'

'Never mind,' said Mr Frisby.

It was a point on which he was sensitive. Much time had passed since then, but he could never quite forget the day when the leading wag of his school had discovered his secret.

'Well, I must be getting along,' said Mr Hoke.

'Do,' said Mr Frisby cordially. 'The air in this office won't be fit to breathe till you've gone and I've had the windows opened.'

'By the way, did you ever hear the story of the two . . .'

'Yes,' said Mr Frisby.

'Well, I'll be getting along.'

'Start now,' said Mr Frisby.

J. B. Hoke pranced out jubilantly, treading on air, and immediately outside the door cannoned into a substantial body.

'Can't you look where you're going?' he demanded, aggrieved.

'Why, hullo, Mr Hoke,' said the body amiably.

J. B. Hoke recognized the young man who might have been described, without stretching the facts, as the founder of his fortunes. It was to this young man that he owed the delightful experience of sitting in T. Paterson Frisby's office and telling T. Paterson Frisby just where he got off. This pleasing reflection assuaged the pain in the toe on which Berry had trodden.

'Why, hello, Mr Conway,' he said genially. 'Have a good cigar.'

'Thanks.'

'And how's every little thing with Mr Conway?'

'I'm fine. How are you?'

'I'm fine.'

'Both fine. Fine!' said Berry.

'Got any more mines to sell?' asked Mr Hoke.

'No. That was the only one. I can do you five thousand shares of Federal Dye, if you like.'

'Not for me, thanks.'

'No,' said Berry. 'I suppose you're satisfied with the Dream Come True.'

Mr Hoke looked grave.

'You stung me good over that,' he said. 'Two thousand five hundred dollars for a patch of sand covered with barrelhead cactus. Well, well, well, you're a business man, all right.'

It seemed to Berry – being, as he was, in a mood of universal benevolence and wishing to see nothing but smiling faces around him – that he ought to say something to indicate a possible silver lining. He, too, considered that Mr Hoke had allowed his native generosity to lead him into a bad bargain.

'Oh, come!' he protested heartily. 'You never know. I shouldn't be at all surprised if there weren't millions to be made out of the Dream Come True.'

The joviality had returned to Mr Hoke's face. It now faded again as if it had been wiped off with a sponge. For the first time, it occurred to him how very near the door Berry had been standing at the moment of their impact.

Could he have overheard that last little conference?

Pallidly, Mr Hoke ran over in his mind the more recent of his companion's remarks. He was horrified to discover, that, read in the light of these new suspicions, they had a sickeningly sinister ring. "I suppose you're satisfied with the Dream Come True," he had said. And, after that, this shattering speech about the possibility of there being millions in the thing. He stared at Berry with eyes like apprehensive poached eggs.

'What makes you say that?' he quavered.

'Oh, it just struck me as a possibility,' said Berry with a pleasant smile.

A smile, that is to say, which would have seemed pleasant to anyone else. To J. B. Hoke it suggested a furtive gloating.

'What were you doing, standing outside that door?' he asked.

'I thought I heard the buzzer.'

'Oh?' said Mr Hoke slowly. 'Well, nobody touched the buzzer.'

'False alarm,' said Berry genially. 'I'll get back to my basket.'

Mr Hoke watched him out of sight. Then he burst into the office and tottering to the desk, placed his lips to Mr Frisby's ear.

'S-s-s-say!' he hissed.

Mr Frisby withdrew his ear austerely and began to dry it.

'Haven't you gone *yet*?' he asked. 'Do you want me to put a bed in here? What time do you like to be called in the morning?'

Sarcastic, of course. Bitter, undoubtedly. But there are times when a man may legitimately be sarcastic and bitter.

'Say, listen,' said Mr Hoke urgently. 'Just outside the door I ran into that secretary of yours. He was standing there.'

'What of it?'

'Well, do you think he could have heard what we were saying? I was talking pretty loud.'

'You always do. It's one of the things that get you so disliked.'

'And he said something – darned significantly, I thought – about wasn't it possible that there might be millions made out of the Dream Come True.'

'He did?'

'He certainly did. Say, listen. If advance information of our little arrangement gets out before we're ready, we're sunk. It wouldn't be difficult for this fellow to raise a bit of money and start in buying up the shares on margin. He might get thousands for next to nothing, and stay sitting pretty while they shot up. And before we know what was happening those shares would be hitting the ceiling and we'd lose our shirts if we tried to buy them. I've known it happen that way before. Years ago, when I was with Mostyn and Kohn in Detroit, the time they were working that A. and C. ramp, there was a bad leakage in the office.'

'There would be, if you were there,' said Mr Frisby.

'I had nothing to do with it,' protested Mr Hoke, and in his voice there was the pain of what-might-have-been. 'I never knew a thing that was going on. But somebody got advance information, and what they did to Mostyn and Kohn was nobody's business. The stock kited sixty points the first day, and Mostyn and Kohn out in the cold, wondering what was happening to them and each of them accusing the other of double-crossing him. Mostyn hit Kohn on the beezer, I remember, and God knows there was plenty of it to hit. Well, that's what's going to happen here if we don't watch out. You ought to fire that fellow, Pat.'

'Don't call me Pat,' said Mr Frisby. 'And where's the sense of firing him?'

'Well, we ought to do something.'

'Why did he say he was standing out there?'

'He put up some story about thinking he had heard the buzzer.'

'H'm!' said Mr Frisby. 'Well, good-bye.'

'Don't you want me to wait?'

'Is it likely that anyone would ever want you to wait? Get out of this, and don't keep coming running in again all the time.'

'Well, I'll tell you. My mind's not easy.'

'A mind like yours,' said Mr Frisby, 'couldn't be.'

For some moments after the door had closed, T. Paterson Frisby sat rocking meditatively in his chair. He was not thinking about Berry. His partner's panic had aroused no responsive thrill in his heart. What did disturb him was the thought that, in a world which they said they were going to make fit for heroes to live in, nobody had started the millennium by lynching J. B. Hoke. It looked like negligence somewhere.

He spent nearly twenty minutes thinking about Mr Hoke. At the end of that period, crystallizing his thoughts, as was his custom, into the telling phrase, he reached for a cuff and wrote on it as follows:

J. B. Hoke is a son of a . . .

In moments of strong emotion the handwriting tends to deteriorate. Mr Frisby's did. So what that last word was we shall never know.

CHAPTER 9

I

The total failure of her brother George to accomplish anything constructive by his trip to Valley Fields had convinced Lady Vera Mace of the truth of the ancient proverb that if you want a thing well done you must do it yourself. Reluctantly, therefore, for she was a woman with many calls on her mind, she caught the six-thirty-four train some days later, and, arriving at the gate of Peacehaven, met her nephew, Lord Biskerton, coming out. Another moment, and she would have missed him.

Had she done so, it would have been all right with the Biscuit. This sudden apparition of a totally unwanted aunt affected him much as the ghost of Banquo on a memorable occasion affected Macbeth.

'Good Lord!' he exclaimed. 'What on earth are you doing down here?'

'I want to have a talk with you, Godfrey.'

'But you can't,' protested the Biscuit. 'I'm not open for being talked to.'

His emotion was understandable. He was just on his way to Castlewood to collect Miss Valentine and take her to the Bijou Palace (One Hundred Per Cent. Talking) at the corner of Roxburgh Road and Myrtle Avenue, the meeting-place of all that is best and fairest in Valley Fields. And, while he knew he was doing this merely because he was sorry for a lonely little girl, a stranger in a strange land, who had few pleasures, the last thing he wanted was a prominent member of the family dodging about the place, taking notes of his movements with bulging eyes.

'I'm busy,' he said. 'Occupied. Full of appointments. I'm just off to the pictures.'

'What I have to say is much more important than any pictures.'

'Not than these. They're showing a film of the life of a Spanish onion. Full of educative value, with a most beautiful theme song.'

'I shan't keep you more than a few minutes. I've got to catch the seven-ten train back to Victoria. I am dining with Lady Corstorphine at Mario's.'

'Ah!' said the Biscuit, relieved. 'That puts a different complexion on the matter. Well, I'll walk to the station with you.'

He hurried her round the corner and into the asphalt-paved, beehive-lined passage that led thither. Only when they were out of sight of Mulberry Grove did his composure return.

'How the dickens did you find out I was living here?' he asked. 'It looks to me as if there had been a leakage somewhere.'

'Your father went round to your flat and made Venner tell him.'

'Ah, that explains it. How is the guv'nor? Pretty fit and insolvent? Still stealing the cat's milk and nosing about in the street for cigar ends?'

'His health and finances are in much the same state as usual.'

'Poor old chap!' said the Biscuit sympathetically. 'Odd how none of our family seem able to get their hooks on a bit of money.'

'He tells me he is hoping to let Edgeling to Mr Frisby for Goodwood. I think it would be an excellent thing. But I did not come here to talk about your father. I want to speak to you about Ann.'

'Yes?' said the Biscuit. 'Good old Ann? How is she?'

'She is very well.'

'Buzzing about a lot and rejoicing in her youth, I suppose? Parties, routs, and revels?'

'She was at home, answering her letters of congratulation, when I left. At least, I think she was.'

'You think? Are there secrets between you?'

'It is quite possible,' said Lady Vera, 'that she was writing to everybody to say that congratulations were unnecessary, as she was no longer engaged.'

The Biscuit gaped.

'Says which?'

'What do you mean by that extraordinary expression?'

'Eh? Oh,' said the Biscuit, momentarily confused, 'I picked it up. From a fellow next door. A man. He's an American. An American man. One of the first families in Great Neck, New York. The phrase implies astonishment and incredulity. Why the dickens should Ann say she was no longer engaged?'

'Because she may be intending to break off the engagement.'

The Biscuit stared.

'What! Give me the push?'

'Yes.'

'You mean, actually slip me the old acid-drop?'

'Yes.'

'But what would she do that for?'

Lady Vera began to deliver the exordium which she had roughed out in the train.

'Your father and I are terribly worried, Godfrey. We both think that you have made the greatest mistake in disappearing like this.'

'But I had to disappear. Didn't the guv'nor explain? I was the hunted fox with the pack in full cry after me. I was the hare that pants for cooling streams when heated in the chase. I couldn't go out of doors without hearing a "Yoicks! Hark For'rard!" from a shirt merchant or a "Tantivy!" from a bespoke tailor.'

'I know all that,' said Lady Vera impatiently. 'Naturally it would have been a fatal thing if you had had to appear in the County Court. But whatever induced you to tell Ann you had mumps?'

'A pal of mine suggested that. You see, I had to give some explanation of why we failed to notice among those present the young and popular Lord Biskerton. Couldn't just disappear without a word.'

Lady Vera did not snort, for she was a woman of breeding. But she uttered a snort-like exclamation.

'It was an insane suggestion. So idiotic that I am surprised that you did not think of it yourself.'

'Harsh words,' said the Biscuit, pained. 'It seemed to me a ruse that met the case most admirably. Mumps are infectious, so Ann wouldn't come calling at the flat and smoothing my pillow and noticing with surprise that the bed was empty and had not been slept in. If you don't think that is a good idea, all I can say, Aunt Vera, is that you are pretty hard to please.'

'Mumps! And Ann a girl who is so painfully romantic and idealistic.'

'What's that got to do with it?'

'Good gracious, Godfrey . . . !'

'What a title for a musical comedy!' said the Biscuit with

enthusiasm. ' "Good Gracious, Godfrey!" Can't you see it on the... But I'm interrupting you,' he broke off courteously, observing in his companion some slight signs of fermentation.

'What I was about to say was this. I think – and your father thinks – that Ann accepted you – well, shall we say without quite knowing her own mind. That being so, the slightest thing may cause her to change it. And you have deliberately put yourself into a position where, every time she thinks of you, it is to picture you with a face like a water-melon.'

'You mean,' said the Biscuit incredulously, 'you actually mean that a sweet girl like Ann would allow herself to be affected...'

'There is something so utterly ridiculous about mumps.'

'Well,' said the Biscuit, bitterly, 'if that is what a woman's heart is like, then all I can say is, a pretty sex! Yes, I mean it. A pretty sex!'

'And, in addition to that, I have every reason to believe that Ann has met some other man and become dangerously attracted by him.'

The Biscuit gasped. This was news, hot off the griddle.

'You don't mean that!'

'I do. She has been behaving in a very odd manner.'

'But, dash it, what can I do?'

'You must come back.'

'But I can't.'

'Yes, you can. You must tell her that you haven't got mumps, after all. And to account for your absence you must say that you have had to go over to Paris. I have been talking it over with your father, and he agrees with me that it would be a very good thing if you did go to Paris. I can afford to pay your expenses, and I think I might manage to take Ann over there for a week or two. She would like Paris.'

'But I shouldn't,' said the Biscuit explosively. 'I can't stand Paris. I hate the place. Full of people talking French, which is a thing I bar. It always seems to me so affected.'

'It is better than talking like an idiot.'

'Besides, I want to stay here.'

Lady Vera looked at him searchingly.

'Why? What is the wonderful attraction about this extraordinary place?'

'I like it,' said the Biscuit stoutly. 'It has a quiet charm. I enjoy strolling in my garden of an evening, drinking in the peace of the gloaming and plucking snails off the young lobelias.'

'Are you flirting with some girl down here, Godfrey?' said Lady Vera tensely.

It is possible that at that moment Valley Fields was full of nephews whom an aunt's suggestion had just outraged to the very core. But none of these could have looked half so appalled as the Biscuit.

'Me?' he cried. 'Me?'

'Well, I don't know if you are or not, but I can tell you one thing. If you don't want to lose Ann, you had better leave Valley Fields at once and show yourself again in civilized surroundings.'

The seven-ten train rolled into the station. Lord Biskerton assisted his aunt into a first-class carriage.

'I have it,' he said jubilantly. 'Here is the solution, sizzling from the pan. Tell Ann I haven't got the mumps, but am in reality in the Secret Service of my country, and am away somewhere on a job the nature of which I am not empowered to reveal. That will bring the roses back to her cheeks. That will make her regard her Godfrey with admiration and esteem.'

The seven-ten rolled out of the station. It bore with it an aunt thinking poorly of her nephew. Lady Vera's opinion of Lord

Biskerton's mentality, never high, had in the last few minutes sunk to a new, low figure. She supposed that she had done something to cause Providence to afflict her with a nephew like that, but she could not recall any offence of the colossal proportions which would justify the punishment. She sighed deeply, and fell back on Woman's only consolation in times of stress. Opening her bag, she produced her puff and began to powder her nose.

As for the Biscuit, he picked up his feet and returned to Castlewood on the run.

II

In Lady Vera's flat in Davies Street, Mayfair, Ann, at the time when this conversation was taking place, had paused in the writing of her letters to have one of her heart-to-heart talks with her Conscience. Ever since the night of the Bassinger Ball at the Hotel Mazarin, this incubus had been making itself more than ordinarily obnoxious.

'Tired?' asked Conscience, with affected solicitude.

'No.'

'Then why have you stopped writing?'

'I don't know.'

'To think, perhaps? To muse, maybe? About that affair at the Mazarin, possibly?'

'Well, why shouldn't I?'

'A pretty disgraceful affair, that,' said Conscience with growing severity. 'A very shady bit of work, indeed, I should describe it as. I wonder you don't try to forget it. I suppose you realize that, if Toddy Malling hadn't come along at that particular moment, that man would have kissed you?'

'Would he?'

'You know he would. And you would have liked it, too. That's the part that sickens me. That's the thing that makes me writhe. That's the aspect of the matter that . . .'

'All right,' said Ann, shortly.

Conscience was not to be silenced.

'A nice girl like you! A girl who has always prided herself on her fastidiousness. A girl who could never understand how other girls in her set could make themselves cheap and let themselves be pawed about – Ugh!' said Conscience witheringly. 'Necker!'

Ann shuddered.

'Yes, Necker! And you engaged to a delightful young man, heir to one of the finest titles in England. And a young man, what is more, who is at this very instant writhing on a bed of pain, his only consolation the thought of you. "This may be agony," he is saying to himself as the spasm catches him, "and I'm not pretending it isn't. But on the other side there is this to be said – Ann loves me. Ann is true to me. Ann is not going about the place on private petting-parties with men she scarcely knows by sight." That's what he's saying, this unhappy young man.'

'But he's got mumps.'

'What of it?'

'It seems so silly.'

'Where the heart has been given, the size of the face should not matter.'

'No-o,' said Ann doubtfully.

There was a pause.

'And this other man,' resumed Conscience. 'What do you know about him? Coming right down to it, how do you know he's worthy of you?'

'He must be with a face like that.'

'Statistics show that fifty per cent. of murderers and other criminals have pleasing faces. You can't go by the face.'

'And he is the only man I have ever met who was really romantic.'

'Romantic! That's the trouble with you,' said Conscience, snatching at the point. 'Do you know what you are? A silly, sentimental schoolgirl. Yes, you are. Romance! The idea! Isn't it romantic enough for you to be the future Countess of Hoddesdon? I'm ashamed of you.'

'I've got to get on with my letters,' said Ann.

She resumed her task. It was one she had found laborious of late. All these idiotic people writing to wish her happiness, when they ought to have known that marrying Lord Biskerton wasn't going to make her ... She checked herself sternly. It was just this kind of reflection which had caused Conscience to maltreat her so much in the last few days.

'*Dear Lady Corstorphine,*' she wrote doggedly. '*How sweet of you to ...*'

'Oh, gosh!' said Ann.

She laid down her pen. She simply couldn't.

'?' said Conscience.

'Oh, all right,' said Ann.

She worked off the Corstorphine one. Two pages of pretty, girlish spontaneity which made her feel as if she were having teeth dragged out of her. Then she picked up the next in order from the pile.

Castlewood,
Mulberry Grove,
Valley Fields,
S.E.21.

Dear Ann,

   I suppose you have quite forgotten me....

Ann looked at the signature.

K. Valentine.

A sensation that was like poignant nostalgia swept over Ann Moon. Kitchie Valentine! The girl who had been such fun on the boat, coming over from America – such ages ago. Ann started guiltily. She was a girl who formed friendships with the eager impulsiveness of a kitten, and she had loved Kitchie. When they had parted at Waterloo Station, they had vowed to have all sorts of good times together.... And here she had been in England weeks and weeks and weeks and had never once given Kitchie a thought.

These steamer friendships!

Reading the letter did nothing to heal her remorse. Poor Kitchie! She seemed to be having a wretched time. This uncle of hers might have been the life and soul of the officers' mess of the Loyal Royal Worcestershires, but he was evidently proving a poor companion for a young girl. True, there was some mention of a man next door, a Mr Smith, who appeared to be agreeable; but there was very little about him and a great deal about the absent Merwyn Flock. Merwyn, it seemed, had not written for nearly a month, and it was this that was distressing Kitchie Valentine almost more than her uncle Everard's habit of falling asleep after lunch and making a noise like a bassoon.

Ann put down her pen. She glowed with altruistic fervour. This letter, happening to coincide with the first free evening she had had for a considerable time, decided her. Tonight, by a curious chance, she was engaged to no hostess. She could, therefore, and would, go straight down to this Valley Fields, wherever it might be, and call at Castlewood, and bring Kitchie back for dinner somewhere. And after dinner they would come back to the flat and have one of their long ship-board talks.

Her two-seater was garaged just round the corner. Ten minutes later, having been informed that the route to Valley Fields was through Sloane Square, Clapham, Brixton and Herne Hill, she was hurrying on her way. Half an hour later, she had pulled up outside Castlewood. Thirty-two minutes later, she was being informed that Miss Valentine was not at home. She had gone to the pictures, Gladys-at-Castlewood said, with Mr Smith from Peacehaven.

'Oh, well, tell her I called.'

Ann could not help feeling a little annoyed. She knew that she ought not to be grudging Kitchie any simple pleasures she might be able to snatch from life, but her relief-expedition had undeniably fallen somewhat flat. Her rush to ameliorate the monotony of life at Castlewood seemed to have been wasted on one who, despite the hard-luck stories she told in her letters, was apparently never without a Smith to help her through the long days.

The gleam of water across the road caught her eye. She walked to the railings and stood looking at the swans. They had little to offer her in the way of entertainment. Twilight was falling on Mulberry Grove, and Egbert and Percy had turned in for the night. Each was floating with his head tucked under the left wing; and if there is any spectacle more devoid of dramatic interest than a swan with its head tucked under its wing, it is two swans in that position. Ann turned away, and, doing so, was aware that her sylvan solitude had been invaded. Over the gate of the house named The Nook a young man was leaning. The smoke of his tobacco floated up towards the smiling sky.

Ann started to walk to her car. There was a cosy smugness about Mulberry Grove which somehow seemed to invest the presence there of two persons of the opposite sex with the suggestion of a *tête-à-tête*, and she disliked this enforced intimacy. She felt almost as if she were shut up in a railway carriage alone with this young man, and had a feeling that he might at any moment open a conversation by asking her if she objected to smoking.

When he did open the conversation, however, it was not to make this inquiry. She had scarcely passed him when he uttered the word 'Gosh!' in a loud and startled voice. And almost simultaneously the gate slammed and he was at her side.

She stopped. She turned. She arranged her features for a withering look – a look which would say 'Sir!' even if she did not say it.

She gave a little gasp. She stared. The withering look went all to pieces, and in its place there appeared one of blank astonishment.

'Oh!' said Ann sharply.

The swan Egbert, roused from his beauty-sleep, uttered a crisp oath and dozed off again.

III

Berry Conway had come out of The Nook to lean on his gate and smoke in no idle spirit of *dolce far niente*. It was not the mere beauty of the summer evening that had drawn him thither. He had come because the Old Retainer had been weeping on his neck indoors and seemed likely, if he remained, to go on weeping indefinitely.

It was immediately on his return from the City that he had first perceived that this woman was not her old, placid self. She appeared to be in the grip of some powerful, though at the moment suppressed, emotion. When she spoke, it was in a low, husky voice. She sniffed once or twice. And as he went upstairs to change his clothes he could feel her eyes fixed on his back in a stare like that of some dumb animal trying to express itself.

This was at six-thirty. Descending the stairs at six-forty-five, he found her waiting in the hall. There could be no doubt now that something momentous had occurred. The Old Retainer was plainly in what, if he had been a cross-word puzzle enthusiast, he would have described as a state of excitement, a flurry, a twitter, tremor, pulsation, palpitation, ruffle, hurry of the spirits, pother, stew (colloq.) and ferment.

At six-fifty it had all come out. Sergeant Finbow, until that morning Police-Constable Finbow, had celebrated his promotion by making her an offer of marriage.

At seven-fifteen she was still saying that she would not dream of deserting Master Berry. At seven-twenty, arguing forcibly, Berry had begun to try to convince her that, even lacking her protective care, he would manage to get along somehow. At seven-thirty, the weeping had set in. And at seven-thirty-five, he had broken from the clinch, lit his pipe, and come out to lean on the gate and adjust his mind to this extraordinary piece of good fortune.

With the Old Retainer satisfactorily settled and off his mind, he could at last begin to come to terms with this business of life. She had always been the great obstacle. The future now opened out before him, rich and splendid. No more Nook. No more

Frisby. He could start fair, with the world as his oyster and an intense and all-conquering determination as his oyster-fork.

He leaned on the gate, planning great things. Mulberry Grove, now that he was so near to parting from it, had taken on quite an attractive air. There was a girl across the road, inspecting the swans. The sight of her turned his thoughts to their favourite theme, and for some moments a mist hid Mulberry Grove and the rest of the world from his sight.

It cleared away, and he saw that the girl was coming towards him.

IV

Ann was the first to speak. She was still feeling a little breathless. She had just become a convert to the doctrine of Predestination, and was finding the experience somewhat overwhelming. It was, she realized, evidently Fate's intention that, wherever she might happen to be, this young man should materialize out of thin air at her side, so there was nothing to be done about it. Conscience could not blame her for what was Fate's fault.

She spoke with a childlike wonder.

'Is there any place where you aren't?' she said.

Berry continued to stare. The idea of Predestination had not yet occurred to him. His theory, as far as he was capable of evolving any theory, was that this extraordinary occurrence had something to do with will-power. His tense meditations about this girl had evidently had the effect of drawing her from somewhere in the centre of London to Mulberry Grove, Valley Fields. Which, considering that the distance was about seven miles, was not bad going.

'Is it really you?' he said.

Ann said it was.

'Well, I suppose all this is happening,' said Berry, 'but I can't believe it. What...?'

'What...?' said Ann, simultaneously.

'I beg your pardon.'

'Go on.'

'I was going to say, "What are you doing here?"'

'So was I. I came to see a friend who lives here.' Ann paused, trying to assimilate an idea. 'Do *you* live here?' she asked, surprised. Of course, one knows that Secret Service men must live somewhere, but one somehow does not associate them with fragrant backwaters in the suburbs.

Berry would have given much to deny it. He glowed with shame for Mulberry Grove. Beastly, smug, placid, prosaic place. Black Joe's opium-dive in Deptford was the only fitting address for the man he would have liked to be.

'Yes,' he admitted.

'But why?'

Berry was frank about it.

'They don't pay us much in the Secret Service,' he said.

'What a shame!' cried Ann. 'Considering all the dangerous things you have to do.'

'Oh, well!' said Berry.

There was another pause.

'What...?' said Ann.

'What...?' said Berry.

'I beg your pardon,' said Berry.

'Go on,' said Ann.

'No, you go on,' said Berry.

'What became of you the other night, at the dance?'

'I was ejected by a man with a walrus moustache, who seemed to be someone in authority.'

'That was your host.'

'Not mine.'

Ann's eyes widened.

'Do you mean to say you were not invited?'

'Only to get out.'

'But why ...?'

'To see you, of course.'

'Oh!' said Ann.

'I was in the lobby. I saw you getting into the lift.'

'The elevator?'

'The elevator,' said Berry, accepting the emendation. 'They told me there was a dance going on upstairs, so I went up.'

An odd shyness had taken possession of Ann. She was annoyed to find herself trembling. A sense of something momentous about to happen was making her feel strangely weak.

To counteract this, she endeavoured to keep the conversation on a light, chatty note.

'What a lot of people there were at that dance,' she said brightly.

'Only one, for me,' said Berry.

The light, chatty note seemed to have failed. And Ann began to see that, if this interview was to be kept within bounds which would meet with the approval of a rigid New England Conscience, she would have to be more adroit than she had been up to the present. She remembered expressing to her Uncle Paterson over the trans-Atlantic telephone some weeks earlier a desire to become acquainted with one of those men who meet a girl and gaze into her eyes and cry 'My mate!' and fold her in their arms. She seemed to have found him.

'I couldn't think what had become of you that night,' she said.

'You mean you missed me?' said Berry hungrily. 'Do you mean you missed me?'

Ann's Conscience, which up till this moment had been standing aside and holding a sort of watching brief, now intruded itself upon the scene.

'I don't want you to think I am always shoving myself forward,' said Conscience frigidly, 'but I should be failing in my duty if I did not point out that you are standing at a Girl's Cross Roads. Everything depends on what reply you make to the very leading question which has just been put to you. I don't know if you have been observing this young man at all closely, but I ought to inform you that there is a gleam in his eye which I don't at all like. The slightest encouragement at this point will obviously be fatal. I would suggest some such answer as "Oh, no" or "What makes you think that?" or even a wordless raising of the eyebrows. But, whatever you do, let me urge upon you with all the emphasis of which I am capable not to drop your eyes and say "Yes."'

'Yes,' said Ann, dropping her eyes. 'Of course I did.' She raised her eyes again and looked straight into his. She was a girl who was lost to all shame. 'You had just begun to tell me something, you see, and naturally I wanted to know what it was.'

Berry clenched his hands. He coughed. And, having coughed, he uttered a sort of high-pitched bark. The swan Percy woke up and hissed an opprobrious epithet at him.

'It was only this,' said Berry, choking over each syllable. 'I've loved you from the very first time I saw you.'

'I thought that was it,' said Ann.

He was gazing into her eyes. He now folded her in his arms. He did not cry 'My mate!' but Ann received the impression that the remark was implied. She hung limply to him. What had become of her Conscience she did not know. It appeared to be dead or unconscious. In a situation where she should have been feeling nothing but shame, she felt only a happiness that seemed to be tearing her asunder. At a moment when the face of Lord Biskerton, swollen and wrapped in flannel, should have been hovering reproachfully before her eyes, she saw only Berry.

She drew away and gave a little sigh.

'I knew this would happen,' she said. 'That's why I ran away that day.'

Berry caught her in his arms again. The swan Egbert turned to the swan Percy and said something in an undertone. Percy nodded and both birds then sneered audibly. Swans, like sub-editors, are temperamentally incapable of understanding love's young dream.

'Of course, we oughtn't to,' said Ann reflectively. 'It's all wrong.'

'It isn't.'

'But I'm engaged,' said Ann. It sounded silly to her, even as she said it. Such a trifling objection.

'I love you,' said Berry.

'I love you,' said Ann.

'I knew I loved you the moment I saw you that day at the Berkeley.'

'I suppose I did, too.'

'Some day I'm going back to the Berkeley and I'm going to ask the management if I can put up a tablet on the wall. When I came out of the inn that afternoon and found you gone, I nearly died.'

'And now you've found me again, you probably will,' said Ann. A happy smile lit up her face. 'The row there's going to be about this!'

'Row?' said Berry. In his exalted mood, it seemed incredible to him that the whole world would not greet this wonderful consummation of all his hopes and dreams with cheers and enthusiasm. 'Do you mean,' he demanded incredulously, 'that you think anyone's going to *object*?'

'I do.'

'Who?'

'My *fiancé*, for one.'

'Oh . . . !' Berry dismissed this negligible unknown with a gesture.

'And my father. And my mother. And my uncle. And—'

Berry laughed scornfully. So might a knight have laughed at a covey of dragons.

'Let 'em,' he said.

Ann's laugh was a contented laugh, a little bubble of happiness breaking from a rainbow.

'I knew you would say that. That's what I love about you. How awful it would be if you were – just ordinary.'

Berry started. Out of a blue sky there seemed to have come the rumbling of distant thunder.

'Ordinary?'

'Like all men I've ever met. They work in offices, and—'

'Work in offices,' said Berry. He spoke dully, and that thunder seemed to him to be coming closer.

But Ann had come closer, too, and that made him forget the thunder. She was holding the lapels of his coat.

'I've just had an idea,' she said.

'What?'

'Why shouldn't we tell each other our names? Think how nice it would be to know who we are.'

'My name's Conway.'

'Well, you don't expect me to call you Mr Conway.'

'Beresford Conway. All my pals call me Berry.'

'All my pals call me Ann. Moon is my other name.'

'Ann Moon?'

'Ann Moon.'

Berry wrinkled his forehead.

'But it's familiar.'

'Is it?'

'I mean I've heard it before somewhere.'

'Have you? Where?'

'I can't remember. Or did I read it somewhere?'

'Perhaps.'

'Ann Moon. Moon. Moon. I know I've heard it before, but I can't place it.'

'Perhaps you're thinking of some other Moon. There are lots of us, you know. June, Oh, Silvery, My California – dozens and dozens.'

Berry became aware that in a futile discussion of names golden moments were running to waste.

'What does it matter, anyway?' he said. 'You're you.'

'And you're you.'

'And here we both are!'

'But we won't stay here. I don't like those swans.'

'*I* don't like those swans,' said Berry, scrutinizing them.

'They're sneering at us.'

'They *are* sneering at us.'

'We'll fool them. We'll get into my car and we'll drive up to London and we'll have dinner somewhere – Mario's is a good place. One needn't dress in the balcony – and then we can talk without having a bunch of birds listening to everything we say.'

'Splendid!'

'That'll make them feel silly.'

'It will make them feel about as silly as two swans have ever felt.'

Egbert looked at Percy. Percy looked at Egbert.

'Well!' said Egbert.

'These young couples!' said Percy. 'Another minute and I should have been sick.'

V

Mulberry Grove slept under the night sky. Up and down it, smoking a thoughtful cigarette, paced Godfrey, Lord Biskerton. He appeared to be in sentimental mood. From time to time he gazed up at the stars and seemed to think well of them.

Rapid footsteps turned the corner. He advanced to meet the new-comer.

'Berry?'

'Hullo.'

'Take a turn along the road with me, laddie,' said the Biscuit. 'I want a word with you.'

Berry would have preferred to slip past and postpone this interview. He was conscious of an extreme discomfort. Since his departure from Mulberry Grove in Ann's car, many things had been made clear to him. He knew now why the name Ann Moon had sounded familiar.

Few things in life are more embarrassing than the necessity of having to inform an old friend that you have just got engaged to his *fiancée*. It is a task that calls for coolness of head and the quiet marshalling of the thoughts, and Berry would have wished to sleep on this thing and go more deeply into it on the morrow.

But the Biscuit, apparently mistrustful of his ability to hold his companion purely by the magic of his conversation, had seized his elbow in a firm grip.

'Yes, old boy,' he said, 'I want your counsel. Where have you been all night?'

'I went out to dinner. At a place called Mario's.'

'I know it well,' said the Biscuit. 'I've taken Ann there.'

It was a cue, and Berry knew that he ought to have accepted it. He did go so far as to open his mouth, but the words refused to come.

'Nobody should go to Mario's,' said the Biscuit, 'without trying the *minestrone*. Did you have *minestrone*?'

'I can't remember.'

'You can't remember?'

'We had some sort of soup, I suppose,' said Berry desperately. 'But I was so—'

'We?' said the Biscuit.

'I was with a girl,' said Berry. It seemed monstrous to refer to Ann in that casual way, but still it was the technical description of her.

'*The* girl?' asked the Biscuit with sudden interest.

'Yes.'

'So you've met her again?'

'Yes.'

'And how's everything coming along?'

Berry plunged. If this thing had to be done, it was best to do it quickly.

'We're engaged,' he said.

'Fine!' said the Biscuit. 'So you're engaged? Well, well!'

'Yes.'

'Just to this one girl, I suppose?'

'What do you mean?'

'You always were a prudent, level-headed fellow who knew where to stop,' said the Biscuit enviously. 'I'm engaged to two girls.'

'What!'

The Biscuit sighed.

'Yes, two. And I'm hoping that you may have a word of advice to offer on the subject. Otherwise, I see a slightly tangled future ahead of me.'

'Two?' said Berry, dazed.

'Two,' said the Biscuit. 'I've counted them over and over again, but that's what the sum keeps working out at. I started, if you remember, with one. So far, so good. A steady, conservative policy. But complications have now arisen. You may have heard me speak of one Kitchie Valentine?'

'The kid next door?'

The Biscuit frowned.

'Don't call her the kid next door. The angel next door, if you like, or the adjoining seraph.'

'Biscuit, let me tell you—'

'No,' said Lord Biskerton with gentle firmness. 'Let *me* tell *you*. I added young Kitchie to the strength tonight. Somewhere near the end of Roxborough Road, under, if I remember rightly, the third lamp-post from Myrtle Avenue. It happened like this.'

'Biscuit, listen—'

'It happened like this,' said Lord Biskerton. 'Until recently she was engaged to a bounder of the almost incredible name of Merwyn Flock. How she ever came to do such a cloth-headed thing, I cannot say, but such are the facts. He's an actor, and some day, if all goes well, I hope to pop over to America, where he performs, and fling a hearty egg at him. The low hound!

He chucked her, Berry,' said the Biscuit, wrestling with rising emotion. 'He took that loving heart in his greasy hands and squeezed it dry and threw it away like an old tube of tooth-paste. She got a letter from him tonight, saying that he had just married some actress or other but hoped they would always be friends. "Can't we be friends?" he said. There's a song with that title. I've sung it in my bath.'

'Biscuit . . .'

'I thought she seemed a bit under the weather when we were starting off for the pictures. Not at all her old bright self, she wasn't. She was depressed during the six-reel feature-film, and the two-reel Mickey Mouse didn't get a smile out of her. On our way home she told me all. And, believe me or believe me not, old boy, I hadn't got more than about halfway through the cheering-up process when I suddenly found that we were linked in a close embrace, murmuring soft words of endearment, and two minutes later I discovered with some surprise that we were engaged. That's Life.'

'Are you fond of her?' was all Berry could find to say.

'Of course I'm fond of her,' said the Biscuit with asperity. 'I love her with a passion that threatens to unseat my very reason. I can see now that it was a case of love at first sight. The moment I set eyes on her, I remember, something seemed to tell me that I had found my mate. Oh, don't make any mistake about it, my lad, we are twin souls. On the other hand, that doesn't alter the fact that I'm engaged to two girls.'

'But you aren't.'

'Tut, tut!' said the Biscuit, annoyed at his friend's denseness. 'Count them for yourself. Kitchie, one. Ann . . .'

'I'm engaged to Ann.'

The Biscuit clicked his tongue.

'No, you're not, old boy,' he said, patiently. 'Don't try to cloud the issue by being funny. You're engaged to this girl of yours, whatever her name is.'

'Her name is Ann Moon.'

'What!' cried the Biscuit.

'You heard.'

'I did hear,' said the Biscuit. 'But I was wondering if I could believe my ears, if I could credit my senses. You mean to tell me that Ann, while engaged to me, heartlessly and callously went off and got engaged to someone else? My gosh! Doesn't this throw a blinding light on the fickleness of woman! That sex ought to be suppressed. I've often said so. You mean – literally – that you and Ann—'

'Yes.'

'Was she the girl whose car you jumped into and said you were a Secret Service man?'

'Yes.'

'Medium-sized girl with grey eyes and a beautiful figure and a way of wrinkling up her nose when she . . .'

'I know her by sight, thanks,' said Berry. 'You needn't describe her.'

'Well, this is the most extraordinary thing I ever heard in my life,' said the Biscuit.

He brooded for a while in stunned silence.

'Perhaps it's all for the best,' he said at length.

'I think so,' said Berry.

'In fact,' said the Biscuit, now definitely perking up, 'you might describe it as a consummation devoutly to be wished.'

'That's just how I was going to describe it.'

'Yes, yes, yes, yes, yes,' said the Biscuit, with growing satisfaction, 'I see now that it is the best thing that could possibly have happened. The momentary spasm of pique and chagrin is over, and I can face facts. I realize now that Ann never did care a damn for me.'

'She likes you. She said so.'

The Biscuit smiled sadly, and emitted five more yes's.

'But we were not affinities. I saw that from the start. She had a way of looking sideways at me suddenly and looking quickly away again as if she hoped I wasn't true but was reluctantly compelled to believe that I was. She would never have been happy with me. It was only the fact that I proposed to her at Edgeling at the exact moment when the sunset and the ivied walls had made her feel all emotional that ever caused her to accept me. Take her, old friend, and my blessing with her. Take her, I say. Take her.'

'All right,' said Berry. 'All right – I'm going to.'

The Biscuit uttered a sharp exclamation.

'But are you?' he said significantly.

'I am.'

'You think you are, which is a very different thing, old boy. Have you considered? Have you reflected? Have you tried to realize your very equivocal position?'

'What do you mean?'

'What do I mean? Why, you've ensnared her heart under false pretences. You must see that for yourself. Dash it, you offer this bird...'

'Don't call her a bird.'

'You offer this charming and idealistic girl a Secret Service man, complete with mask and gun and dripping with romance, and she books you on those terms. What's she going to say when she finds that you are in reality an inky devil with paper cuff-protectors who works in a City office?'

'Yes,' said Berry dismally.

'What do you mean, yes?'

'I mean I had thought of that.'

He stared unhappily through the railings at the ornamental water. It looked cold and depressing. A breeze had sprung up, and was sighing through the trees with what an hour ago he would have considered a lovely whispering, but which now seemed to bring with it the suggestion of a sneer. Forlornness had suddenly come into the night.

'You think she will be annoyed when she finds out?'

'Annoyed?' said the Biscuit. 'I should think she would chew your head off.'

'I shouldn't mind that,' said Berry, 'if she didn't refuse to have anything more to do with me.'

There was a silence.

'I am going to chuck my job with old Frisby tomorrow,' said Berry. 'Then I shall go off somewhere – to America or some-where – and try do to something worth while.'

The Biscuit, a sympathetic soul, became encouraging.

'An excellent idea. Go West, young man, shoot a couple of Mexicans and send her the skins, and, who knows, all may yet be well. The main thing is that on no account must she ever know that you were her uncle's office-boy.'

'You wouldn't tell her?'

'Tell her!'

'I hate the feeling that I'm lying to her.'

'It would be fatal, fatal, absolutely fatal, old boy,' said the Biscuit vehemently. 'At the present stage of affairs, utterly fatal.'

'But she's got to find out some time.'

'Some time, yes. But let it be later, when the links forged by the laughing Love God have grown stronger. You haven't studied the sex as I have, laddie. I know women from beads to shoe-sole. Never confess anything to a girl till you have consolidated your position with her. A girl learns that a comparative stranger has been fooling her, and she hits the ceiling. But later on, it is different. Later on, she simply says to herself "Oh, well, Hell! It's only old George or whatever the name may be. I always did think him a bit loony, and now I know." And she curses him for about twenty minutes, just for the good of his soul and to show him who's boss, and then the forgiveness, the reconciliation, and the slow fade-out on the embrace.'

'There's something in that,' said Berry, brightening.

'There's everything in that. Once a man has made himself solid with a girl, he has nothing to fear. She may appear to the casual eye to be madder than a wet hen, but, if he's made himself solid, he can always bring her round. He can plead. He can grovel on the floor and tear his hair. He can apply the salve and give her the old oil. And, provided she has got used to seeing him around and has allowed him to dig himself well into the wood-work, he can always talk her over. But for the time being not a word. Secrecy and silence. Don't dream of confessing anything till the moment is ripe.'

'I won't!'

Berry drew a deep breath.

'Thanks, Biscuit,' he said with fervour. 'I'm glad I asked your advice.'

'Always ask my advice,' said the Biscuit handsomely. 'Always come to me with your little troubles and perplexities. I like all my young friends to feel that they have someone they can lean on in Uncle Godfrey.'

'I feel a lot better now.'

'I'm not feeling so bad myself,' said the Biscuit. 'I confess that there was a moment this evening when the thought that I was one *fiancée* over the odds more or less disturbed me. I should say now that God was in His heaven and all pretty well right with the world. I think we must celebrate this, old boy. How about lunch tomorrow in the City somewhere? I could go to the City without having Dykes, Dykes and Pinweed jumping on my neck. I'll call for you at the office at about one-thirty.'

VI

Lord Hoddesdon had spent this momentous evening dining luxuriously at his club. He had eaten all the things his doctor had told him to avoid, and had drunk a bottle of wine which his doctor insisted was poison to him. There are occasions which have to be observed with fitting solemnities, in the teeth of the whole medical profession; and one of these had just come to brighten Lord Hoddesdon's life. He had just let Edgeling Court to Mr Frisby for Goodwood Week and another month after that, and a cheque for six hundred pounds was even now on its way to exhilarate a banker who had almost given up hope.

At the inception of the campaign, Lord Hoddesdon had feared that he would never be able to bring the thing off. Shown photographs of Edgeling, T. Paterson Frisby had at first merely grunted. Becoming more vocal, he had wished to be informed what the heck his companion supposed he could possibly want with a house in the country the size of the Carlton Hotel. And when Lord Hoddesdon had dangled Goodwood races temptingly before his eyes, Mr Frisby had remarked with some asperity that if his lordship imagined that he was one of those fools who take pleasure in playing the ponies, he was under a grave misapprehension.

Later, however, he had wobbled from this firm standpoint. He had asked to see the photographs again. He had requested time to consider. And today he had fallen completely, justifying the capitulation by saying that he wasn't sure, after all, but what a house-party for Goodwood might not be a nice sort of thing for his niece, Ann. Be able to entertain all her friends and repay hospitality and that, said Mr Frisby.

Lord Hoddesdon did not believe that this was his true motive. An observant man, he had witnessed the growing alliance between Mr Frisby and Lady Vera Mace, and he fancied that Vera must have used her influence with the financier. If so, reflected Lord Hoddesdon, sipping Benedictine and smoking a Corona-corona, it was dashed sporting of her. Yes, dashed sporting. There had been times when he had found himself unable to think of his sister without a rising feeling of nausea, but tonight he approved of her *in toto*.

He decided to toddle round to Davies Street and give her a head of the family's blessing. A just man, he believed in encouraging sisters, when deserving. He finished his cigar, donned hat and coat, and set out.

There was nobody in the flat but the maid when he arrived. He seated himself comfortably, and gave himself up to opalescent meditations on the subject of the six hundred pounds. Presently a latch-key clicked in the door, and the next instant Lady Vera had hurried into the room.

'George!' she cried, and there was relief in her voice. 'Thank goodness you are here. I was just going to telephone to your club to ask you to come round at once.'

This sisterly affection touched Lord Hoddesdon. That

anything untoward could have occurred never crossed his mind. In a world where people handed you cheques for six hundred pounds, untoward occurrences were impossible.

'Were you, old girl?' he said jovially. 'Well, here I am. And I've got news.'

'*I've* got news,' said Lady Vera, sinking into a chair like a tragedy queen. 'The worst possible news.'

'Oh, my Lord!' said Lord Hoddesdon, deflated. He was feeling that he might have counted on Vera to spoil his evening.

Lady Vera had sprung from her chair and was now standing on the rug, panting at him. Lord Hoddesdon ground a heel into the carpet. There were moments when his sister reminded him of a rocketing pheasant; and, while he liked rocketing pheasants at the proper time and in their proper place, he strongly objected to amateur imitations of them in a small drawing-room.

'What *is* it?' he demanded irritably.

Lady Vera found speech.

'George, I've just come from dining with Lady Corstorphine.'

'Well?'

'At Mario's.'

'Well?'

'And what do you think?'

'What on earth do you mean, what do I think?'

'Ann was there.'

'Why shouldn't she be?'

'Not with us. She was up in the balcony.'

'Well?'

Lady Vera held her brother with a glittering eye, and delivered her thunderbolt.

'She was with a man, George!'

Lord Hoddesdon made one last feeble attempt to clutch at

the vanishing skirts of Happiness. But he knew, even as he spoke, that the effort was futile.

'No harm in that,' he said, though quaveringly. 'Can't see any harm in that. Girls nowadays . . .'

'Don't be a fool, George,' said Lady Vera curtly, shattering his last hope. 'If it had been Toddy Malling or Bertie Winch or any of the men she goes dancing with, do you suppose I should be upset? This was a man I had never seen before. It was obviously *the* man!'

'Not the one Jane Venables said she saw with her in her car that day!'

'It must have been.'

'You can't be certain,' pleaded Lord Hoddesdon faintly.

'I can make certain,' said Lady Vera. 'Here is Ann. I will ask her.'

A latch-key had turned in the front door, and from the hall there came the voice of a girl. She was singing softly to herself.

'She sounds happy!' said Lord Hoddesdon apprehensively.

'And she looked happy in the restaurant,' said Lady Vera. Her voice was grim. 'They were staring into each other's eyes.'

'No!'

'And holding hands.'

'No, dash it!'

'I saw them, I tell you.'

The door opened.

'Ah, Ann, my dear,' said Lady Vera. 'So you've got back.'

Ann's gaiety had waned. No girl enjoys a disagreeable scene, and she knew that there was one before her. Anything like subterfuge was foreign to Ann Moon's nature. She had no intention of concealing what had happened. The only thing that was perplexing her was the problem of how best to reveal it. Some people, she knew, preferred their bad news broken to them gently. Others would rather that you poured it over them like a pail of water and got it done with.

She was still debating within herself the comparative merits of the two methods, when Lady Vera went on speaking and she knew that neither would be needed.

'Who was your friend?' asked Lady Vera.

'Fellow you were dining with,' added Lord Hoddesdon, underlining the point. 'Fellow,' he went on, removing the last trace of ambiguity, 'who was up in the balcony with you at Mario's?'

'Yes,' said Lady Vera, in a voice of the purest steel. 'You were holding his hand, if you remember, and gazing into his eyes.'

It was a situation in which a nice girl should have quailed. An exceptionally nice girl might even have burst into tears and covered her face with her hands. Ann, after an uncontrollable start, was unfortunate enough to see the ludicrous side of the affair. Before she could check it, a happy laugh was echoing through the room.

Lord Hoddesdon's views on happy laughs were identical with his views on rocketing pheasants. At the proper time nobody enjoyed them more than himself. At a moment like this, and from a girl who had been playing fast and loose – yes, dash it, fast and loose with his only confounded son, he resented them keenly.

'Don't *giggle!*' he cried.

Ann became grave.

'I'm sorry,' she said. 'Only it seemed so funny that you should have been looking on all the time.'

'The humorous aspect of the matter,' said Lady Vera heavily, 'is not the one that appeals to me.'

'I'm sorry,' said Ann. 'I shouldn't have . . . It was too bad of me. . . . But you know how it is when you're nervous.'

'Nervous!' Lord Hoddesdon snorted. 'You nervous? If ever I've seen a girl calmer and more – er – what's the word? – more – ah – begins with a b. . . .'

'George,' said Lady Vera, 'be quiet.'

Lord Hoddesdon subsided into his chair. He seemed to be wishing that he had brought his Dictionary of Synonyms along with him this evening.

'I'm sorry,' said Ann for the third time, 'and if I had known about it sooner I would have told you sooner, but I am afraid I am not going to marry Godfrey.'

Lord Hoddesdon heaved slightly, like a volcano erroneously supposed to be extinct. His sister, noting the symptoms, raised a compelling hand.

'George!'

'Aren't I to say a word?' demanded Lord Hoddesdon with pathos.

'No.'

'Oh, very well. I'm the head of the family. Biskerton is my only son. This girl comes calmly in and tells us that she proposes to throw him over like a – like a – well, to throw him over. And I am not to say a word. I see. Precisely. Quite. I suppose,' said Lord Hoddesdon witheringly, 'that you would have no objection to my amusing myself with a game of solitaire while you two discuss this affair – this affair in which I, of course, have no interest whatever. Ha!' said his lordship, feeling, in spite of himself, a good deal better.

Lady Vera turned to Ann.

'Perhaps you will explain?'

'I don't think there is anything to explain.'

'Of course not,' said Lord Hoddesdon heartily, addressing a china cat which stood on a small table at his elbow. 'Certainly not. Nothing to explain. Quite so. Very bad form of us to be inquisitive. But let me tell you . . .'

'George!'

'Oh, all right,' said Lord Hoddesdon.

'I mean,' said Ann, 'if you saw me at Mario's, you must know that . . .'

'I know, what apparently seems to you the only point worthy of discussion, that you propose to jilt my nephew in favour of this man you were dining with tonight. But I think that, as you have been put in my charge by your parents and that I am, therefore, in a position of trust and responsibility, I am entitled to ask . . .'

'Who the devil is the mouldy feller?' said Lord Hoddesdon, rising suddenly to the surface.

Lady Vera tightened her lips. The question was, in essence, the high spot to which her speech was tending, though she would have phrased it differently. But she liked to ask her own questions for herself. She directed at her brother a glance which sent him back into the recesses of his chair, and turned to Ann expectantly.

'Yes,' she said. 'Who is he?'

'His name is Conway.'

'And what is he?'

'He is in the Secret Service.'

Lord Hoddesdon, though crushed, could not let this pass.

'Secret Service?' he said. 'Secret Service? Secret Service? Never heard such nonsense in my life.'

'George!'

'Yes, but dash it . . .'

'George!'

'Oh, all right!'

'He is in the Secret Service, is he?' said Lady Vera, ignoring a low rumbling from the volcano. 'He told you that?'

'Yes.'

'Tonight?'

'No. When we first met.'

'When was that?'

'About a week ago.'

'A week! A week! A week!...'

'George!'

'Oh, all right.'

'So you have known this young man you intend to marry as long as a week?' said Lady Vera. 'Fancy! Might I ask how you made his acquaintance?'

'He jumped into my car.'

'He – what? Why did he do that?'

'He was chasing The Sniffer....'

'I'm afraid I don't understand this modern slang. What do you mean by chasing The Sniffer?'

'He was trying to catch a criminal called The Sniffer. Only he wasn't. I mean, it wasn't The Sniffer after all. But he thought it was, and he jumped into my car and I drove him down to Esher. And then I met him again.'

'Where?'

'At the Bassingers' dance.'

'Oh!' Lady Vera was a little shaken. 'He knows the Bassingers, does he?'

Ann was her honest self.

'No,' she said.

'But you say he was at their dance?'

'He came there because he saw me going up in the elevator. He wasn't invited.'

The Volcano erupted. An eye-witness, who had been present on both occasions, would have been irresistibly reminded of the Mont Pelee horror.

'Wasn't invited? Wasn't invited? A gate-crasher! You hear that? My only son isn't good enough for the girl, so she goes out and picks up a blasted gate-crasher!'

The revelation had moved Lady Vera so deeply that she could not even spare the time to say 'George!'

'Well!' she said, drawing in her breath sharply.

'I thought it was very sporting of him,' said Ann defiantly.

'Sporting!'

'Well, it was. To do a thing like that just because he wanted to see me so much. It isn't very pleasant for a man to be turned out of a dance.'

'So he was turned out? I see. Charming! And when did you meet him again?'

'Tonight.'

'And ...'

'He kissed me,' said Ann stoutly, wishing, for she was a self-respecting modern girl, that she had been able to refrain from blushing. 'And I kissed him. And he told me he loved me. And I told him I loved him. And then we went off to dinner.'

There was a silence, broken only by a noise from Lord Hoddesdon like the bubbling of molten lava.

'And you know nothing about him,' said Lady Vera, 'except that he says he is in the Secret Service and is not *persona grata* at the Bassingers' dances? Has this remarkable person any fixed abode? Or does he just wander about the streets jumping into girls' cars?'

'He lives,' said Ann softly, breathing the address in a devout voice, for it was sacred to her, 'at The Nook, Mulberry Grove, Valley Fields.'

'What!' cried Lady Vera.

'What!' cried Lord Hoddesdon.

'Why, what's the matter?' asked Ann, surprised.

'Nothing,' said Lady Vera.

'Nothing,' said Lord Hoddesdon.

'If you're thinking that people have no right to live in the suburbs,' said Ann, once more with defiance in her voice, 'he has to, because they don't pay you much in the Secret Service.'

'I see,' said Lady Vera silkily. 'This young man is not well off. How lucky he has decided to marry money.'

'What do you mean?' cried Ann. 'Are you suggesting . . . ?'

Lady Vera's manner changed. She became so intensely motherly that her brother, rumbling in his chair, stared at her, awed.

'My dear child,' she said, and her smile was a composite of all of the smiles of all the mothers in filmdom, 'of course I know just how you are feeling about this man, but you really must use your intelligence. It is not as if you were a stupid, unsophisticated girl. You have seen quite enough of the world to know that life is not a fairy-story.'

'Or a twopenny novelette,' said Lord Hoddesdon.

'Or a twopenny novelette,' said Lady Vera. 'You know what big cities are like. London is full of adventurers, as I suppose New York is. This man is one of them.'

'He isn't!'

'My dear child, of course he is. And you could see it for yourself if you were not blinded by infatuation. Jumping into girls' cars! Honest men don't jump into girls' cars.'

'*I* don't,' said Lord Hoddesdon, mentioning a case in point. 'Never jumped into a girl's car in my life.'

'I am talking to Ann, George,' said Lady Vera gently. 'We are not interested in your autobiography. What you don't realize, dear,' she proceeded, 'is that you are a very well-known girl. Your photograph has been in all the weekly papers. You have been seen about everywhere. There are a dozen ways in which this man could have got to know you by sight. Obviously he must have marked you down; and when he saw you in your car that day he seized his opportunity. He knew how it would appeal to an imaginative girl, a man jumping in beside her and asking her to help him pursue a criminal. He knew that you are the daughter of a very rich man...'

Ann had had sufficient.

'I'm not going to listen to any more,' she said pinkly.

'There isn't any more to listen to,' said Lady Vera. 'I have told you the whole story. And, if you have any sense at all, you will realize for yourself...'

'Good night,' said Ann, and went out with her chin up.

She left behind her an electric silence. Lord Hoddesdon was the first to break it.

'Well?' he said.

'What on earth do you mean by "Well?"' retorted Lady Vera. She was still tingling with the battle-spirit, and it rendered her irritable.

'What do you make of it?'

'What do I make of what?'

'I mean, do you suppose you have convinced her about this fellow? Being an adventurer and all that?'

'At least I have given her something to think about.'

Lord Hoddesdon pulled at his moustache.

'Odd about that address.'

'My dear George,' said Lady Vera, with the same patient contempt with which another great mind was wont to say 'My dear Watson', 'I really cannot see why you should consider it odd.'

'Well, dash it,' protested his lordship, 'the coincidence – you can't say it's not a coincidence. Mulberry Grove, Valley Fields, is where Godfrey is living.'

'Exactly. And I have no doubt that this man has somehow managed to scrape acquaintance with Godfrey. Godfrey, who has no idea of reticence but babbles all his most private affairs into the ear of the first person who comes along, must undoubtedly have told him who he was and, I suppose, showed him Ann's photograph and mentioned that she was a very romantic girl. And when the man found her sitting alone in her car, he saw his chance.'

'I see. I've often thought,' said Lord Hoddesdon, with a father's sad earnestness, 'that Godfrey ought to be in some sort of mental institution. He has gone and messed things up thoroughly now. Is there anything we can do, do you think?'

'Of course there is something we can do. You don't imagine that I am going to sit quietly and see this man ruin Ann's life? I should imagine that the thing will resolve itself into a question of money. Mr Frisby must buy him off.'

'You think he would?'

'Of course he would. He will be just as anxious as we are to free Ann from this entanglement.'

'Why?'

'His sister, Ann's mother, is, I understand, the sort of woman who would make herself exceedingly unpleasant if Ann were to marry the wrong man.'

'Ah!' said Lord Hoddesdon, enlightened. He knew all about unpleasant sisters.

'So,' said Lady Vera, 'you had better go down to Valley Fields tomorrow morning and see this man. I'll get Mr Frisby to give you a cheque.'

Lord Hoddesdon started violently. Until this moment he had been looking on the affair in a spirit of easy detachment. He had never dreamed that there would be any suggestion of his undertaking the negotiations. The mere idea of paying a return visit to the stamping-ground of the disciple of Stayling and running the risk of renewing his acquaintance with that extra-ordinarily belligerent little person with the eyeglass and the vocabulary appalled him.

'Go to Valley Fields!' he cried. 'I'm dashed if I do.'

'George!'

'No,' returned Lord Hoddesdon, reckless of the lion-tamer's gleam in his sister's eye, 'I will not. You aren't going to get me down to that hell on earth, not if you argue all night.'

'George!'

'It's no good saying "George"! I'm not going. I don't like Valley Fields. There's something about the place. It's unlucky.'

'Don't be absurd.'

'Absurd, eh? Well, look what happened last time. I went down there in a grey top-hat that I had meant to see me through another half-dozen Ascots, and I only just managed to escape with my life in a cloth cap with purple checks. And that wasn't all. That wasn't half of it. I had to run – run like a hare, dash it! to escape being murdered by a beer-swilling native. I had to gallop into back gardens and leap through windows. And you calmly ask me to go over all that again! I can see myself! No,' said Lord Hoddesdon, firmly, 'I approve of the idea of offering this bounder money to release Ann, but I decline to be appointed paymaster. Do the thing in a regular and orderly manner, I say. Go to your friend Frisby and tell him to send his lawyer to interview this fellow. It's a lawyer's job. Good night, Vera!'

And, seizing his hat, Lord Hoddesdon sprang for the door. He could have lingered, had he wished, to hear what his sister had to say in reply to this ultimatum, but he did not wish.

CHAPTER 10

I

Although the little luncheon arranged by Lord Biskerton and his friend Berry Conway had been designed primarily as a celebration of their joint felicity, they had scarcely settled themselves at the table before it lost this carefree aspect and became undisguisedly a discussion of ways and means. The peculiar complexity of their position had escaped neither of them. Each had been doing solid thinking overnight, and the business note was struck almost immediately.

'What it all boils down to,' said the Biscuit, when the waiter had left them and it was possible to deal with matters more intimate than the bill of fare, 'is where do we go from here?'

Berry nodded. This was, he recognized, the problem.

'I am not saying,' proceeded the Biscuit, 'that this isn't the maddest, merriest day of all the glad new year, because it is. We love. Excellent! We are loved. Capital! Nothing could be sweeter. But now the question arises, how the dickens are we going to collect enough cash to push the thing through to a happy conclusion? We must not fail to realize that between us we have got just about enough to pay for one marriage ceremony. And we shall need a couple.'

Berry nodded again. He had not failed to realize this.

'Because,' said the Biscuit, 'there is none of that one-portion-between-two stuff with clergymen. Each time the firing-squad assembles, even though it be on the same morning and with a breathing-space of only a few minutes, the vicar wants his little envelope. So we are faced by the eternal problem of Money and how to get it. Who,' he asked, looking across the room, 'is the red-faced bird who has just waved a paternal hand at us? I don't know him. One of your City friends?'

Berry followed his gaze. At a table near the door a stout and florid man was sitting, obviously doing himself well. J. B. Hoke, that obese double-dealer, always made of his lunch almost a holy rite and as a temple in which to perform it he usually selected this particular restaurant. For here he could get soup that was soup, a steak that was a steak, and in addition that wholehearted affection which restaurateurs bestow on clients who come regularly and are restrained from giving of their best neither by parsimony nor by any of these modern diet fads.

J. B. Hoke had never dieted in his life. Nor was there at the present point in his career any reason for him to stint himself from motives of economy. Things were going well with Mr Hoke. He had unloaded all his Horned Toad Copper at four shillings, and the *Financial News* informed him this morning that it was down to one shilling and sixpence. At his leisure he proposed to buy it in again, possibly when it had sunk to a shilling, and then the information of the discovery of the new reef would be made public and he would have nothing to do but sit pretty and watch her shoot skywards. The future was looking to Mr Hoke as rosy as his face.

He regarded Berry with eyes that bulged with greed and good-will. The thought that he was about to make a large fortune out of a property for which he had paid this young man five hundred pounds diverted Mr Hoke. He bestowed upon his steak a look that was somehow deeper and more reverent than that which he usually accorded to steaks, though his manner toward them was always respectful. He was pleased to see that today the white-aproned *chef* had excelled himself. J. B. Hoke had chosen that steak in person after a good deal of careful thought, and justice had been done to it in the cooking.

'That,' said Berry, 'is Hoke. The fellow who bought my mine.'

'Is it?' The Biscuit scrutinized the philanthropist with interest. 'Bought the mine, did he? Odd. He doesn't look like a mug. You don't think it's possible . . .'

'What?'

'I was just wondering whether that mine was quite such a dud as you thought it. I don't like Hoke's looks. I suspect the man. He has the air of one who would be pretty rough with the widow and the orphan if he got a chance. What's become of this mine? Is he using it as a summer camp or something?'

'I believe it has been absorbed into a thing old Frisby owns – Horned Toad Copper.'

'How does Frisby get mixed up with it?'

'Hoke's a friend of his.'

'Is he?' The Biscuit snorted. 'Well, that damns him properly. What honest man would be a friend of old Frisby? A bounder,' said the Biscuit bitterly, 'whose only niece gets engaged to an admirable young man of good family and who, in spite of being given every opportunity of coming across with a small gift, sits tight and does nothing. You take it from me, Berry, these hounds have done you down.'

'Well, it's too late to worry about it now.'

'I suppose it is.'

'What we had better think about is how we are going to raise a bit of money.'

The Biscuit frowned.

'Money!' he said. 'Yes. You're right. What a rotten thing this business of money is. Half the best chaps in the world are crippled for want of it. And the fellows who have got it haven't a notion what to do with it. Take old Frisby, for instance. Worth millions.'

'I suppose so.'

'And is a bloke with a face like a horse and a spending capacity of about twopence a day. On the other hand, take me. You know me, Berry, old man. Young, enthusiastic, dripping with *joie de vivre*, only needing a balance at the bank to go out and scatter light and sweetness and – mark you – scatter them good. If I had money, I could increase the sum of human happiness a hundredfold.'

'How?'

'By flinging purses of gold to the deserving, old boy. That's how. And here I am, broke. And there is your foul boss, simply stagnant with the stuff. All wrong.'

'Well, don't blame me.'

'What ought to happen,' said the Biscuit, 'is this. If I had the management of this country, there would be public examinations held twice a year, at which these old crumbs with their hoarded wealth would be brought up and subjected to a very severe inquisition. "You!" the Examiner would say, looking pretty sharply at Frisby. "How much have *you* got? Indeed? Really? As much as that, eh? Well, kindly inform this court what you do with it." The wretched man, who seems to feel his position acutely, snuffles a bit. "Come on, now!" says the Examiner, rapping the table. "No subterfuge. No evasion. How do you employ this very decent slice of the needful?" "Well, as a matter of fact," mumbles old Frisby, trying to avoid his eye, "I shove it away behind a brick and go out and get some more." "Is that so?" says the Examiner. "Well, upon my Sam! I never heard anything so disgraceful in my living puff. It's a crying outrage. A bally scandal. Take ten million away from this miserable louse and hand it over to excellent old Biskerton, who will make a proper use of it. And then go and ask Berry Conway how much he wants." We'd get somewhere then.'

He contemplated dreamily for a while the Utopia he had conjured up. Then he looked across the room again, and clicked his tongue disapprovingly.

'I'll swear Hoke swindled you over that mine,' he said. ' I can see it in his eye.'

'There must be dozens of ways of making money,' said Berry, reflectively. 'Can't you suggest anything?'

The Biscuit withdrew his gaze from Mr Hoke, and gave his mind to the problem.

'How about winning the Calcutta Sweep?' he asked.

'Fine!' said Berry. 'Or the Stock Exchange Sweep.'

'Why not both?'

'All right. Both, if you like.'

'Still,' said the Biscuit, pointing out the objection frankly, for he was not a man to allow himself to build castles in the air, 'we shan't be able to do that for about another ten months or so, and what we need is cash down and on the nail. We will ear-mark the Calcutta and Stock Exchange sweeps for a future date, but in the meantime we must be thinking of something else – something that will bring the brass in quick. Any ideas?'

'Invent a substitute for petrol.'

'Yes. We might do that. It would be simpler, though, to save some old man from being run over by a truck. He would turn out to be a millionaire and would leave us a fortune.'

'That would mean waiting,' Berry pointed out.

'So it would. Possibly for years. I had overlooked that. It seems to me that every avenue is closed. We might try the old Secret game, of course.'

'I don't know that.'

'Yes, you do. I recollect telling you. The two blokes – Bloke A. and Bloke B. Bloke A. goes up to Bloke B. and says, "I know your secret!" And Bloke B.—'

'I remember now. But suppose your second bloke hasn't got a secret?'

'My dear old boy, everybody has a secret. It's one of the laws of Nature. When you get back to the office, try it on old Frisby and watch him wilt. Become a gentlemanly blackmailer and earn while you learn.'

'Talking of Frisby,' said Berry, looking at his watch, 'I suppose I ought to be getting along. He's had another of his dyspeptic attacks and didn't come to the office this morning. He 'phoned to say he wanted me to bring the mail up to his flat in Grosvenor House. Rather convenient.'

'Why convenient?'

'Well, for one thing, I want to see him, to tell him I'm chucking my job. And then,' said Berry, 'I shall be near the Park. I promised to meet Ann at the Tea House. We're going to feed the ducks on the Serpentine.'

'My God!'

'Well, we are,' said Berry doggedly. 'And if you don't like it, try to do something about it. Are you coming along?'

'No. I shall sit here and think. I must think. I must think – think. How the dickens, with your whole future clouded with the most delicate financial problems, you can waste your time feeding ducks—'

'I don't look on it as a waste of time,' said Berry. 'So long. See you tonight.'

He walked to the door, and was hailed in passing by Mr Hoke.

'And how's Mr Conway?' asked Mr Hoke.

'I'm all right, thanks,' said Berry.

'Who's your friend?'

'Man who lives next door to me down at Valley Fields.'

'What were you talking about so earnestly?'

Berry wanted to hurry on.

'Oh, various things. The Dream Come True, among others.'

'The Dream Come True, eh?'

'Yes. He seemed interested in it. Well, I must rush.'

'Pleased to have seen you,' said Mr Hoke.

He returned to his steak, and for some moments became absorbed in it. Then a shadow fell on the table, and, looking up, he perceived his old friend, Captain Kelly.

II

Mr Hoke was not glad to see Captain Kelly. Indeed, he had been going to some little trouble of late to avoid him. But his mood was too radiant to allow him to be depressed by this encounter.

''Lo, Captain,' he said amiably.

Captain Kelly pulled a chair back and lowered himself into it with a tight-trousered man's slow caution.

'Lunch?' said Mr Hoke.

'No,' said Captain Kelly.

His manner was undeniably on the curt side, and a man with a more sensitive conscience than Mr Hoke possessed might have been troubled. J. B. Hoke's military friend was looking across the table at him in an odd, stony way. Never effusive, he seemed now even less cordial than his wont. His lips were set in a straight line: and even when speaking he scarcely opened them.

Mr Hoke gathered that his old crony had been hearing things. The fact did not disturb him. Sooner or later, he told himself philosophically, there was bound to be a show-down. He was glad that it had come now, when he was feeling in particularly good form and able to cope with a dozen injured Captains.

'Want a word with you,' said Captain Kelly.

J. B. Hoke cut off a generous piece of steak, dipped it in salt, smeared it with mustard, bathed it in Worcester Sauce, placed a portion of potato on it, added cabbage and horse-radish, and raised the complete edifice to his mouth. Only when it was safely inside did he reply, and then only briefly.

'Yeah?' he said.

The Captain continued to eye him fixedly.

'Begin by saying,' he went on, 'that of all the dirty, swindling hounds I've ever met you're the worst.'

Hard words never broke Mr Hoke's bones. He smiled indulgently.

'What did you have for breakfast, Captain?'

'Never you mind what I had for breakfast. I had a brandy and soda, if you want to know.'

'I guess it disagreed with you,' said Mr Hoke, detaching another portion of steak and occupying himself once more with the building operations.

Captain Kelly was plainly in no mood for persiflage.

'You know what I'm talking about,' he said. 'What about that mine?'

'What mine?'

'The Dream Come True I'm talking about.'

'What about the Dream Come True?'

'Yes, what about it?' said the Captain.

Mr Hoke engulfed his mouthful, and sat champing placidly. The spectacle appeared to infuriate his friend.

'See here,' said Captain Kelly, his face, educated by a thousand poker-games, still expressionless save for a little vein below the temple which swelled and throbbed, 'wasn't the agreement that you and I should buy that mine together? Wasn't it? And didn't you go off and buy it for yourself? It's no use trying to deny it. Bellamy was there when you did it, and he told me. You Jonah!'

'Judas,' corrected Mr Hoke. He liked to get these things right.

He smeared mustard amiably.

'Bless your heart,' he said, with gentle amusement, 'I'm not trying to deny it.'

'Ah,' said Captain Kelly.

'You want to watch your step when you're doing business,' said Mr Hoke. 'If you don't, you find yourself side-tracked, and there you are, out in the cold, and nothing to be done about it.'

'Nothing to be done about it?'

'Not a thing,' said Mr Hoke, 'to be done about it.'

Captain Kelly breathed softly through his nose.

'Ah!' he said again.

'Say "Ah" just as often as ever you like,' said Mr Hoke, generously. 'It won't make any difference.' He swallowed another mouthful of steak. 'I'm sorry for you, Captain. If it's any consolation to you to know it, I'm sorry for you. You've let yourself be out-smarted. It's the fortune of war. That's all there is to it. Happens all the time. You today, me tomorrow.'

Captain Kelly crumbled bread. It was Mr Hoke's bread, but its owner made no complaint. A man in his position could afford to take the big, broad view about bread.

'What do you expect to make out of this deal?' asked the Captain.

Mr Hoke had no objection to answering that question.

'Thousands and thousands,' he said. 'And thousands.'

'And I might have had half,' sighed Captain Kelly.

'And you,' agreed Mr Hoke, 'might have had half.'

The Captain sighed again. There was a long silence.

'I could have done with a bit of money just now,' said the Captain.

'I bet you could,' said Mr Hoke cordially.

'I've a lot of expenses just at present.'

'We all have,' said Mr Hoke.

'You see, it costs money to entertain these fellows,' said the Captain pensively.

Mr Hoke cut steak.

'What fellows?' he asked.

'A couple of lads from Chicago have come over with a letter of introduction from a friend of mine in America. He's a man I'm under obligations to, so it's up to me to take care of them. And they seem to think,' said Captain Kelly, sighing once more, 'of nothing but pleasure. That's why I want to find some money.'

'I suppose so,' said Mr Hoke.

'You'd be surprised what a lot it runs into, taking these fellows around London and showing them the sights. The best is none too good for them. Three times to Madame Tussaud's in the last week.'

'Ah,' said Mr Hoke. 'They live high, those boys.'

'Of course, there's the other side. They're grateful to me. They look on me like an elder brother. They said yesterday that there wasn't anything in the world they wouldn't do for me.'

'That's fine,' said Mr Hoke heartily. 'A nice spirit.'

'You'd have laughed if you had heard what their idea of doing something for me was,' proceeded the Captain. 'They asked me if there wasn't anybody I wanted bumped off. If there was, they would be proud and happy to do it for me free of charge, just to show their gratitude and keep their hand in.'

Mr Hoke may have laughed, but, if so, he did it inaudibly. He was in the act of raising another portion of steak: but though his mouth now opened slowly, as if to receive the *bonne bouche*, he did not insert it. He lowered his fork, and gazed at his companion in a rather strained way.

'Bumped off?' he said, in a thin voice.

'Bumped off,' said the Captain. 'Didn't I mention,' he went on, with a glance of mild surprise at his companion's drooping jaw, 'that they were gunmen?'

'Gug?' said Mr Hoke.

'Yes. And rather well known, I believe, over on the other side. What they call Chicago gorillas. Extraordinary chaps!' said the Captain, reflectively. 'Children of Nature, you might say. Just a couple of great, big, happy schoolboys. Fancy wanting to repay hospitality by coshing somebody who had done your host a bad turn. It amused me.'

He chuckled, to show that he still found the pretty fancy entertaining. He had a curious way of chuckling. His mouth lifted itself slightly on one side, the lips remaining tightly closed. His eyes during the performance retained their normal aspect, which was that of a couple of bits of light blue steel. Mr Hoke found it interesting, but not attractive.

'Well, I mustn't waste the whole day talking to you,' said Captain Kelly, rising.

'Hey!' said Mr Hoke. 'Wait!'

'Something you want to say?' asked the Captain, resuming his seat.

Mr Hoke swallowed painfully.

'Guys like that ought to be in gaol,' he said, with feeling. 'In gaol, that's where they ought to be.'

Captain Kelly nodded lightly.

'They were for a day or two,' he said, 'that time they shot Joe Frascati in Chicago. They let them out, though. Still, they had to come here till it blew over.'

'Shush-shot him?' quavered Mr Hoke.

'Bless you,' said the Captain, 'that's nothing in Chicago. You ought to know that, coming from the other side. Well, as I was saying, they wanted to oblige me, and by a bit of bad luck I happened to mention the way you had done me down. You never saw two fellows so worked up. Big-hearted, that's what they are. You can say what you like about these gunmen, but they stick up for their friends. *You* were one of the things they wanted to stick up,' said Captain Kelly, chuckling at the pleasantry. His spirits seemed to have improved.

Mr Hoke became vociferous.

'Stick me up? What for? I've not done nothing. You don't suppose I was really planning to do you down, do you – an old friend like you? I was just kidding you, Captain, to get your goat. I wanted to see how you'd take it.'

'Well, you saw,' said the Captain briefly. 'And now I really must be going. I promised to meet those two at the club.'

'Wait!' said Mr Hoke. 'Wait! Wait!'

He gulped.

'You get your half share all right,' he said. 'I'll give you a letter to that effect, if you like. Write it now, if you want me to.'

Something that was very near to being a pleased smile flitted across the Captain's face.

'I should,' he said. 'I know it would please those boys. The waiter will bring you ink and paper.'

'I've a fountain-pen,' said Mr Hoke thickly. 'And here's a bit of paper that will do.'

He scribbled feverishly. Captain Kelly examined the document, seemed contented with it, and put it carefully away in his pocket.

'I'll be at the club all the afternoon,' he said, rising. 'Only got to look in at Somerset House to get this stamped.'

He walked in a leisurely manner to the door. And Mr Hoke, his appetite no longer what it had been, stopped eating steak and called for coffee and a double brandy.

Then, lighting a large cigar, he gave himself up to meditation. The sunshine which so recently had bathed his world had vanished. There had been a total eclipse.

III

It was as he reached the point in his cigar where a good smoker permits himself the first breaking of the ash that J. B. Hoke became aware that his privacy had once more been invaded. Standing beside his table was the young man who had been lunching with Berry Conway. This young man was eyeing him meaningly.

It disturbed Mr Hoke.

Mentally, at this moment, J. B. Hoke was a little below par. His nervous system had lost tone. He was in the state where men start at sudden noises and read into other people's glances a sinister significance which at a happier time they would not attribute to them. And, as he met the Biscuit's eye, there came to him abruptly the recollection that this was the man who, according to young Conway, had shown such an interest in the Dream Come True.

'Well?' said Mr Hoke belligerently. He found the other's scrutiny irritating. 'Well?'

The young man's gaze narrowed.

'Hoke,' he said in a low, steady voice, 'I know your secret!'

CHAPTER 11

I

Prone on the sofa in his palatial apartment on the second floor of Grosvenor House, T. Paterson Frisby lay and stared at the ceiling. It seemed to him that they had been painting it yellow. The walls were yellow, too: and some minutes previously, when he had risen with the idea of easing his agony by pacing the floor, he had noticed this same gamboge *motif* in the sky. The fact is, extraordinary things were happening inside Mr Frisby. He had been eating roast duck again.

There was once a devout and pious man who, irresistibly impelled by his carnal appetites, sat down in the middle of Lent to a mutton chop. Hardly had he taken his first mouthful when there was a roll of thunder and the heavens were rent by a great flash of lightning. He paled, and pushed his plate away. But, though alarmed, he was peevish.

'What a fuss,' he said, 'about a mutton chop!'

Mr Frisby might have echoed his cry, substituting for chop the words roast duck. It seemed to Mr Frisby that his punishment was out of all proportion to his crime. Just one brief period of self-indulgence, and here he was, derelict.

What was going on in T. Paterson's interior resembled in some degree a stormy Shareholders' Meeting. Nasty questions were being asked. Voices were being raised. At times it seemed as though actual violence had broken out. And the pepsine tablets which he kept swallowing so hopefully were accomplishing nothing more than might on such an occasion the bleating 'Gentlemen, please!' of an inefficient Chairman.

'Ouch!' said Mr Frisby, as a new spasm racked him.

He had but one consolation. In all the dark cloud-rack there was only one small patch of blue sky. At any moment now his secretary would be arriving with the mail, and he looked forward with something approaching contentment to the thought of working off some of his venom on him. Minus roast duck, he was not an unkindly man: but under its influence his whole nature changed, and he became one of those employers who regard a private secretary as a spiritual punching-bag.

It was in this unpromising frame of mind that Berry found him.

Berry was feeling a little disturbed himself. The pleasure of the Biscuit's society had caused him to prolong his luncheon beyond its customary limits: and on his return to the office there had been a succession of visitors, anxious to see Mr Frisby. These he had had to deal with, and it had taken time. There was only another fifteen minutes before the hour of his tryst with Ann at the Hyde Park Tea House. As he entered the room, he was looking fussily at his watch.

'Well. . . .' began Mr Frisby, half rising from his bed of pain.

It had been his intention to continue the speech at some length. What it was in his mind to say was that when he telephoned to the office for his mail to be brought to Grosvenor House after lunch, he meant after lunch and not five minutes before dinner-time. He would have gone on to inquire of Berry if he had lost his way, or if he had been entertaining himself between Pudding Lane and Grosvenor House by rolling a peanut along the sidewalk with a tooth-pick. To this he would have added that if Berry supposed that he paid him a weekly salary simply because he admired his looks and liked having something ornamental about the office, he, Berry, was gravely mistaken.

For Mr Frisby, as we have seen, could, when moved, be terribly sarcastic.

All these things the stricken financier would have said, and many more: and the saying of them would undoubtedly have brought him much relief. But even as he uttered that 'Well. . . .' his visitor spoke.

'I can only give you a minute,' he said.

It affords a striking proof of the superiority of mind over matter that at these words Mr Frisby completely forgot that he was a sick man. A sudden lull fell on that Shareholders' Meeting inside him. So great was his emotion that he sprang from the sofa like a jumping bean.

Mr Frisby had once had a secretary who had startled him by coming into the office one afternoon in a state of smiling intoxication and falling over a chair and trying to take dictation with his head in a wastepaper basket. And until this moment this had always seemed to him to constitute what might be called the Furthest North of secretarial eccentricity.

But now that episode paled into insignificance. Between a pie-eyed secretary who fell over chairs and a curtly impatient secretary who looked at his watch and said he could only give him a minute there was no comparison whatever.

'I'm sorry,' said Berry, 'but I've promised to go and feed the ducks on the Serpentine.'

It was undoubtedly that fatal word 'ducks' that struck Mr Frisby dumb. Nothing else could have withheld him from the most eloquent address that had ever scorched a private secretary's ears. But at the sound of that word, as once had happened in a palace in Fairyland at the sound of a kiss dropped on the brow of Sleeping Beauty, everything inside him seemed suddenly to come alive again. The Shareholders' Meeting was on once more in all its pristine violence.

Mr Frisby sank back on to the sofa, and reached feebly for the pepsine bottle.

'As a matter of fact,' proceeded Berry, 'I only looked in to tell you that I was resigning my position. But you will be all right,' he added kindly. 'You can 'phone to an agency to send you up a stenographer to attend to these letters, and you can always get another secretary in half an hour. And now,' he said, 'I'm afraid I really must rush. I've got to be at the Tea House in the Park in five minutes.'

He hurried out, feeling that he had conducted the delicate business of resignation in a tactful and considerate manner. In a way, he was fond of Mr Frisby, and wished that he had had more time to spare him: but the necessity of being punctual at the tryst was imperative. He raced for the door of the suite, and reached it just as it was being opened by Mr Frisby's man for the admittance of a new visitor.

The new arrival was no stranger to him, though he supposed he was to her. It was Lady Vera Mace. Berry was never quite sure how he stood with Lady Vera in the matter of bowing or smiling or other form of intimacy. Eleven years ago she had visited her nephew, Lord Biskerton, at school, and he, Berry, as the Biscuit's best friend, had been included in the subsequent festivities: but, though in his own memory this affair still remained green, the party of the second part had evidently forgotten it entirely. On the one occasion when they had met since that distant date, in Mr Frisby's outer office when she had called to discuss the chaperoning of Ann, she had given no sign of recognition.

So now he claimed no acquaintance. He did not bow, but stood to one side in a courtly manner, to allow her to pass. And as she passed her eyes fell on him and he was surprised to see them light up suddenly, as if in recognition. And what surprised him more was that the light in those eyes was not merely that of recognition but of fear and dislike. Why, if Lady Vera remembered him at all, she should remember him as something obnoxious, Berry could not understand. At the age of fifteen he had probably not been exactly fascinating, but he was astonished to find that he had been so repulsive as to cause this woman, eleven years later, to shudder at the sight of him.

It was rather maddening, in a way. But he had no time to worry himself about it now. Lady Vera had passed on and was entering the room where Mr Frisby and his interior organism were conducting their silent battle. Berry dismissed the matter from his mind, and ran down the corridor to the stairs. All he was thinking of now was that in another five minutes he would be meeting Ann again. A man with a thing like that before him had no time to worry about his unpopularity with the sisters of earls.

Lady Vera Mace was a dignified woman: and, like all women who are careful of their dignity, she seldom hurried. But such was the emotion with which the sight of Berry had filled her that, as she crossed the threshold of Mr Frisby's sitting-room, she was positively running. The desire to receive some explanation of the presence in the financier's suite of one whom she had come to look upon as London's leading adventurer accelerated her movements to an extraordinary degree. Daughter of a hundred earls though she was, she charged in like a greyhound on the track of an electric hare. She trembled with curiosity and with that horror which good women feel when they have just met members of the Underworld face to face in a narrow passage. And she was just about to pour forth a rain of questions when she perceived that her host was sitting doubled up in a chair, uttering sounds as of one in pain.

Lady Vera stopped, concerned. Accustomed to making up her mind quickly, at a very early date in their acquaintance she had decided quite definitely that later on she would marry T. Paterson Frisby. At their very first meeting she had recognized him as one who needed a woman to look after him and when, in the course of their conversations she had discovered that the post was vacant, she had determined to fill it.

So now she gazed upon him with something stronger than the detached womanly pity which she would have bestowed on a mere stranger whom she had found tying himself into knots.

'Whatever is the matter?' she asked.

'Ouch!' said Mr Frisby.

Lady Vera had that splendid faculty which only great women possess of going instantly to the heart of a problem. At their first encounter this man had been in very much the same condition, and he had confided to her then his hidden secret.

'Have you been eating duck again?' she asked keenly.

She saw him writhe, and knew that her diagnosis had been correct.

'Wait!' she said.

A woman of acute perception, she realized that this was no time for advising the patient to think beautiful thoughts, to recommend him to fancy himself a bird upon a tree and to seek relief in song. The thing had gone too far for that. Cruder and swifter remedies were indicated.

She went to the telephone and was almost immediately in communication with the druggist on the main floor of the building. She spoke authoritatively and as one having knowledge: and presently there was a ring at the bell and a small boy appeared, bearing a brimming glass full of some greyish liquid.

'Drink this,' said Lady Vera.

Mr Frisby drank, and instantly it was as if some strong man had risen in the Meeting of Shareholders, dominating all. The shouts died to whispers, the whispers to silence. Peace reigned. And T. Paterson Frisby, licking his lips, spoke in a low, awed voice.

'What was it?'

'It is something my husband used to recommend. He suffered as you do. But after lobster. He said it was infallible.'

'It is,' said Mr Frisby. 'Have you ever tried it on a corpse? I should say it would work.'

A great surge of emotion had risen within him. He looked at Lady Vera Mace with glowing eyes, and a voice seemed to whisper to him that now was the moment for which he had been waiting so long. On a score of previous occasions T. Paterson Frisby had contemplated the idea of laying his widowed heart at the feet of this woman, of putting his fortune to the test, to win or lose it all: but always he had refrained. He had lacked the necessary courage. She had seemed so aloof, so statuesque. Now, as she stood there radiating gentle sympathy, she became approachable: and that inner voice seemed to say to him 'Go to it!'

He cleared his throat. What there had been in that stuff which he had just swallowed, he could not say: but its effect had been to bring him to the top of his form. He felt confident. And he would undoubtedly have expressed himself in a series of telling phrases, calculated to win the heart of any woman, had not Lady

Vera abruptly remembered that ten minutes ago she had hurried into this room in a spirit of research and inquiry. Even as Mr Frisby was shaping his opening sentence, she shattered his whole scheme of thought with an agitated exclamation.

'That man!' she cried.

'Eh?' said Mr Frisby.

'What was that man doing here?'

Regretfully, T. Paterson Frisby recognized that the golden moment had passed. The subject had been definitely changed. He saw now that his visitor's mind was not in a condition to be receptive to the voice of Love. She seemed to want to know something about some man, and it was plain that no other topic would interest her. He swallowed his emotion, therefore, and sought enlightenment.

'Man?' he said. 'What man?'

'The man I met as I came in. What was he doing here?'

Mr Frisby was puzzled. She seemed to be referring to his late secretary.

'He came to bring me my mail,' he said.

'Your mail?' Lady Vera's eyes widened. 'Do you *know* him?'

A warm gleam came into Mr Frisby's eye. Subsequent occurrences had dimmed the memory of that remarkable interview with Berry Conway, but now it came back to him. He quivered a little.

'I thought I did,' he said. 'Yes, sir! But he certainly surprised me just now. The young hound! "I can only give you a minute!" He said that. To me! And off he went to feed ducks!'

Mr Frisby paused, wrestling with a strong emotion.

'But who is he?'

'He is – was – my secretary.'

'Your secretary?'

'That's right. His name's Conway. And until today I'd always found him an ordinary, respectful . . .'

Lady Vera uttered an exclamation. She saw all.

'So that's how he came to know Ann!'

Mr Frisby found himself puzzled again.

'Ann? My niece Ann? He doesn't know Ann.'

Lady Vera hesitated. It seemed cruel to let the thing descend on this man suddenly, like an avalanche.

'He does,' she said.

'I don't think so,' said Mr Frisby.

'I saw them dining together last night. Mr Frisby,' said Lady Vera, unequal to the task of breaking the news gently. 'I have had a talk with Ann. An awful thing has happened. She has broken off her engagement with my nephew, and says she is resolved to marry this man Conway. That is why I came here this afternoon to see you. We must decide what to do about it.'

Mr Frisby uttered an exclamation. He, too, saw all.

'So that's why he was so fresh!'

There was something not unlike satisfaction in his voice. All he could think of for the moment was that a mystery had been solved which might have vexed him to his dying day. Then, like an icy finger on his spine, came the realization of what this meant.

'Marry him?' he gasped. 'Did you say marry him?'

'She said she intended to marry him.'

'But she can't!' wailed Mr Frisby. 'My sister Josephine would never give me a second's peace for the rest of my life.'

He stared at his visitor, appalled, and was stunned to perceive a soft smile upon her face. What anyone could find to smile at in a world where his sister Josephine's daughter was going about marrying penniless ex-secretaries was more than Mr Frisby could understand.

'Why, of course!' said Lady Vera. 'How foolish of me not to have seen it directly you told me.'

'Eh?'

'Everything is going to be quite simple,' said Lady Vera. 'If this man Conway is really your secretary, the problem solves itself.'

'Eh?' said Mr Frisby again.

'But I didn't tell you, did I? You see, Mr Frisby, what has happened is this. This man, as far as I can gather from her story, seems to have swept Ann off her feet by telling her a lot of romantic stories about himself. Well, surely, when she finds that he has been lying to her and is nothing but a miserable secretary, she will realize the sort of man he is and will give him up of her own accord.'

Mr Frisby looked doubtful.

'Told her romantic stories, did he?'

'He said he was a Secret Service man. You can imagine the effect that that would have on an impressionable girl like Ann. But when she finds out...'

Mr Frisby shook his head.

'A bird as smooth as that,' he said, 'is going to be smooth enough to jolly her along even when she does find out.'

'Then what you must do,' said Lady Vera with decision, 'is simply to send your lawyer down to his house to offer him money to give Ann up.'

'But would he give her up?' Mr Frisby drooped despondently. He could see the flaw in the idea. 'Why would he take money to give her up, when he could get more money by standing pat?'

Lady Vera over-ruled the objection.

'When your lawyer explains to him that Ann will be sent back to America immediately, out of his reach, if he refuses to come to terms, I am sure that he will be only too glad to take whatever you offer.'

The gloom passed from Mr Frisby's face, he gazed reverently at this woman of infinite sagacity.

'You're dead right,' he said. 'I never thought of that. I'll get on to Robbins on the 'phone right away.'

'Yes, do.'

'I'll tell him to start the bidding at a thousand pounds.'

'Or two?'

'Yes, two. You're right again. He'll drop sure for two thousand. Two thousand is big money.'

'What I would have done without you,' said Lady Vera, 'I don't know. Some men in your position would have ruined everything by being niggardly.'

Mr Frisby glowed and expanded beneath her approbation. Once more that voice seemed to be whispering in his ear that it would be well to go to it. He simply needed an opening. The emotion was there, all ready to be poured out. All he required was a cue.

'Nothing niggardly about me,' he said, with modest pride.

'No.'

'I'm fond of money – I don't deny it – but...'

'Isn't everybody?'

'What?'

'Fond of money.'

'Are you?'

'Of course I am.'

'Have mine,' said Mr Frisby.

He strode to the telephone, unhooked the receiver, and barked into it to cover a certain not unnatural confusion. If his cheeks had not been made of the most durable leather, they would have been blushing. What he had said was not what he had been intending to say. He had planned something on tenderer and more romantic lines. Still, that was the way it had come out. The proposition had been placed on the agenda, and let it lay, was Mr Frisby's view.

'Chancery 09632? Robbins? Come right round to Grosvenor House, Robbins. Yes, at once. Want to see you.'

Lady Vera was contemplating his rigid back with a kindly smile. She was experienced in the matter of inarticulate proposals. The late Colonel Archibald Mace had grabbed her hand at Hurlingham one summer afternoon, turned purple, and said 'Eh, what?' Compared with him, Mr Frisby had been eloquent.

'Well?' said T. Paterson Frisby, replacing the receiver and turning.

'You go with it, I suppose?' said Lady Vera.

Mr Frisby nodded curtly.

'There is that objection,' he said.

Lady Vera smiled.

'I don't consider it an objection.'

'Vera!' said Mr Frisby.

'Paterson!' said Lady Vera.

'Don't call me Paterson,' said Mr Frisby, breathing devoutly down the back of her neck. 'It's a thing I wouldn't mention to anyone but you, and I hope you won't let it get about, but my first name's Torquil.'

II

To Berry Conway, hurrying across its verdant slopes to where the Tea House nestled among shady trees, Hyde Park seemed to be looking its best and brightest. True, the usual regiment of loafers slumbered on the grass and there was scattered in his path the customary assortment of old paper bags: but this afternoon, such is the magic of Love, these objects of the wayside struck him as merely picturesque. Dogs, to the number of twenty-seven, were barking madly in twenty-seven different keys: and their clamour sounded to him like music. If he had had time, he would have pursued and patted each separate dog and gone the rounds giving sixpences to each individual loafer. But time pressed, and he had to forgo this piece of self-indulgence.

If anyone had told him that his manner during their recent chat had been of a kind to occasion Mr Frisby pain, he would have been surprised and wounded. He was bubbling over with universal benevolence, and the five children who stopped him to ask the correct time received, in addition to the information, a sort of bonus in the form of a smile so dazzling that one of them, less hardy than the rest, burst into tears. And when, coming in view of the Tea House, he perceived Ann already seated at one of the tables, his exhilaration bordered on delirium. The trees seemed to dance. The sparrows sang with a gayer note. The family at the next table, including though it did a small boy in spectacles and a velvet suit, looked like a beautiful picture. Many a person calmer than Berry Conway at that moment had been accepted – and with enthusiasm – by the authorities of hospitals as a first-class fever patient.

He leaped the railings and covered the remaining distance in two bounds.

'Hullo!' he said.

'Hullo,' said Ann.

'Here I am!' he said.

'Yes,' said Ann.

'Am I late?' asked Berry.

'No,' said Ann.

A just perceptible diminution of ecstasy came to Berry Conway. He felt ever so slightly chilled. Nearly eighteen long hours had passed since he and this girl had last met, and he could not help feeling that something more in the key of drama should have signalized their reunion. Of course, in a public place like Hyde Park girls are handicapped in the way of emotional expression. Had Ann sprung from her seat and kissed him, the small boy at the next table would undoubtedly have caused embarrassment by asking in a loud voice, 'Mamah, why did she do that?' No, he could quite see why she did not spring and kiss him.

But – and now he saw what the trouble was – there was nothing whatever to prevent her smiling and – what is more – smiling with a shy, loving tenderness. And she had not done so. Her face was grave. If he had been in a slightly less exalted mood, he might have described it as unfriendly. There was not a smile in sight. Her mouth was set, and she was not looking at him. She was concentrating her gaze – letting her gaze run to waste, as it were – on a small, hard-boiled-looking Pekingese dog which had wandered up and was sitting by the table, waiting for food to appear.

Love sharpens the senses. Berry realized now what the matter was.

'I *am* late,' he said, contritely.

'Oh, no,' said Ann.

'I'm most frightfully sorry,' said Berry. 'I had to see someone on my way here.'

'Oh?' said Ann.

Even a man with Berry's rosy outlook could not blink the fact that the thermometer was falling. He cursed himself for not having been punctual. This, he told himself, was the way men rubbed the bloom off romance. They arranged to meet girls at five sharp at Tea Houses, and then they loitered and dallied and didn't arrive till five-one or even five-two. And, meanwhile, the poor girls waited and waited and waited, like Marianas in Moated Granges, longing for their tea...

Now he saw. Now he understood. Tea! Of course. All he had ever heard and read about the peril of keeping women waiting for their tea came back to him. And he was conscious of a great surge of relief. There was nothing personal about her coldness. It did not mean that she had been thinking things over and had decided that he was not the man for her. It simply meant that she wanted a spot of tea and wanted it quick.

He banged forcefully on the table.

'Tea,' he commanded. 'For two. As quick as you can. And cakes and things.'

Ann had stooped, and was tickling the Peke. Berry decided for the moment, till the relief expedition should arrive with restoratives, to keep the conversation impersonal.

'Lovely day,' he said.

'Yes,' said Ann.

'Nice dog,' said Berry.

'Yes,' said Ann.

Berry withdrew into a cautious silence. Talking only made him feel that he had been thrown into the society of a hostile stranger. He marvelled at the puissance of this strange drug, tea, the lack of which can turn the sweetest girl into a sort of trapped creature that glares and snaps. Amazing to think that about two half-sips and a swallow would change Ann into the thing of gentleness and warmth that she had been last night.

He sat back in his chair, and tried to relieve the strain by looking at the silver waters of the Serpentine. From its brink a faint quacking could be heard. Ducks. In a very short while he and a restored, kindly Ann would be scattering bits of cake to those ducks. All that was needed now was...

'Ah!' said Berry.

A tray-laden waitress was approaching.

'Here comes the tea,' he said.

'Oh!' said Ann.

He watched her fill her cup. He watched her drink. Then, reassured, he braced himself to make his apology as an apology should be made.

'I feel simply awful,' he said, 'about keeping you waiting like that.'

'I had only just arrived,' said Ann.

'I had to go and see someone...'

'Who?'

'Oh, a man.'

Ann detached a piece of cake and dropped it before the Peke. The Peke sniffed at it disparagingly, and resumed its steady gaze. It wanted chicken. It is the simple creed of the Peke that, where two human beings are gathered together to eat, chicken must enter into the proceedings somewhere.

'I see,' said Ann. 'A man? Not a gang?'

Berry started. The tea sprang from his cup. The words had been surprising enough, but not so surprising as the look which accompanied them. For, as she spoke, Ann had raised her head and for the first time her eyes met him squarely. And her eyes were like burning stones.

'Er – what?'

'A gang, I said,' replied Ann. Her eyes were daggers now. They pierced him through and through. 'I thought that, whenever you had a spare five minutes, you spent it rounding up gangs.'

In the distance ducks were quacking. At the next table the small boy had swallowed a crumb the wrong way and was being pounded on the back by abusive parents. Sparrows twittered, and somewhere a voice was calling to Ernie to stop teasing Cyril. Berry heard none of these things. He heard only the beating of his heart, and it was like a drum playing the Dead March.

He opened his mouth to speak, but she stopped him.

'No, please don't bother to tell me any more lies,' she said.

She leaned forward, and lowered her voice. What she had to say was not for the ears of the family at the next table.

'Shall I tell you,' she said, 'how I spent the afternoon? When I got home last night, I had a talk with Lord Biskerton's aunt, who is chaperoning me while I am over here. She had seen you and me dining at Mario's, and she had a lot to say about it. I wanted to discuss things with you, so I went down to Valley Fields in my car, and called at The Nook. You were out, but there was an elderly woman there with whom I had quite a long chat.'

It seemed to Berry that he had uttered a sudden, sharp wail. But he had done so only in spirit. He sat there, staring silently before him, his whole soul in torment. She had met the Old Retainer! She had had quite a long chat with the Old Retainer! He shuddered at the thought of what she must have heard. If ever there was a woman who could be relied on to spill the beans with a firm, unerring hand, that woman was the Old Retainer.

Ann continued speaking in the same low, even voice.

'She told me that you were the last person to do anything as nasty and dangerous as that, because you had always been so quiet and steady and respectable. She told me that you were my uncle's secretary and had never done anything adventurous or exciting in your life. She told me that you wore flannel next to your skin and bed-socks in winter. And,' said Ann, 'she told me that scar on your temple was not caused by a bullet, but that you got it when you were six years old by falling against the hat-stand in the hall because you forgot to scratch the soles of your new shoes.'

She rose abruptly.

'Well, that's all,' she said. 'Why you took so much trouble to make a fool of me, I don't know. Good-bye.'

She was walking away – walking out of his life: and still Berry found himself unable to move. Then, as she disappeared round the angle of the Tea House, he seemed to come out of his trance. He sprang to his feet, and was hurrying after her to explain, to plead, to give her the old oil, to clear himself at least of the charge of wearing bed-socks, when a voice arrested him.

'Jer want your bill, sir?'

It was the waitress, grim and suspicious. She disapproved of customers who developed a sudden activity before they had discharged their financial obligations.

'Oh!' Berry blinked. The waitress sniffed. 'I was forgetting,' said Berry.

He found money, handed it over, waved away the change. But the delay, though brief, had been fatal.

He vaulted the railings and stood peering about him. Hyde Park basked in the summer sunshine, green and spacious. The dogs were there. The loafers were there. The paper bags were there. But Ann had gone.

The ducks in the Serpentine quacked on, unfed.

III

In the smoking-room of the low and seedy club which was his haunt, Captain Kelly was listening with an expressionless face to an agitated Mr Hoke.

'He said he knew your secret?'

'Yes.'

J. B. Hoke mopped his forehead. Emotion, coupled with the four double brandies which he had taken to restore himself after the shock of his recent interview with the Biscuit, had made him more soluble than ever. He had become virtually fluid.

'Which secret?' asked the Captain.

'About the Dream Come True, of course.'

'Why of course? You must have a hundred, each shadier than the other.'

Mr Hoke was not to be consoled by this kindly suggestion. He shook his head.

'This fellow's a friend of young Conway. He lives next door to Conway. He was lunching with Conway. They were talking about the Dream Come True. Conway told me so. I thought right from the start that Conway had been listening at the door that day, and I was right.'

The Captain considered.

'Maybe,' he said. 'On the other hand, this red-headed chap may have been bluffing you.'

'I'm not so easy to bluff,' said Mr Hoke, bridling despite his concern.

'No?' said Captain Kelly. He smiled a twisted smile. 'Well, you were easy enough for me to bluff. You took in that story of mine about the gorillas without blinking. And you signed away half your cash on the strength of it.'

A hideous suspicion shot through Mr Hoke. He trembled visibly.

'The gorillas!' he gasped. 'Do you mean to say—?'

'Of course I do. Gorillas! There aren't any gorillas. What would I be doing spending my money on gorillas? I made them up. It flashed into my mind. Just like that. You know how things flash.'

Mr Hoke was breathing stertorously. It was as if this revelation of a friend's duplicity had stunned him.

'And you fell for it,' said Captain Kelly with relish. 'I'd never have thought it of you. Going to cost a lot, that is.'

Mr Hoke recovered. He spoke venomously.

'Is it?' he said. 'You think you're on to a good thing, do you?'

'I know it.'

'Well, let me tell you something,' said Mr Hoke. 'Do you know how many shares of Horned Toad Copper I hold at the present moment?'

'How many?'

'Not one. Not a single solitary darned one. That's how many.'

The Captain's face stiffened.

'What are you talking about?'

'I'll tell you what I'm talking about. I sold all my holdings at four, and I was going to buy them back when I felt they'd gone low enough. And then we would have spilled the info' about the new reef, and everything would have been fine. But now where are we? What is to prevent that red-headed young hound getting together some money and starting buying directly the market opens? What's to prevent him buying up all the shares there are?'

Something of his companion's concern was reflected on Captain Kelly's face.

'H'm!' he said. He paused thoughtfully. 'You really think he knows?'

'Of course he knows. He said "I know your secret." And I said "What secret?" And he said "Ah!" And I said "About the Dream Come True?" And he said "That's the one."'

Captain Kelly eyed his friend unpleasantly.

'And you said you weren't easy to bluff! I wish I'd been there.'

'What would you have done?'

'I'd have soaked you with a chair before you could start talking. Can't you see he didn't really know anything?'

'Well, he knows plenty now,' said Mr Hoke sullenly. Recalling the scene, he sat amazed at his simplicity. He could not believe that it was he, J. B. Hoke, who had behaved like that. He put it down to the fact that those phantom gorillas had been preying on his mind to such an extent that he had become incapable of clear thought.

'What are you going to do about it?' asked Captain Kelly.

Mr Hoke regarded him with cold reproach.

'What can I do about it?' he said. 'I'll tell you what I *was* going to do about it, if you like. I came here to ask you to send those two gorillas of yours down to Valley Fields where this guy lives, and attend to him.'

'Cosh him?'

'There wouldn't have been any need to cosh him. All that's necessary is to keep Conway and that red-haired bird away from the market long enough to let me buy back that stock. They can't do anything today, because the market's closed. But, if they aren't stopped, they'll be there bright and early tomorrow morning. I was going to tell you to send these gorillas down to keep them bottled up at home till I was ready to let them out. They could have flashed a gun at them, and made them stay put.

I only need a couple of hours tomorrow to clean up that stock. But what's the use of talking about it now?' said Mr Hoke disgustedly. 'There aren't any gorillas.'

He brooded disconsolately on this shortage. Captain Kelly was also brooding, but his thoughts had taken a different turn.

'It's a good idea,' he said at length. 'I wouldn't have expected you to think of it.'

'What's a good idea?'

'Bottling these fellows up.'

'Yeah?' said Mr Hoke. 'And how's it going to be done?'

Captain Kelly smiled one of his infrequent smiles.

'We'll do it.'

'Who'll do it?'

'You and I'll do it. We'll go down there and do it tonight.'

Mr Hoke stared. His potations had to a certain extent dulled his mental faculties, but he could still understand speech as plain as this.

'Me?' he said, incredulously. 'You think I'm going to horn into folks' homes with a gat in my hand?'

'Ah!' said Captain Kelly.

'I won't.'

'You will,' said the Captain. 'Or would you rather let these two chaps get away with it?'

Mr Hoke quivered. The prospect was not a pleasant one.

'You've said yourself what will happen,' proceeded the Captain, 'if these fellows aren't stopped. They'll get hold of all that stock, and somebody will suspect something, and the price will go up, and when we try to buy we'll have to pay through the nose.'

Mr Hoke nodded pallidly.

'I remember M.T.O. Nickel opening at ten and going to a hundred and twelve two hours later on a rumour,' he said. 'That was five years ago. It'll be the same with Horned Toad. Once start fooling around with these stocks and you never know what won't break.' He paused. 'But go down to Valley Fields and wave gats!' he said, shaking gently like a jelly. 'I can't do it.'

'You're going to do it,' said Captain Kelly firmly. 'Have you got a gat?'

'Of course I haven't got a gat.'

'Then go and buy one now,' said Captain Kelly, 'and meet me here at nine o'clock.'

IV

Captain Kelly regarded Mr Hoke censoriously. He did not like the way his friend had just tumbled into his car. Like a self-propelling sack of coals, the Captain considered.

'Hoke,' he said, 'you're blotto!'

Mr Hoke did not reply. He was gazing good-humouredly into the middle distance. His eyes were like the eyes of a fish not in the best of health.

'Oh, well,' said the Captain resignedly, 'maybe the fresh air will do you good.'

He took his seat at the steering-wheel, and the car moved off. Nine o'clock struck from Big Ben.

'Got gat,' said Mr Hoke, becoming chatty.

'Shut up,' said Captain Kelly.

Mr Hoke laughed softly and nestled into his seat. The car slid on towards Sloane Square. Mr Hoke nodded at the policeman on point-duty.

'Got gat,' he informed him as one old friend to another.

CHAPTER 12

I

When the poet Bunn (1790–1860) spoke of the heart being bowed down by weight of woe, he spoke, of course, as poets will, figuratively. Fortunately for the security of our public vehicles, grief has no tonnage. If the weight of human sorrow had been a thing of actual pounds and ounces, the Number Three omnibus which shortly before 8.30 p.m. set Lord Biskerton down at the corner of Croxleigh Road, Valley Fields, could never have made its trip from London. It must have faltered and stopped, and its wheels would have buckled under it. For the Biscuit was a heavy-hearted young man.

All through the long summer afternoon, starting about ten minutes after the conclusion of his interview with Mr Hoke, his gloom had been deepening. And with reason.

'What,' J. B. Hoke had asked, in a fine passage, 'is to prevent that red-headed young hound getting together some money and starting buying directly the market opens?'

The Biscuit could have informed him. The obstacle that stood between himself and anything in the nature of big buying in the market was the parsimony, the incredulity, the lack of broad vision displayed by the fellow human beings. Offered a vast fortune in return for open-handedness, they had declined to be open-handed. One and all, they had shrunk from entrusting him with the loan that would enable him to invade the market on the morrow and cash in on the private information he had received concerning the imminent boom in Horned Toad Copper.

Of all sad words of tongue or pen, the saddest are these – 'He knew something good, but could not make a touch.'

The whole matter of borrowing money is extraordinarily complex, and no publicist has yet been able to explain why it is that A. can do it, while B. can't – or taking another case, that of C. and D., why C. can bite the ear at will for thousands, while D., though a certainty for a fiver, is never able to soar above that sum. The nearest one can get to a solution is to say that, in order to borrow on a large scale, one has to be a firm of some kind.

If the Biscuit had been the Pernambuco and Fiji Trading Co., or Gold Bricks and Perpetual Motion Ltd, he would, no doubt, have been returning to his little home this evening with his pockets bulging with specie. But he had conducted his campaign as an individual – and, what is more, as an individual who was known to be in the fiver class. He had made his name in that division. When people saw Lord Biskerton coming, they automatically dipped into their note-cases for fivers. They refused, to a man, to encourage him to go out of his class by giving him a thousand pounds, which was what he wanted now.

He had tried prospects likely and unlikely. Dogged to the last, the fine old Crusading spirit of the Biskertons had taken him even into the lair of the Messrs Dykes, Dykes and Pinweed. And all Dykes, Dykes and Pinweed had done had been to babble nastily of their account. And finally, when young Oofy Simpson, notoriously the richest property at the Drones, had failed to develop pay-ore, the Biscuit gave the thing up.

He made his way to Mulberry Grove with slow and dragging feet. His was a tortured soul. He writhed every time he thought of what he was missing. Once, at school, he had made six shillings that R. B. (Tape-Worm) Blenkinsop could eat ten macaroons during the eleven o'clock intermission: and until now he had always looked on that as the softest snap of his career. But it was as nothing compared with the one with which Fate was tantalizing him just now. This was the real thing. This was money for jam. And he could not grab it.

Breathing heavily, the Biscuit reached Mulberry Grove and turned in at the gate of The Nook. He wanted sympathy, and Berry Conway could supply it. Hope, moreover, not yet quite dead, whispered that Berry might possibly be able to raise a bit of money. That bird Attwater – he had once lent Berry two hundred pounds, and Berry had paid it back. Surely this must have inspired Attwater with confidence.

Becoming almost cheerful for a moment, the Biscuit tapped at the window of the sitting-room.

'Berry,' he called.

Berry was in, and he heard the tap. He also heard his friend's voice. But he did not reply. He, too, was in the depths and, much as he enjoyed the Biscuit's society as a rule, he felt unequal to the task of chatting with him now. The Biscuit, he feared, would start rhapsodizing about his Kitchie, and every word would be a dagger in the heart. A man who has recently had his world shattered into a million fragments by a woman's frown cannot lightly entertain happy lovers in his sitting-room.

So Berry crouched in the darkness, and made no sign. And the Biscuit, with a weary curse, turned away and sat on the front steps and smoked a cigarette.

Presently, finding no solace in nicotine, he rose, and, going to the gate, leaned upon it. He surveyed the scene before him. Darkness was falling now, but the visibility was still good enough to enable him to perceive the swan Egbert floating on the ornamental water, and he speculated idly on the possibility of picking him off at this distance with a bit of stick. When the soul is bruised, relief can sometimes be found in annoying a swan. The Biscuit stooped and possessed himself of a sizeable twig.

He was just poising this, trying to gauge the necessary trajectory, when between him and his objective there inserted itself a body. A tall, thin man of ripe years had come round the corner and was regarding him as if he had been the tombstone of a friend.

'Good evening, Mr Conway,' said this person, in a sad voice that reminded the Biscuit of his bank manager regretting that in the circumstances it would be inconvenient – nay, impossible – to oblige him with the suggested overdraft. 'This is Mr Conway, I suppose? My name is Robbins.'

II

The error into which the senior partner of the legal firm of Robbins, Robbins, Robbins and Robbins had fallen was not an unnatural one. He had been despatched by Mr Frisby to Valley Fields to deal with an adventurer residing at The Nook, Mulberry Grove, and he had reached the gate of The Nook, and here was a young man standing inside looking out. It is scarcely to be wondered at that Mr Robbins considered that he had reached Journey's End.

'I should be glad of a word with you, Mr Conway,' he said.

The interruption of his sporting plans annoyed the Biscuit.

'I'm not Mr Conway,' he said, curtly. 'Mr Conway's out.'

Mr Robbins held up a gloved hand. He had expected this sort of thing.

'Please!' he said. 'I can readily imagine that you would prefer to avoid a discussion of your affairs, but I fear I must insist.'

Mr Robbins had two manners – both melancholy but each quite distinct. When having a friendly talk with a client on a matter of replevin or the like, he allowed himself to ramble. When dealing with adventurers, he was crisp.

He spoke coldly, for he disliked the scoundrel before him.

'I represent Mr Frisby, with whose niece, I understand, you are proposing to contract an alliance. My client is fully resolved that this marriage shall not take place, and I may say that you will gain nothing by opposing his wishes. An attitude of obduracy and defiance on your part will simply mean that you lose everything. Be reasonable, however, and my client is prepared to be generous. I think you will agree with me, Mr Conway – here *in camera*, as one might say, and with no witnesses present – that heroics are unnecessary and that the only aspect of the matter on which we need touch is the money aspect.'

The Biscuit had not allowed this address to be delivered without attempted punctuation. He had had far too much to put up with that afternoon to be willing to listen meekly to gibberers. The other's white hairs, just visible under his top-hat, protected him from actual assault: or he would have squashed that top-hat in with a single blow of the fist. However, he had endeavoured to speak, only to find the practised orator riding over him and taking him in his stride. Now that his companion had paused, and he had an excellent opportunity of reiterating that a mistake had been made, he did not seize it. The thought that at the eleventh hour Fate had sent him a man who talked about money

– vaguely at present, but nevertheless with a sort of golden promise in his voice – held him dumb.

'Come now, Mr Conway,' said Mr Robbins. 'Are we going to be sensible?'

The Biscuit choked. The twig dropped from his nerveless hand.

'Are you offering me money to ...'

'Please!'

'Let's get this straight,' said the Biscuit. 'Is there, or is there not, money on the horizon?'

'There is. I am empowered to offer ...'

'How much?'

'Two thousand pounds.'

Mulberry Grove swam before the Biscuit's eyes. The swan Egbert looked like two swans, twin brothers.

'Yes, think it over,' said Mr Robbins.

He adjusted his coat, draping it about him so as more closely to resemble a winding-sheet. The Biscuit leaned on the gate in silence.

'When do I get it?' asked the Biscuit at length.

'Now.'

'Now?'

'I have a cheque with me. See!' said Mr Robbins, pulling it out and dangling it.

He had no need to dangle long.

'Gimme!' said the Biscuit hoarsely, and snatched it from his grasp.

Mr Robbins regarded him with a sorrowful loathing. He had expected acquiescence, but not acquiescence quite so rapid as this. Despite the fact that he had stressed his disinclination for heroics, he had not supposed that this deal would have been concluded without at least an attempt on this young villain's part to affect reluctance.

'I think I may congratulate the young lady on a fortunate escape,' he said, icily.

'Eh?' said the Biscuit.

'I say I may congratulate...'

'Oh, ah,' said the Biscuit. 'Yes. Thanks very much.'

Mr Robbins gave up the attempt to pierce this armoured hide.

'Here is my card,' he said, revolted. 'You will come to my office tomorrow and sign a letter which I shall dictate. I wish you good evening, Mr Conway.'

'Eh?' said the Biscuit.

'Good evening, Mr Conway.'

'What?' said the Biscuit.

'Oh, good night,' said Mr Robbins.

He turned, and walked away. His very back expressed his abhorrence.

The Biscuit stood for a while gaping at the ornamental water. Then, walking slowly and dazedly to Peacehaven, he mixed himself the whisky and soda which the situation seemed to him so unquestionably to call for.

In the intervals of imbibing it, he sang joyously in a discordant but powerful baritone. The wall separating the sitting-room of Peacehaven from the sitting-room of The Nook was composed of one thickness of lath and plaster, and Berry Conway, wrestling with his tragedy, heard every note.

He shuddered. If that was how Love was making his neighbour feel, he was glad that he had been firm and had paid no attention to his knocking on the window.

III

It was some twenty minutes later that the car containing Captain Kelly and his ally, Mr Hoke, turned into Mulberry Grove.

'Here we are,' said the Captain. 'Get out.'

Mr Hoke got out.

'Now,' said Captain Kelly, having, in his military fashion, surveyed the *terrain*, 'this is what we do, so listen, you poor sozzled fish. You go round to the back and stay there. I'll stick here, in the front. And, remember, no one is to leave either of those two houses. And, if anyone goes in, they've damn' well got to stay there. Do you understand?'

Mr Hoke nodded eleven times with sunny goodwill.

'Got gat,' he said.

CHAPTER 13

I

A diet of large whiskies and small sodas, persisted in through the whole of a long afternoon and evening and augmented by an occasional neat brandy, is a thing which cuts, as it were, both ways. It had had the effect of bringing J. B. Hoke to the back-garden of The Nook with a revolver in his hand – a feat which he could never have achieved purely on lemonade: and so far may have been said to have answered its purpose. But it had also had the effect of blurring Mr Hoke's faculties.

As he stood, propping himself up against The Nook's one tree and breathing the sweet night air of Valley Fields, his mind was not at its best and clearest. He had a dim recollection of a confused conversation with his friend, Captain Kelly, in the course of which much of interest had been said: but it had left him in a state of uncertainty on three cardinal points.

These were:

        (a) Who was he?
        (b) Where was he?
        (c) Why was he?

To the solution of this triple problem he now proceeded to address himself.

In a way, it was the sort of thing Marcus Aurelius used to worry about. But Mr Hoke had an advantage over the Roman Emperor. The latter sought for some explanation of his presence in the great world of men. J. B. Hoke simply wanted to know why he was leaning against a tree in what appeared to be a suburban garden.

Obviously, he felt, he must be there for some good purpose; and he fancied that, if he only remained perfectly quiet and concentrated, it would all come back to him.

So, for a space, Mr Hoke stood and meditated on first causes. And he was still meditating when Fate assisted him by causing the hand which rested against the tree to slip. Mr Hoke, thrown off his balance, fell sideways and sustained a painful blow on the left ear. The shock accomplished what mere thought had been unable to effect. Sitting on the ground and rubbing the injured spot, he found Memory returning to her throne.

Now he recollected. Now everything was clear. The Captain had stationed him in this garden to prevent, by force if necessary, the exodus of young Conway and his red-headed friend. Mr Hoke rose and dusted his trousers with an air of determination. He was still conscious of a slight swimming of the head, but at least he had found the answer to the great fundamental problem.

Instinctively feeling that it would be sure to come in useful, J. B. Hoke had provided himself for this expedition with a large pocket-flask. He now produced this, and drank deeply of its contents. And his mood, which had begun by being one of amiable vacuity and had changed to one of self-pity, changed again. If somebody had come along and flashed a light on Mr Hoke's face at this moment, he would have perceived on it an expression of sternness. He was thinking hard thoughts of Berry and his friend. Trying to sneak out and slip something across a good man, were they? Ha! thought Mr Hoke.

With a wide and sweeping gesture, designed to indicate his contempt for and defiance of all such petty-minded plotters, he flung an arm dramatically skywards. Unfortunately, it was the arm which ended in the hand which ended in the fingers which held the flask; and the fingers, unequal to the sudden strain, relaxed their grip. The next moment, the precious object had vanished into the night, with its late owner in agonized pursuit.

Mr Hoke had never been a reader of poetry. Had he been, those poignant words of Longfellow:

> I shot a flask into the air:
> It fell to earth, I knew not where.

would undoubtedly have flashed into his mind, for they covered the situation exactly. The night was dark, and the grounds of The Nook, though not large compared with places like Blenheim or Knole, were quite large enough to hide a flask. For many long and weary minutes Mr Hoke traversed them from side to side and from end to end like a hunting dog. He poked in bushes. He went down on hands and knees. He scrutinized flower-beds. But all to no avail. The garden held its secret well.

J. B. Hoke gave it up. He was beaten. Sadly he rose from the last flower-bed: and, turning, he was aware that there was light in one of the ground-floor windows, where before no light had been. Interested by this phenomenon, he hurried across the lawn and looked in.

The young man, Conway, was there, eating cold ham and drinking whisky.

The discovery that he was on the point of perishing of thirst and hunger had come quite suddenly to Berry as he sat nursing his sorrow in the darkened sitting-room. At first, he had repelled it: for the mere thought of taking nourishment was, in his present frame of mind, odious to him. Then, as the urge grew greater, he had succumbed. He had gone to the larder and foraged. And now he was setting to with something like enthusiasm.

Mr Hoke, crouching outside the window, eyed him wistfully. He could have done with a slice of that ham. He could have used that whisky. He flattened his nose against the pane and stared wolfishly. A yearning for his lost flask tormented him.

Suddenly he observed the banqueter stiffen in his chair and raise his head, listening. Mr Hoke heard nothing, and was not aware that the front door bell had rung. But Berry had heard it, and a wild, reasonless hope shot through him that it was Ann, come to tell him that in spite of all she loved him still. True, she had given at their parting no indication of the likelihood of any such change of heart, but the possibility was enough to send Berry shooting out of the door and down the hall. Mr Hoke found himself looking into an empty room.

Empty, that is to say, except for the ham on the table and the whisky bottle beside it. These remained, and J. B. Hoke found in their aspect something magnetic, something that drew him like a spell. He tested the window. It was not bolted. He pushed it up. He climbed in.

What with the tumult of his thoughts and the necessity of drinking his courage to the sticking-point, Mr Hoke tonight had for perhaps the first time in his life omitted to dine, preferring to concentrate his energies on the absorption of double whiskies. He was now ravenously hungry, and he assailed the ham with a will. He also helped himself freely from the whisky bottle.

A man who is already nearly full to the top with mixed spirits cannot do this sort of thing without experiencing some sort of spiritual change. At the beginning of the meal, J. B. Hoke had been morose and particularly unkindly disposed towards Berry. By the time he had finished, a gentler mood prevailed. He was feeling extraordinarily dizzy, but with the dizziness had come a strongly marked benevolence and a keen desire for the society of his fellows.

He rose. He went to the door. From the direction of the sitting-room came the buzz of voices. Evidently some sort of social gathering was in progress there, and he wanted to be in it.

He zig-zagged down the passage, chose after some hesitation the middle one of the three handles with which a liberal-minded architect had equipped the sitting-room door, and, walking in, gazed on the occupants with a smile of singular breadth and sweetness.

There were two persons present. One was Berry. The other was a distinguished-looking man of middle life with a clean-cut face and a grey moustache. Both seemed surprised to see him.

''Lo!' said Mr Hoke spaciously.

Berry, in his capacity of host, answered him.

'Hullo!' said Berry. The apparition had not unnaturally startled him somewhat. 'Mr Hoke!'

'Hic-coke,' replied Hoke, endorsing the statement.

Berry had now arrived at a theory which seemed to him to cover the facts. He assumed that after admitting Lord Hoddesdon a short while back he had forgotten to close the front door, and that his latest visitor, finding it open, had come in. It was a thing that might quite easily have happened, for his lordship's arrival, puzzling him completely, had taken his mind off all other matters. At any rate, here Hoke was, and he endeavoured politely to discover what had brought him there.

'Do you want to see me about something?' he asked.

'Got gat,' said Mr Hoke pleasantly.

'Cat?' said Berry.

'Gat,' said Mr Hoke.

'What cat?' asked Berry, still unequal to the intellectual pressure of the conversation.

'Gat,' said Mr Hoke with an air of finality.

Berry tentatively approached the subject from another angle.

'Hat?' he said.

'Gat,' said Mr Hoke.

He frowned slightly, and his smile lost something of its effervescent *bonhomie*. This juggling with words was giving him a slight, but distinct headache.

Lord Hoddesdon, too, seemed far from genial. The interruption coming at a moment when he had begun to talk really well, annoyed him.

Considering that he had stated so firmly and uncompromisingly to his sister Vera that nothing would induce him ever to return to Valley Fields, the presence of Lord Hoddesdon in Berry's sitting-room requires, perhaps, a brief explanation. Briefly, he had changed his mind. It is the distinguishing mark of a great man that he is never afraid to change his mind, should he see good reason to do so. And Lord Hoddesdon, thinking things over in his club, had seen excellent reason.

Lady Vera's revelations on the previous night had shaken him to the core. If Ann Moon was really planning to jilt his son and marry this Conway, the matter was serious. Although nothing in the millionaire's behaviour so far had indicated a desire to part with money, it had seemed to Lord Hoddesdon, always an optimist, that, once the girl was married to his son, he would surely be in a position to work Mr Frisby for a small loan. He and T. Paterson would then, dash it, be practically relations.

It was vital, accordingly, that this Conway be firmly suppressed by one in authority.

Conscious, therefore, of the fact that he now had six hundred pounds in his account at the bank, he had come to The Nook to buy the fellow off. He had come by night, because in his opinion Valley Fields was safer then. And he had just been in the act of talking to him as a head of the family should have talked, when this disgusting interruption had occurred. Right in the middle of one of his best sentences the door had opened and in had staggered a large, red-faced inebriate.

Conscious that the spell had been broken and that further discussion of a delicate matter must be postponed, and feeling bitterly that this was just the sort of friend he might have expected the man Conway to have, Lord Hoddesdon rose.

'Where is my hat?' he said stiffly.

'Gat,' said Mr Hoke, his annoyance increasing. It seemed to him that these people were deliberately affecting to misunderstand plain English.

He regarded Lord Hoddesdon, now making obvious preparations for departure, with a hostile eye. For some little time he had been allowing his mind to wander from his mission, but now Captain Kelly's words came back to him. 'No one is to leave either of these houses,' the Captain had said. 'And if anyone goes in, they've dam' well got to stay there.' The grey-moustached stiff had gone in. Very well. Now he would stay here.

'You thinking of leaving?' asked Mr Hoke.

Lord Hoddesdon raised his eyebrows. Impecuniosity and the exigences of a democratic age had combined to cause his lordship to be sparing of the *hauteur* which so often goes with blue blood: but he employed it now. He stared at J. B. Hoke like a *seigneur* of the old *régime* having a good look at a vassal or varlet.

'I haven't the pleasure of knowing who you are, sir ...'

Berry did the honours.

'Mr Hoke – The Earl of Hoddesdon—'

Mr Hoke's severity waned a little.

'Are you an Oil?' he said, interested.

'... but, in answer to your question, I *am* thinking of leaving,' said Lord Hoddesdon.

Mr Hoke's momentary lapse into amiability was over. He was the strong man again, the man behind the gun.

'Oh, no!' he said.

'I beg your pardon?' said Lord Hoddesdon.

'Granted,' said Mr Hoke. He produced the gat, of which they had heard so much, and poised it in an unsteady but resolute grasp. 'Hands up!' he said.

II

In the sitting-room of Peacehaven, meanwhile, separated from the sitting-room of The Nook by only a thin partition, events had been taking place which demand the historian's attention. It is to Lord Biskerton and his affairs that the chronicler must now turn his all-embracing eye.

At about the moment when Mr Hoke was climbing over the dining-room window-sill of The Nook, intent on ham and whisky, the Biscuit, seated in an armchair next door, had begun to gaze at a photograph of Miss Valentine on the mantelpiece, thinking the while those long, sweet thoughts which come to a young man with love in his heart and a cheque for two thousand pounds in his pocket. The burst of song in which he had indulged on returning home after the departure of Mr Robbins had continued for the space of perhaps ten minutes. At the end of that period, he had abated the nuisance and turned to silent musing.

He gazed at the photograph of Kitchie. To have won the love of a girl constructed on those lines might have been considered luck enough for any ordinary man. But not for Godfrey Edward Winstanley Brent, Lord Biskerton, Fortune's Favourite. To him had been vouchsafed in addition one of the red-hottest tips that ever emanated from the Stock Market and, as if that were not sufficient, a miraculous shower of gold which would enable him to profit by it.

From his earliest years, the Biscuit had nourished an unwavering conviction that Providence was saving up something particularly juicy in the way of rewards for him, and that it was only a question of time before it came across and delivered the goods. He based this belief on the fact that he had always tried to be a reasonably bonhomous sort of bird and was one who, like Abu Ben Adhem, loved his fellow-men. Abu had clicked, and Lord Biskerton expected to click. But not in his most sanguine moments, not even after a Bump Supper at Oxford or the celebration of somebody's birthday at the Drones, had he ever expected to click on this colossal scale. It just showed that, when Providence knew it had got hold of a good man, the sky was the limit.

Furthermore, while benefiting him, Providence would also put good old Berry on Easy Street. Lavish. That is what the Biscuit considered it. Lavish. Nestling in his chair, he felt almost dizzy. Joy-bells seemed to be ringing in a world where everything, after a rocky start, had suddenly come abso-bally-right.

Presently, as he sat, there came to him the realization that on one point he had made a slight and pardonable error. Those were not joy-bells. What was ringing was the one at the front door. A caller had apparently come to share with him this hour of ecstasy. Hoping that it was Berry, fearing that it might be the Vicar, he went to the door and opened it. And, having opened it, he stood on the mat, staring with a wild surmise.

He had been prepared for Berry. He had been prepared for the Vicar. He had even been prepared for somebody selling brooms, cane-bottomed chairs, or aspidistras. What he had not been prepared for was his late *fiancée*, Ann Moon.

'Hul-lo!' said the Biscuit, blinking.

She was gazing at him with large eyes, and she seemed a little breathless. Her face was flushed, and her lips were parted. Extraordinarily pretty – not that it mattered, of course – it made her look, the Biscuit felt.

'Hullo!' he said blankly.

'Hullo,' said Ann.

'You!' said the Biscuit.

'Yes,' said Ann. 'May I come in?'

'Come in?'

'Yes.'

'Oh, rather,' said the Biscuit, roused to the necessity of playing the host. 'Of course. Certainly.'

Still stunned, he led the way to the sitting-room.

'Would you like to take a seat, or anything of that sort?'

'May I?'

'Certainly,' said the Biscuit. 'Of course. Oh, rather.'

Ann sat down, and there followed a pause of some length. It is not easy for a girl who has broken her engagement with a man and who has called at his house to suggest that, her outlook on things having altered, that engagement shall be resumed, to know exactly how to start.

Ann's mind, like that of her host, was in a distinctly disordered condition. She had come here on one of those sudden impulses on which she was too prone to act. She told herself that she hated and despised Berry, and this had led to a conviction that she had treated the Biscuit very badly and must make amends. But it was not easy to open the subject.

'Cigarette?' said the Biscuit.

'No, thanks.'

What made it so particularly difficult was that her mind was divided against itself. It was all very well for her to tell herself that she hated and despised Berry. So she did. But how long would this attitude last after the first spasm of righteous indignation had ceased to hold control? At present, she was still in the full grip of that burning fury which comes to every girl who has been made a fool of and who is compelled to face the sickening fact that Mother – or, at least, her chaperon – was right. Lady Vera had said that Berry was a mercenary impostor, and a mercenary impostor he had proved.

So far, as the Biscuit would have said, so good.

But all the while there was something deep down in her which was whispering that, impostor or not, he was the man she loved and always would love. For years she had been plagued by a meddling and interfering Conscience; and now that at last she seemed to be acting on lines of which Conscience approved, up popped an inconvenient Subconscious Self to make her uneasy. Look at it how you liked, it was a pretty tough world for a girl.

She forced herself to crush down this new assailant.

'Godfrey,' she said.

'Hullo?'

'I want to speak to you.'

'Shoot,' said the Biscuit.

'I—' said Ann.

She stopped. It was even more difficult than she had thought it would be.

Silence fell again. The Biscuit raked his mind for conversational material. He had always been fond of Ann but he was bound to admit that he had liked her better before she contracted this lock-jaw or aphasia or whatever it was. Put it this way. A merry, prattling girl – excellent. A girl apparently suffering from the dumb staggers – no good to a fellow whatever. If Ann had come all the way to Valley Fields merely to gulp at him, he wished she would go.

As a matter of fact, he wished she would go, anyway. He was an engaged man, and an engaged man cannot be too careful. Kitchie might resent – and very properly resent – this entertaining of attractive females in his home.

However, he had to be courteous. It being impossible to take her by the scruff of the neck and bung her out, something in the nature of polite chit-chat was indicated.

'How are you?' he said.

'I'm all right.'

'Pretty well?'

'Yes, thanks.'

'You're looking well.'

'*You're* looking well.'

'Oh, I'm all right.'

'So am I.'

'That's good,' said the Biscuit. 'I wonder if you'd mind if I took a small snort? The old brain feels as if it had come a bit unstuck at the seams.'

'Go ahead.'

'Thanks. You?'

'No, thanks.'

'Well, best o' luck,' said the Biscuit, imbibing.

He felt more composed now. It occurred to him that a major mystery still remained unsolved.

'How did you know I was living here?' he asked.

'Lady Vera told me.'

'Ah!' said the Biscuit. 'I see. *She* told you?'

'Yes. By the way, did she tell you?'

'That I live here?'

'About her engagement.'

The Biscuit goggled.

'Her engagement?'

'She's going to marry my uncle.'

'What! Old Pop Frisby?'

'Yes.'

'My . . . stars!'

'I was surprised, too. I hadn't thought of Uncle Paterson as a marrying man.'

'Any man's a marrying man that a woman like my Aunt Vera gets her hooks on,' said the Biscuit profoundly. 'Well, I'm dashed! So my family is keeping your family in the family, after all. Knock me down with a feather, that's what you could do.'

He mused awhile. Things were growing clearer.

'So that's why you came down here?'

'No.'

'How do you mean, no?'

'I mean, no.'

'You mean, you didn't come here just to tell me this bit of news?'

'No.'

'Then why,' demanded the Biscuit, putting his finger squarely on the centre of this perplexing matter, 'did you come? Always glad to see you, of course,' he added, gallantly. 'Drop in any time you're passing and all that. Still, why did you come?'

Ann felt that the moment had arrived. With a slight tingling of the spinal cord and other evidences of embarrassment in the shape of the glowing cheek and the foot drawing patterns on the floor, she braced herself to speak.

'Godfrey,' she said.

'Carry on,' said the Biscuit encouragingly, after an adequate pause.

'Godfrey,' said Ann, 'you got a letter from me, didn't you?'

'Breaking the engagement? Rather.'

'I came here,' said Ann, 'to tell you I was sorry I wrote it.'

The Biscuit was insufferably hearty.

'Not at all. A very well-expressed letter. Thought so at the time and think so still. Full of good stuff.'

'I . . .'

The Biscuit clicked his tongue remorsefully.

'By the way,' he said, 'can't think what I was doing, not touching on the topic before, but wish you happiness, and all that sort of rot. Berry Conway told me you and he had signed up.'

'Do you know him?' cried Ann, astonished.

'Of course I know him. And I ought to have extended felicitations and so forth long ago. What with life being tolerably full, and one thing and another, I overlooked it. Dashed sensible of you both, I consider. There's no one I would rather see you engaged to than old Berry.'

'We are not engaged.'

'Not?'

'No.'

'Then,' said the Biscuit, aggrieved, 'I have been misinformed.

My leg has been pulled, and – what makes it worse – by a usually reliable source.'

'I've broken it off,' said Ann shortly.

The Biscuit stared.

'Broken it off?'

'Yes.'

'Why?'

'Never mind why.'

'My dear old soul,' said the Biscuit paternally, 'I would be the last man to butt in on other people's affairs, but, honestly, don't you think you're rather overdoing this breaking-off business? I mean to say, twice in under a week. Goodish going, you must admit. I don't know what the European record for engagement-breaking is, but I should say you hold it. Twice! Great Scott!'

Ann clenched her hands.

'It needn't be twice,' she said, speaking with difficulty, 'unless you like.'

'Eh?'

'I came here,' said Ann, 'to suggest that, if you felt the same, we might consider that letter of mine not written.'

The Biscuit gasped. They were coming off the bat too quick for him today. First Hoke, then old Robbins, and now this. He began to feel slightly delirious.

'Do you mean,' he asked, 'that you're suggesting that you and I . . . ?'

'Yes.'

'That our engagement . . .'

'Yes.'

'That we shall . . . ?'

'Oh, yes, yes, yes!' said Ann.

There was a long silence. The Biscuit walked to the window,

and looked out. There was nothing to see, but he remained there, looking, for some considerable time. He perceived that all his tact and address would be needed to handle this situation.

'Well?' said Ann.

The Biscuit turned. He had found the right words.

'Look here, old soul,' he said apologetically, 'I'm afraid I've a rather nasty knock for you, and, if you take my advice, you'll have a drink to brace yourself. I'd do anything in my power to oblige, but the fact is I can only be a sister to you.'

With a sorrowful jerk of the thumb, he indicated the mantel-piece.

'Like Dykes, Dykes and Pinweed,' he said, 'I'm bespoke.'

Ann caught her breath in sharply.

'Oh!' she said.

She got up. Never since the day when, a child of eleven, she had been pushed on to the platform to assist a conjurer at a children's party, had she felt so supremely foolish: but she held her head high. She went to the mantelpiece and examined the photograph thoughtfully.

'She's pretty,' she said.

'She *is* pretty,' agreed the Biscuit.

'Why, I know her!' exclaimed Ann.

'You do?'

'It's Kitchie Valentine. I came over in the boat with her.'

The Biscuit had half a mind to say something about this bringing them all very close together, but he was not quite sure how it would go. It might go well, or it might not go well. He decided to keep it back.

'She lives next door, doesn't she?' said Ann. 'I had forgotten.'

'That's right,' said the Biscuit. 'Next door. We did most of our coo-and-billing across the fence.'

'I see. Well, I hope you'll be very happy.'

'Oh, I shall,' the Biscuit assured her.

'I think I'll be going,' said Ann.

The Biscuit held up a compelling hand.

'Wait!' he said. 'Just one moment. I want to get to the bottom of this business of old Berry.'

'I don't want to talk about him.'

'This lovers' tiff...'

'It wasn't a lovers' tiff.'

'Then what was it? Good heavens!' said the Biscuit, warming to his subject. 'If ever there were a couple of birds made for one another, it's you and Berry. I mean to say, you're one of the sweetest things on earth, and he's a corker. His life was gentle, and the elements so mixed in him that Nature might stand up and say to all the world "This was a man!" I always remember that bit,' said the Biscuit. 'Had to write it out a hundred times at school for bunging an orange at a contemporary and catching my form-master squarely in the eyeball, he happening to come unexpectedly into the room at the moment. If you've really gone and given old Berry the push, you must be cuckoo. It's no good telling yourself that there'll be another one along in a minute, because there won't. You won't find another fellow like Berry in a million years. He's all right. And what they think of him in the Secret Service!' added the Biscuit, belatedly remembering. 'The blokes up top have got their eye on him all right. I can tell you!'

Ann laughed shortly.

'Secret Service!'

'Why,' asked the Biscuit, 'do you say "Secret Service" in that nasty, tinkling voice?'

'I know all about him, thanks,' said Ann. 'There's no need for you to lie to me. He did all of that that was necessary.'

'Oh?' said the Biscuit reflectively. 'Oh, ah! Ah! Oh!'

He began to understand.

'He's my uncle's secretary,' said Ann, with scorn.

'In a measure,' admitted the Biscuit reluctantly, 'yes. But,' he went on, brightening, 'what of it?'

'What of it?'

'What difference does it make?'

Ann's eyes blazed.

'You don't think it makes any difference? You don't think that a girl's feelings are likely to change towards a man when she finds he has been lying to her and making a fool of her and pretending to be fond of her just because . . .' She choked. '. . . just because she happens to be rich?'

The Biscuit was shocked.

'My dear young prune,' he said, 'you aren't asking me to believe that you think that a fellow like Berry was after your money?'

'Yes, I am. Lady Vera said he was.'

'Admitting,' said the Biscuit, 'that what my Aunt Vera doesn't know about cash-chivvying isn't worth knowing, I deny it *in toto*. Aunt Vera was talking through her hat. Listen, you poor mutt. I was at school with old Berry for a matter of five years, and I know him from caviare to nuts. He's the squarest bird on earth. And that's official. You don't suppose a man can be mistaken about another man after five years at school with him, do you? Berry's all right.'

'Then why did he lie to me?'

'I'll tell you about that,' said the Biscuit. 'Give you a good laugh, this will. He saw you at the Berkeley that day and fell in love with you, and then he saw you in your car, and the only way he could think of to get to know you was to jump in and say he was a Secret Service man. That's the sort of chap he is. Weak in the head, but fizzing with romance. And in *re* his being your uncle's secretary. You don't imagine he stuck on as secretary to old Pop Frisby because he enjoyed it, do you? He was left without a penny in the world, and some lawyer cove lent him a couple of hundred quid to give him a start, and he had to get a job and hold it down till he had paid the stuff back. And all the time he was yearning to roll to 'Rio or go to Arizona and do something or other to rocks – he told me what it was, but I've forgotten. Blackjacking, it sounded like. And, talking of Arizona, let me tell you something, and you'll see what a young muttonhead you've been to think that it was your money he was after. He's got money himself, thousands and thousands of pounds of it. Or he will have tomorrow. Me, too. We've come into a fortune.'

Ann was silent. Then she drew her breath in with a long sigh.

'I see,' she said.

'It's no good saying you see. What are you going to do about it?'

'I've made a fool of myself,' said Ann.

'You've made a gosh-awful fool of yourself,' agreed the Biscuit enthusiastically. 'You've acted like a poop and a pip-squeak. What steps, then, do you propose to take?'

'Shall I write to him?'

'Not a bad idea.'

'I'll go home and do it now.'

'Excellent.'

'Well, I'll be going, Godfrey.'

'Perhaps it would be as well,' said the Biscuit. 'I mean, delighted you were about to come, and so on, but you know how it is.'

'I suppose I ought to try to thank you,' said Ann, at the front door.

'Not a bit necessary. Only too pleased if any little thing I may have said has been instrumental. . . .'

'Well, good-bye.'

'Good-bye,' said the Biscuit. 'I shall watch your future career with considerable interest. Hullo, who's this bird?'

The bird alluded to was the redoubtable Captain Kelly, who had suddenly manifested himself out of the darkness and intruded on this farewell.

'Just a moment,' said Captain Kelly.

Ann stared at him, alarmed. With his hat pulled down over his eyes, the Captain was a disquieting figure.

'All hawkers, bottles, and street cries should go round to the back door,' said the Biscuit, with a householder's austerity. 'Unless, by any chance,' he said, an alternative theory crossing his mind, 'you're the Vicar?'

'I'm not the Vicar.'

'Then who are you?'

'Never mind who I am,' said Captain Kelly shortly. 'All I want to say is that you don't leave here tonight, and this young lady doesn't leave here tonight.'

'What!' cried the Biscuit.

'What!' cried Ann.

'See this?' said the Captain.

The light from the hall shone on a businesslike-looking revolver. Ann and the Biscuit gazed at it, fascinated.

'I'll be waiting outside if you try any funny business,' said Captain Kelly.

'But what's it all about?' demanded the Biscuit.

'You know what it's all about,' said the Captain, briefly. 'In you get now, and don't try to come out, unless you want the top of your head blown off. I mean it.'

Inside the hall, the Biscuit stared at the closed door as if he were trying to see through it.

'The suburbs for excitement!' he said.

Ann uttered an exclamation.

'But I can't stay here all night!' she cried.

The Biscuit quivered as if an electric shock had passed through him.

'You jolly well bet you can't!' he agreed vehemently. 'I don't know if you happen to know it, but poor little Kitchie's faith in Man is pretty wobbly these days. She had a bad shock not long ago, administered by a worm of the name of Merwyn Flock. If she finds that you and I have been camping out here.... My gosh!' groaned the Biscuit, 'all will be over. No wedding-bells for me. She's as likely as not to go into a convent or something.'

'But what's to be done? Who is that man?'

'I don't know. No pal of mine.'

'He must be mad.'

'He's absolutely potty. But that doesn't make it any better. Did you see that gun?'

'Well, what are you going to do?'

'Take another small snort.'

'What's the good of that?'

'I'll tell you what's the good of it,' said the Biscuit. 'It will clear my mind, enable me to grapple more freely with a problem to which as yet I can see no answer. I'm a pretty quick fellow, as a rule, but when it comes to homicidal lunatics in the front garden, I am not ashamed to confess myself temporarily baffled. The one thing certain is that somehow or other, by what means I cannot say, you have got to be eased out of here as soon as possible.'

He led the way back to the sitting-room, and reached abstractedly for the decanter. He was thinking . . . thinking.

III

In a prosaic age like the one in which we live anything that seems to border on eccentricity is always judged harshly. We look askance at it, and draw damaging conclusions. Deviate ever so little from the normal behaviour of the ordinary man, and you meet inevitably with head-shakings and suspicion from a censorious world.

The actions of both Captain Kelly and J. B. Hoke had been, as we have seen, dictated by careful and reasonable reflection. They were based on solid common-sense. Yet, just as Ann and the Biscuit, in the sitting-room of Peacehaven, had come to the conclusion that the Captain was unbalanced and even potty, so now did Berry and Lord Hoddesdon, on the other side of the partition, take a snap judgement and condemn Mr Hoke on the same grounds.

Lord Hoddesdon was the first to clothe this thought in words. He had been watching Mr Hoke's pistol with a fascinated eye and a sagging jaw, and now he spoke.

'Who is this lunatic?' he asked.

Berry was more soothing.

'It's quite all right, Mr Hoke,' he said. 'You're among friends. You remember me, don't you? Conway?'

'The man's a raving madman,' proceeded Lord Hoddesdon. 'Keep your dashed finger off that trigger, sir, confound you!' he added, with growing concern. 'The thing will be going off in a minute.'

'Hands up,' said Mr Hoke, muzzily.

'Our hands are up,' said Berry, still with that same elder-brotherly sweetness. 'You can see they're up, can't you? Look! Right up here.'

And, to emphasize the point, he twiddled his fingers. Mr Hoke stared at them, with an air of dislike, blinked, and rose to a point of order.

'Hey!' he observed. 'Quit that!'

'Quit what?'

'That twiddling,' said Mr Hoke. 'I don't like it.'

It reminded him somehow of spiders, and he did not wish to think of spiders.

'I'll tell you what,' said Berry. 'Put that pistol away and just sit back quite quietly, and I'll go and make you a nice cup of tea.'

'Tea?'

'A nice, hot, strong cup of tea. And then we'll all sit down and have a good talk, and you shall tell us what it is that's on your mind.'

Mr Hoke regarded him owlishly. He seemed to be considering the suggestion.

'I had a mother once,' he said.

'You did?' said Berry.

'Yes, sir!' said Mr Hoke. 'That's just what I had. A mother.'

'The man's a dashed, drivelling, raving, raging lunatic,' said Lord Hoddesdon.

Mr Hoke started. Something in his lordship's words had caused a monstrous suspicion to form itself in his clouded mind. It seemed to him, if he had interpreted them rightly, that Lord Hoddesdon was casting doubts on his sanity. He resented this. He would have been the first to admit that he had taken perhaps one over the eight and that his mental powers had lost, in consequence, something of their usual keen edge: but he was deeply wounded to think that anyone should consider him *non compos*.

'Think I'm crazy?' he said.

'Not *crazy*,' said Berry. 'Just...'

'He's as mad as a hatter,' insisted Lord Hoddesdon, who objected to paltering with facts and liked to call a spade a spade. 'Will you stop fingering that trigger, sir! Do you want a double murder on your hands?'

'I'm not crazy,' said Mr Hoke. 'No, sir.'

'I'm sure you're not,' said Berry. 'Just the tiniest bit over-excited. Why not lay that pistol down – look, there's a table where it would go nicely – and tell us all about your mother?'

Mr Hoke's mind was still occupied with his grievance. He objected to this attempted side-tracking of the conversation to the topic of mothers. Plenty of time, he felt, to talk about mothers when he had proved to these sceptics that he was as sane as anybody. He proceeded to give his proofs.

'You want to know why I'm acting this way?' he said. 'You don't know, do you? Oh, no, you don't know. Can't imagine, can you? That red-headed pal of yours hasn't been telling you what I told him about the Dream Come True, has he? Oh, no. He hasn't come and handed you the dope, has he? Oh, no. You and your mothers! Don't try to put me off by talking about your mother, because I know what I'm doing, and if your mother doesn't like it, she can do the other thing.'

To Lord Hoddesdon, chafing impotently, these strong remarks on the subject of dreams and mothers seemed but further evidence, if such were needed, that he stood in the presence of one of the most pronounced lunatics who ever qualified for the restraint of a padded cell. Gibbering, pure and simple, his lord-ship considered Mr Hoke's last speech. But to Berry there came dimly, as through a fog, a sort of meaning.

'What about the Dream Come True?' he asked.

'You don't know, do you?' asked Mr Hoke, witheringly.

He moved cautiously across the room, the better to keep his eye upon his prisoners, and sat with his back against the wall, surveying them keenly.

'You don't know, do you?' he said. 'That red-head didn't tell you, did he? And you weren't listening outside old Frisby's door that day, when him and me were talking about keeping it under our hats that there had been a new reef located? Well, if you think you're going to get up to London tomorrow and start in buying Horned Toad stock, you've another guess coming. You're going to stay right here, that's what you're going to do.'

He turned a glazing eye on Lord Hoddesdon.

'And that goes for you, too, Oil,' he said.

Berry uttered a sharp cry. It was as if a great light had shone upon him. What Mr Hoke's maunderings about the Biscuit meant, he was unable to gather: but from the welter of the other's words there had emerged the broad, basic fact that the Dream Come True had been a valuable property, after all, and that old Frisby and this inebriated viper had known it all along. And they had tricked him into selling it for the mere song its name suggested.

A wave of helpless fury flooded over him.

'So you knew there was copper there?' he cried.

'Knew it all along,' said Mr Hoke. 'And I'm going to clean up big. You'll see Horned Toad up in the hundreds before the end of the week.'

A whistling sigh escaped Lord Hoddesdon. His arms were aching, and this meaningless exchange of remarks was making his head ache still more. Dreams and mothers, and now horned toads.... It was too much for a nobleman of limited intellect to be expected to endure with composure.

283

Berry's hands had begun twitching again, and Mr Hoke commented on the fact.

'Don't twiddle!' he said.

He leaned against the wall, and endeavoured to steady his faithful gat. He did not like the expression on Berry's face. For the matter of that, he did not like the expression on Lord Hoddesdon's face. And he was about to say as much, when without any warning there was a loud, splintering crash and quite a lot of the wall fell on top of his head.

'Hell!' cried Mr Hoke, mystified.

There is always a reason for the most perplexing occurrences. To J. B. Hoke this sudden dissolution of what had appeared to be a solid wall seemed to step straight into the miracle class. He thought, as far as he was capable of thinking at all, of earthquakes.

His mind also toyed for an instant with the theory that possibly this was the end of the world. And all it was, in reality, was Berry's next-door neighbour, Lord Biskerton, endeavouring to take a short cut from Peacehaven to The Nook.

We left the Biscuit, it will be recalled, in the act of thinking. A brain of that calibre cannot go on thinking long without some solid result. Scarcely had the Biscuit swallowed one stiffish whisky and soda and begun another, rather milder, when the solution of the problem with which he was confronted flashed upon him. Suddenly a thought came like a full-blown rose, flushing his brow; and, charging down stairs to the cellar, he came racing up again, armed now with the pick-axe used by suburban householders for breaking coal.

His train of thought may be readily followed. The more he caught the eye of the photograph of his betrothed on the mantelpiece, the more clearly did he perceive that something must be done to dissolve this enforced *tête-à-tête* between Ann and himself on the premises of Peacehaven. Captain Kelly's strongly expressed views had shown him that it was impossible for her to leave by the ordinary route, and so he had adopted the only alternative one. Let him get through into Berry's sitting-room, he felt, and the thing would at least become a threesome. Good enough, was the Biscuit's verdict.

He swung his weapon vigorously, and was delighted to find that it met with little resistance. Architects of suburban semi-detached villas do not build party-walls with an eye to this sort of treatment. Encouraged, he redoubled his efforts.

Lord Biskerton, as we have said, was delighted. But it is rarely in this world that we find everybody happy at the same time, and it would be idle to pretend that his exhilaration was shared by Mr Hoke. What he was going to do about it, beyond uttering a reproving 'Hey!' Mr Hoke did not know: but he knew that he did not like it.

He backed away from the centre of disturbance with a pop-eyed stare of concern; and it was at this moment that Berry, grateful for the opportunity, sprang forward and with a dexterous flick of the foot kicked the pistol out of his hand. He and Mr Hoke then went into conference on the floor.

Lord Hoddesdon, lowering his aching arms, possessed himself of a stout chair and stood by the rapidly widening hiatus in the wall, awaiting developments. He was feeling warlike, but not surprised. The rigours of life in the suburbs, experienced first by day and now by night, had hardened Lord Hoddesdon's soul. Just as the traveller to Alaska learns the lesson that there's never a law of God or man runs north of 'fifty-three, so had his lordship become aware that every amenity of civilized life must automatically be considered suspended, once you found yourself in the S.E. 21 postal district of London.

It was not, therefore, Lord Hoddesdon, the well-known club-man, not Lord Hoddesdon, the saunterer round the Royal Enclosure at Ascot, who now stood with raised chair in Berry Conway's sitting-room. It was a throw-back to Lord Hoddes-don's fighting ancestors, a sort of primitive Lord Hoddesdon who, steeled to the realization that in any given house in this infernal suburb a man had got to expect to find homicidal lunatics popping out of every nook and cranny, was prepared to sell his life dearly.

The gap in the wall widened, and Lord Hoddesdon's face grew grimmer. Like his great forebear who had done so well at the Battle of Agincourt, he intended, if necessary, to die fighting.

Round and about the imitation Axminster carpet, meanwhile, the catch-as-catch-can struggle between Berry and his visitor was proceeding briskly and with considerable spirit. J. B. Hoke might have been injudicious in the matter of refreshment that day; he might, during his retirement in London, have allowed the enervating conditions of a peaceful life to spoil his figure and impair his wind; but in his hot youth he had been a pretty formidable bar-room scrapper, with an impressive record of victories from the Barbary Coast of San Francisco to the Tender-loin district of New York: and much of the ancient skill still lingered. You could tell by the way he kicked Berry on the shin and attempted to get tooth-hold on his left ear that this was no novice who sprawled and wriggled on the floor.

Berry perceived this himself, and he put his whole soul into the fray. And for a space the issue hung doubtful. Then Mr Hoke made the grave strategic blunder of rising to his feet.

It was not a thing his best friends would have advised. The

mother of whom he had spoken so feelingly would have clicked her tongue and shaken her gentle head, had she seen her boy committing this obvious error. J. B. Hoke was essentially a man who should have stuck to the more free and easy conditions of carpet warfare. Standing up, he offered a too prominent target. Where, on the ground, he had seemed all feet and teeth, he became revealed now as the possessor of a stomach. Berry saw this. He hit Mr Hoke twice, solidly, in the midriff. And Mr Hoke, with a defeated gurgle, folded up like an Arab tent and lay prone. And Berry, jumping for the gat which had been the gage of battle, picked it up and stood, panting.

He was attempting to recover some of the breath of which the recent struggle had deprived him, when a crash from behind, followed by a sharp howl, caused him to turn.

His old friend, Lord Biskerton, was sitting on the floor, nursing a wounded wrist, while his old friend's father, Battling Hoddesdon, stood gazing at his handiwork with surprise and concern.

'Godfrey!'

'Hullo, guv'nor. You here?'

'Godfrey,' cried Lord Hoddesdon. 'I've hurt you, my boy!'

'Guv'nor,' replied the Biscuit, 'you never spoke a truer word. If I hadn't happened to get an arm up in time, the peerage would never have descended through the direct line.'

At this moment, Ann stepped through the hole in the wall.

IV

'Come right in, Ann,' said the Biscuit cordially. 'And thank your stars it wasn't a case of Ladies First. Otherwise you would have caught it on the napper properly. The guv'nor's just been doing his big tent-pegging act.'

This was only Ann's third visit to Valley Fields, and she had, in consequence, but a slight acquaintance with the wholesome give-and-take of life in the suburbs of London. Lord Hoddesdon, entering a sitting-room in Valley Fields and finding two bodies on the floor, would have accepted the phenomenon with philosophic resignation as a perfectly normal and ordinary manifestation of suburban activity. Ann, on the other hand, was surprised.

'What has been happening?' she gasped.

Lord Hoddesdon answered the question with the stolidity of an old *habitué*.

'Lunatic,' he explained. 'Dangerous. Mr Conway overpowered him.'

Ann gazed at Berry emotionally. Her heart was throbbing with all the old love and esteem. One of his eyes was closed, as eyes will close when smartly jabbed by an elbow, and there was blood trickling down his cheek; but she stared at him as at a beautiful picture.

'Why, it's Hoke,' said the Biscuit, interested. 'When did old Hoke go off his onion? He seemed sane enough at lunch.'

Berry laughed unpleasantly.

'He isn't off his head, Biscuit,' he said. 'He knows what he's doing. Biscuit, you were right. He did do me down over that mine. He's just been telling me all about it.'

'Yes, he told me, too. Do you realize what this means, Berry?'

'Are you hurt, Berry, darling?' said Ann.

Berry stared at her.

'What did you say?'

'I said, are you hurt?'

'You said "darling".'

'Well, of course,' said Ann.

'But...'

'Sweethearts still,' explained the Biscuit. 'Recent remarks on her part *re* never wanting to see you again were made under a misapprehension. The scales have fallen from her eyes.'

'Ann!' said Berry.

'Come here,' said Ann, 'and let mother kiss the place and make it well.'

'But... here... dash it!'

It was Lord Hoddesdon who spoke. Affairs of greater urgency had caused him to forget for a while the mission which had brought him down to this house, but he remembered it now, and he gazed with consternation at the horrid picture of Ann – the heiress – old Frisby's niece – so obviously going out of the family. He looked piteously round at his son, as if seeking support, but the Biscuit had other things on his mind.

'Just a moment,' said the Biscuit. 'Are you aware, Berry, that Horned Toad Copper, now quoted at one-and-six or something like that, is going to shoot up shortly into the hundreds?'

'I am,' said Berry bitterly. 'Hoke told me. That's why he came here. He sat and held me up with a gun, to prevent me getting to London to buy the stock. Not knowing, poor chump, that I couldn't have bought the stock if he'd sent a motor to fetch me.'

'Why couldn't you?'

'I haven't any money.'

'Yes, you have. You've got two thousand quid, and here it is. Cheque requires endorsement.'

Berry regarded the slip of paper, astounded.

'How did you get this?'

'Never mind. I have my methods.'

'It's signed by Frisby's lawyer.'

'Never mind who it's signed by, so long as he's good for the stuff. Endorse it, and lend me half. A vast fortune stares us in the eye, laddie. Guv'nor,' said the Biscuit, 'if you've any means of collecting a bit of money tomorrow or the next day, bung it into Horned Toad Copper and clean up. It's a pinch.'

Lord Hoddesdon gulped.

'Frisby gave me a cheque for six hundred pounds only yesterday.'

'He did? One of the most pleasing aspects of this whole binge,' said the Biscuit, 'is that that old buccaneer seems to be financing our little venture. Seething the kid in its mother's milk, is what I call it.' He paused, and a look of despairing gloom came into his face. 'Oh, golly!' he moaned.

'What's the matter?'

The Biscuit's exuberance had vanished.

'Berry, old man,' he said, 'I hate to break it to you, old bird, but in the excitement of the moment I forgot.'

'What?'

'We can't get out of here. We're cornered.'

'Why?'

'Hoke's pal's waiting outside.'

Berry snorted.

'I'll soon fix him!'

'But he's got a gun.'

'So have I.'

'Ah,' said Mr Hoke, making his first contribution to the conversation, 'but it isn't loaded.'

'What?'

Berry tested the statement, and found it correct.

'Knew all along,' said Mr Hoke, 'there was something I'd forgotten. And that was it.'

'Tie that blighter up, guv'nor,' said the Biscuit severely, 'and bung him in the cellar. And I hope the mice eat him.'

He regarded Mr Hoke with growing disapproval. Thanks to his slip-shod methods, the garrison of The Nook was helpless. The curse of the age, the Biscuit felt, was this sloppy, careless way of doing things. You would have expected something better from a businessman like J. B. Hoke, even if he had been getting steadily plastered all the afternoon. That was how the Biscuit felt, and the thought depressed him.

In the mind of Mr Hoke, on the other hand, there was nothing but sunshine. All, he realized, was not lost. In fact, nothing was. He himself had been put out of action, but there still remained his excellent friend, Captain Kelly, and Captain Kelly could handle the situation nicely.

'That's all right about tying me up,' he said. 'What good's that going to do you?'

Berry was making for the door.

'Berry!' cried Ann. 'Where are you going?'

Berry stopped.

'Where am I going?' he repeated. 'I'm going to knock the stuffing out of that fellow.'

'And I'd join you,' said the Biscuit warmly, 'only the guv'nor's gone and smashed my arm. Perhaps you'd care to go along, guv'nor, and lend a hand?'

Lord Hoddesdon thought not. The old Crécy spirit had begun to ebb.

'It's young man's work,' he said.

'Berry!' cried Ann.

But Berry had gone.

In the pause that followed, little of note was said, except by Mr Hoke. Mr Hoke, in spite of the Biscuit's well-meant efforts to repress him by kicking him in the ribs, struck an almost lyrical vein on the subject of his partner.

'He's a gorilla,' said Mr Hoke. 'He never misses.'

He subsided for a moment into a thoughtful silence.

'It seems a pity,' he said. 'A nice young fellow like that.'

A scuffling sound outside broke in on his meditations.

'Ah,' said Mr Hoke pensively. 'This'll be the body coming back.'

Through the doorway came Berry. He was not alone. Resting on his shoulder was the form of Captain Kelly.

The Captain appeared to have sustained a wound from some blunt instrument.

'Now,' said Berry, 'put these two fellows in the cellar, and don't let them out till we've done our bit of business tomorrow.'

'I'll guard them,' said Lord Hoddesdon.

'How did you manage it, old man?' cried the Biscuit.

Berry was silent for a moment. He seemed to be thinking.

'I have my methods,' he said.

'Berry!' cried Ann.

Berry regarded her fondly. He had only one eye with which to do it, but it was an eye that did the work of two.

'Shall I see you to your car?' he said.

'Yes, do.'

'Want me to come along?' asked the Biscuit.

'No,' said Berry.

CHAPTER 14

'Darling,' said Berry.

'Yes, darling?' said Ann.

She was seated at the wheel of her car, and he stood, leaning on the side. Mulberry Grove was dark and scented and silent.

'Ann,' said Berry, 'I've something I want to tell you.'

'That you love me?'

'Something else.'

'But you do?'

'I do.'

'In spite of all the beastly things I said to you in the Park?'

'You were quite right.'

'I wasn't.'

'I did lie to you.'

'Well, never mind.'

'But I do mind. Ann.'

'Yes?'

'I've something I want to tell you.'

'Well, go on.'

Berry looked past her at the ornamental water.

'It's about that fellow.'

'What fellow?'

'Hoke's friend.'

'What about him?'

'You've been saying how brave I was.'

'So you were. It was the bravest thing I ever heard of.'

'You're looking on me as a sort of hero.'

'Of course I am.'

'Ann,' said Berry, 'I've something I want to tell you. Do you know what happened when I got out?'

'You jumped on him and stunned him.'

'Ann,' said Berry, 'I did not. When I got out, I found him lying on the ground with his head in a laurel bush.'

'What!'

'Yes.'

'But . . .'

'Wait, I'll tell you. You remember my housekeeper, Mrs Wisdom?'

'The nice old lady who told me about your bed-socks?'

Berry quivered.

'I've never worn bed-socks,' he said vehemently. 'She thinks I do, but I don't.'

'Well, what about Mrs Wisdom?'

'I'll tell you. She is engaged to a local policeman, a man named Finbow.'

'Well?'

'She and Finbow had been to the movies in Brixton.'

'Well?'

'She came back,' proceeded Berry doggedly, 'and she found a strange man lurking in our front garden.'

'Well?'

'She thought he was a burglar.'

'Well?'

'So,' said Berry, 'she hit him on the head with her umbrella and knocked him out, and all I had to do was to carry him in. Now you know.'

There was a silence. Then Ann leaned quickly over the side of the car and kissed the top of his head.

'And you thought I would mind?'

'I thought you would wish you hadn't made quite such a fuss over my reckless courage.'

'But still you told me?'

'Yes.'

Ann kissed the top of his head again.

'Quite right,' she said. 'Mother always wants her little man to tell her the truth.'

THE END

P. G. Wodehouse

IN ARROW BOOKS

If you have enjoyed *Big Money*, you'll love
Hot Water

FROM

Hot Water

I

THE town of St Rocque stood near the coast of France. The Château Blissac stood near the town of St Rocque. J. Wellington Gedge stood near the Château Blissac. He was reading his letters on the terrace outside the drawing-room.

A passer-by, given the choice between looking at Mr Gedge and at the view beneath him, would have done well to select the latter, for this tubby little man constituted the only blot on an impressive landscape. The Château was on a hill, and from its terrace the ground descended sharply through many-coloured gardens and shrubberies till it reached the lake. Beyond the lake lay sand-dunes, and beyond these glittered the harbour, dotted with boats at anchor.

The town itself was to the left, a straggling huddle of red roofs and white walls in the centre of which, raising a golden dome proudly skywards, stood the building which had made the place the popular resort it was – the Casino Municipale. For St Rocque, once a tiny fishing village, has become in recent years a Mecca for those who enjoy watching their money gathered in with rakes by sad-eyed croupiers.

Mr Gedge, reading his correspondence, did not see the

spreading prospect. Nor did he wish to. He was not fond of St Rocque, and this morning it would have seemed less attractive to him than ever, for three of his letters bore Californian postmarks and their contents had aggravated the fever of his homesickness. Ever since his marriage two years ago and the subsequent exodus to Europe he had been pining wistfully for California. The poet speaks of a man whose heart was in the Highlands, a-chasing of the deer. Mr Gedge's was in Glendale, Cal., wandering round among the hot dogs and filling-stations.

To him, grieving, there entered a trim and personable young woman whom, after a moment of blinking, he identified as Medway, his wife's maid.

'Moddom would like to see you, sir.'

'Eh?' said Mr Gedge. He had already paid his morning visit to the Big Chief. 'Why?'

'I fancy moddom has decided to take the afternoon boat to England to-day.'

Mr Gedge started.

'What!'

'Yes, sir.'

'How long is she going to be gone?'

'I could not say, sir.'

It was a point on which Mr Gedge was anxious to obtain early and authoritative information, for much depended on it. St Rocque, normally, he found a boring spot, but there is one day in the year when it pulls itself together and gives of its best. This is on the occasion of its founder's birthday, which is piously celebrated by a Costume Carnival of impressive proportions. The Festival of the Saint was due next week, and until this moment Mr Gedge had had not even a faint hope of contributing his mite to the revels. Now, for the first time, it seemed as if something might be done about it. He stuffed his letters in his pocket and hurried into the Château.

A lover of the old and quaint would have admired the Château, dating as it did from the late fourteenth or early fifteenth century. The only feeling it gave Mr Gedge was that its architect must have been cock-eyed. Mouldering stone with spiky turrets stuck on all over it was not his idea of a house. And while its interior had been modernized, or what these French called modernized – electric light and two bathrooms – it was not at all what he had been accustomed to in Glendale, California.

He found Mrs Gedge in the Venetian Suite, a large apartment with a heavily carved ceiling which always looked as if it were going to come down and bean you. She was sitting up in bed, dictating letters to Miss Putnam, her social secretary, a thin, colourless feather-weight with horn-rimmed spectacles and an air of quiet respectability.

Mrs Gedge herself would have fought in the light-heavy division. She was a solidly built, handsome woman a few years younger than her husband, and you could see from a glance at her why he always did what she told him to. Even in repose, her manner was forceful. Of her past life before their marriage, except that she was the widow of a multi-millionaire oil man named Brewster who had left her all his multi-millions, Mr Gedge knew nothing. He sometimes thought she might have been a lion-tamer.

With a slight gesture of her hand she caused Miss Putnam to melt into thin air, and raised herself on the pillows.

'What,' asked Mr Gedge, taking the chair vacated by the secretary, 'is all this about your going to England? Medway tells me you're sailing on the afternoon boat.'

'I have had a letter from my lawyer in London. There has been some trouble about English Income Tax, and he says he must see me.'

'How about your ticket?'

'Miss Putnam is attending to that. I want you to run down to the drug store and buy me some seasick remedy. You had better get Philipson's Mal-de-Mer-o.'

'All right.'

There was a pause. Mr Gedge coughed nonchalantly.

'Going to be gone long?'

'About a week.'

'Ah!' said Mr Gedge.

A purposeful gleam lit up his prominent eyes. There and then he had resolved that he would attend the Festival of the Saint, and not only attend it but attend it right. For if anybody thought that he couldn't lay his hands on a pair of pyjama trousers and one of his wife's blouses and wrap a scarf round his head and present a life-like picture of an Oriental potentate, whoever was of that opinion, felt Mr Gedge, was mistaken in the last degree.

'Well, sir,' he said, 'I guess it's going to be lonesome without you. Yessir, it'll be lonesome all right. But I'll make out somehow,' he added bravely, for the Glendale Gedges have the right stuff in them.

'You won't be lonesome. Didn't I tell you?'

'Tell me what?'

'I have invited some people to stay at the Château. They will be arriving the day after to-morrow.'

Something of Mr Gedge's quiet happiness left him. He was not one of those men who enjoy playing the host. A lot of nosy visitors about the place, moreover, might hamper his movements.

'Quite a small party. Senator Opal and his daughter. . . .'

'Old Opal!'

'...and the Vicomte de Blissac.'

'What!'

'I have never met him, but I believe he is a very charming young man.'

Mr Gedge corrected this view.

'A very charming young wild Indian. Never sober, they tell me.'

'I know all about that, and I have given orders that no alcohol is to be served in the Château during his visit. His mother's main reason for sending him to us is that she wants him to have a few weeks of complete abstinence.'

'Say, what is this joint? A Keeley Cure Institute?'

'I am very glad the Vicomte is able to come. There are several things about this house that I wish to discuss with a representative of the family. The Vicomtesse gave me to understand that the plumbing was in good repair. It isn't. It's terrible. And there's that leaky cistern upstairs.'

'So when he arrives,' said Mr Gedge morosely, 'I suppose I meet him on the doorstep and say, "Come right on in, Vicomte. We can't offer you a drink, but step up and take a look at our leaky cistern." That'll make a big hit with him.'

He rumbled wordlessly for a while. Then a sudden and unpleasant idea seemed to strike him.

'What is all this?' he asked suspiciously. 'What's the big idea back of it all? Filling up the place with Vicomtes and Senators – there's something behind it that I don't get. Why the Vicomte? How come the Senator?'

Mrs Gedge was silent for a moment. Into her manner there had crept a sort of strained alertness, like that of a leopard crouching for the spring.

'It is all quite simple,' she said. 'The Vicomte's mother has great influence with the French Government.'

'What of it?'

'Any friend of hers would be welcomed by them.'

Mr Gedge, who had no intention of spending a week-end with the French Government, said so.

'And Senator Opal is so powerful in Washington that he can practically dictate appointments.'

'What appointments?'

'Well, for instance, the appointment of American Ambassador to France.'

'Who's going to be Ambassador to France?' said Mr Gedge, mystified.

He could not have asked a more convenient question. It enabled Mrs Gedge to place the salient facts before him crisply and without further preamble.

'You are,' she said.

Visit our special P.G. Wodehouse website
www.wodehouse.co.uk

Find out about P.G. Wodehouse's books now
reissued with appealing new covers

Read extracts from all your favourite titles

Read the exclusive extra content and immerse
yourself in Wodehouse's world

Sign up for news of future publications
and upcoming events

arrow books